Rainbow
Overalls

T0000581

RAINBOW OVERALLS

by

Maggie Fortuna

2024

RAINBOW OVERALLS

ISBN 13: 978-1-63679-606-2

THIS TRADE PAPERBACK ORIGINAL IS PUBLISHED BY
BOLD STROKES BOOKS, INC.
P.O. BOX 249
VALLEY FALLS, NY 12185

FIRST EDITION: APRIL 2024

CREDITS
EDITOR: ANISSA MCINTYRE
PRODUCTION DESIGN: STACIA SEAMAN
COVER DESIGN BY INKSPIRAL DESIGN

Acknowledgments

Thank you to everyone at Bold Strokes Books for recognizing something in my work and for welcoming me into your community. The opportunity to share this book is a glory beyond estimation.

To my editor, Anissa McIntyre, thank you for your insight and support through the daunting task of editing the inside of my brain into something understandable to the outside world. I greatly appreciate every thoughtful comment and edit you gave me in the pursuit of the ideal version of this book.

To my parents, thank you for encouraging and supporting my creativity, and for giving me space to be myself.

To my sister Susan, thank you for being my friend, confidant, supporter, and partner in creativity since the day I was born. I get to be my most intellectual self and my silliest self with you, and every moment of sharing and dissecting art together has shaped me into the artist and the person that I am now. Thank you for letting me bombard you with anxiety, giving your best advice about every little text or email, and for always committing to the bit.

This book is a love letter to my time in college. Though this version of the place and the people comes from my imagination, every bit of love and acceptance Ginny and Nat feel from their community comes from my experience of the real place. To all the wonderful people who made up that community for me: Every day in Vermont meant more than I can express. To those who helped me through the tumult I dealt with in those years (the tremulous, unsteady moments in particular): My love and gratitude for you is boundless.

I paint with the colors and patterns of all the art I have had the privilege to witness. I would not be myself nor know myself without the stories I have loved. So, lastly, thank you for reading, and thereby helping me make my own contribution to that vast prismatic world of queer art.

For everyone and everything
that made my own time in Vermont so special,
without which the version of me that wrote and shared this book
would never have existed.

If we had a keen vision and feeling of all ordinary human life, it would be like hearing the grass grow and the squirrel's heart beat, and we should die of that roar which lies on the other side of silence.

George Eliot
Middlemarch, A Study of Provincial Life, 1871–1872

CHAPTER ONE

Ginny

Have you ever gone so long without being alone that you've forgotten what solitude feels like? I'm talking about forgetting on a completely subconscious, cellular level. You've spent so much time with others that you no longer realize all the little things you would do differently if you were alone. The awareness of the people around you has seeped into your bones. You know they see you, so your consciousness of their perception of you becomes part of how you carry yourself, and the You you are around these other people starts to feel like the *only You*.

I think that's what happened to me over the last few days, though I'm only noticing it right now. Now that I'm alone again.

This week has been one of the busiest of my life. College orientation. I haven't been alone for longer than a bathroom break or a quick shower in five days. Even now, this peace won't last very long. My roommate Jess had her first class at eight this morning, so when I woke up at nine thirty, she was already gone. I almost wish I'd gotten up earlier to bask in the quiet paradise of solitude (but not really, because *sleep*).

When my eyes opened and I became aware enough to note Jess's absence, tension slipped from my shoulders that I had no idea I was holding. I've been overwhelmed this week, of course, but apparently, I hold that stress even in my sleep, which is a *fun*—meaning stressful and surprising yet altogether par for the course—new development. My first class starts at ten thirty, so the solitude would have ended soon enough anyway.

I guess that's my life now; tiny little moments of time to myself interspersed in a busy college student schedule. I know a more overwhelming version of my life exists, but right now my brain has lost the ability to imagine something more intimidating than my reality.

Maybe that's how everyone feels when they're immersed in a new community. Or maybe it's just an experience reserved for mega-introverts like me. I'm used to a lot of time on my own. Time to recover from every anxiety-provoking social interaction, time to recharge for the next one, and time to spare. Not that I don't have friends back home, or a passable relationship with my parents, but being alone has become my default.

But now it's almost ten and my new roommate is bound to return any minute. It's not that I don't like Jess—she actually seems pretty awesome so far. She's the kind of unflappable person I find almost confusing. I'm sure she has as many moods as everyone else, but so far, she always seems to be happily going with the flow. I was *completely* intimidated by that when we first met, but she's funny, open, and kind, and I think we've started to get along relatively well after this week's crash course in bonding.

I'm clicking the strap on my overalls into place when the door bangs open. Jess comes in and flops on her bed face first. Despite her eternally cool composure, she seems to have a penchant for throwing the door open like it weighs a thousand pounds. She's going to put a dent in the wall soon enough.

"Hey." Her voice is muffled in her purple duvet. "Good morning."

"Good morning." I check myself out in the mirror. I've chosen a pair of overalls over a T-shirt from my favorite coffee shop back home. Overalls always make me feel prepared, and the shirt makes me feel comfortable. A perfect first day combination. "How was your class?"

She flips over to face the ceiling and shrugs. "It was okay. I'm excited about it but also, it's just, like, *so* much work."

I smile. That's the part of college I'm really looking forward to. I've always been a total nerd, but I may finally be somewhere where *nerd* is the goal. I had a difficult time convincing my parents to let me go to a tiny liberal arts college in Vermont, but this is exactly the kind of environment I want to learn in.

We chat about the presentation she has already been assigned for her environmental science class until I tell her I have to leave. She tilts her head back to look at me, dyed-green hair falling over the edge of her bed. I would love to dye my hair, but it's the kind of thing I don't think I'll ever have the courage to do.

"I like your overalls." I think she's smiling, but it's hard to tell upside down. "They're a vibe."

"I—" I have no idea what that means. "Thanks." I smooth them out, suddenly self-conscious. I don't envy Jess's style, exactly, but I envy the confidence with which she wears it, so a compliment from her feels important. She wrinkles her brow at me. I must be acting strange in some way or another.

"Are you really bad at taking compliments, or do you think I'm, like, hitting on you or something?"

I blink at her directness. "Bad at taking compliments."

She nods. I *didn't* think she was hitting on me, but surprise made me hesitate. Last I heard, she was in a committed—although apparently doomed—relationship. The day we met, Jess confided in me as I helped her put up some photos.

"I shouldn't even be hanging these. Basically, all of them have my girlfriend in them, and we're probably gonna break up soon." When I'd stuttered my condolences for her future break-up, she shook her head. "No worries. We both suck at long-distance, but we're also both optimistic idiots, so here we are."

She'd laughed, so I did too, and we'd moved on. I don't think she noticed how the calm confidence with which she'd said *girlfriend* had left me in awe. Now Jess looks at me with her brows pulled down and a slight frown on her lips, and I feel like I've done something wrong.

"Ginny, you're not, like…" She forms her words slowly, which I haven't seen her do before. *Is she going to ask me if I'm queer?* My heartbeat accelerates and the tips of my ears go hot. "*Not* cool with the gay thing, right? You just seem a little shocked by that question."

"No!" I shake my head vehemently. "No, no, of course not." She must see how nervous I am, but I'm surprised she's mistaken it for *that* kind of discomfort. I'm uncomfortable with *myself*, not Jess.

"Cool." She's less skeptical but not entirely un-skeptical. Her phone dings and she turns her attention to it, fingers flying at lightning speed as she texts.

This is my chance. My easy, totally ordinary opportunity to say I'm bisexual. Jess won't judge. She's nice, calm, and one of the most go-with-the-flow people I've ever met. Not to mention gay herself. And if I don't say it now, it'll be so much harder to say it later. But I've never said it out loud to someone before—assuming I don't count my own reflection in the mirror—so the words don't come easily.

It's almost funny how awful never having told anyone feels now, given how normal it used to seem. Just a short while ago I thought I was settled with that part of myself, and that people knowing wouldn't change anything. I knew from the time I was thirteen I liked girls, but when I kissed a boy for the first time at fourteen, I knew I liked guys, too. So, I thought maybe I'd only ever date men. The liking-girls part of me could just stay private, and I'd never have to share *that* part of me with my religious and over-involved parents. But over the last six months or so, something changed. Not telling stopped feeling like privacy and started feeling like a big, bad secret.

It's not that my home situation is even that bad. My parents wouldn't be thrilled, but I'm pretty sure they wouldn't do anything too drastic. They would probably learn to accept it someday. It's always been *me* who couldn't accept myself. I never felt secure enough in my sexuality to tell anyone, and I always hoped, as silly as it sounds now, I could find a way to accept myself without it ever having a real effect on my life.

When I got into college, I promised myself I wouldn't let my sexuality feel like a secret here. I wouldn't hide things. I wouldn't build up the walls of shame and denial I lived with at home. I would be honest. I promised myself I'd be out. And if I'm going to follow through on that, now is the best time to start.

Determination rushes over me, combating my anxiety. I pretend to look for something in my backpack so I don't have to make eye contact with Jess as I speak.

"Actually…" I clear my throat quietly, doing my best to sound completely nonchalant. "I'm bi."

"Oh."

I can't stand it anymore and glance up to see her expression. She's looking me over but doesn't seem too surprised. Her expression clears and she nods.

"I see that for you." Then she frowns. "Now I feel like I have to clarify that I really *wasn't* hitting on you. I was joking."

"I know."

"Cool." She smiles and turns back to her phone, and that's it. She's moved on already.

I told someone, and nothing changed.

I smile at my backpack as I zip it shut, then sling it over my shoulder. We exchange byes as I leave, and the tension in my shoulders feels even lighter than it did when I was alone.

❖

My Gothic Literature course meets on Monday and Thursday mornings. I'm not sure why our term starts on a Thursday, but I'm happy my first ever college class is a literature course. I have absolutely no idea what I want to study here, but I've always had a passion for reading.

I put on my headphones while I walk. The campus is beyond tiny, so I barely enjoy two songs before I arrive in the small seminar room. I grab a random desk, take out a notebook and a pencil, and people-watch as other students slowly file in.

Two minutes before class begins, a group of three people come in together, laughing. They choose seats right across from me in the circle of desks, so it is almost natural to watch them. In particular, the girl directly across from me catches my eye. She listens to one of her friends tell a story, and I watch her brown eyes sparkle as she laughs. The easy confidence with which she carries herself is magnetic. She looks at her friends with endless focus and affection, like there isn't a single sight in the world she'd rather bear witness to, and I'm mesmerized by the force of her attention. I'd look to see how they've drawn such intent focus, but then I'd have to look away from her. She pulls one leg up onto her chair, resting an arm on her knee.

I'm being a total creep. I force my gaze away.

Then I hear her laugh—loud and delighted. *Screw it.* I let myself look at her again.

She's so hot. I am tentative saying those kinds of words about women aloud, but I've had a lot of practice thinking them.

She has high, prominent cheekbones and a strong jaw. Her dark brown hair is bleached blond except for her roots. It's cut relatively short, like a long pixie cut, and she messes with it periodically. She shifts it from one side to the other, then lets it fall over her eyes just a bit when she looks down.

One of her friends—a Black student wearing a crop top I'd die to be able to pull off with confidence—says something and the girl bursts out laughing again. Her smile is wide, easy, and kind of goofy.

She radiates that I'm-queer-and-I'm-happy-with-myself energy I've always been drawn to and am more than a little jealous of. Not that I *know* she's queer, but the hair and the rainbow laces on her Doc Martens are good clues, if I listen to stereotypes. I covertly study her outfit. She's wearing a simple T-shirt and jeans with a hole in one knee. The light denim jacket draped over the back of her chair is practically covered in pins and patches. I squint to try to see what they are without being too obvious. One patch is a word in rainbow lettering, but I can't make out what it says. Do straight people wear more than one rainbow item? I mean, they *can*, but multiple rainbows must suggest something.

God. I've been looking at her for a couple minutes and I'm already invested in her sexuality. I guess I can have a crush on her even if she isn't queer, given I can't imagine doing anything about it anyway. I promised myself I'd be out, not that I'd act on any possible feelings. I can only muster so much bravery.

She looks toward the door, and I follow her gaze.

The professor bustles in holding a mountain of papers. She announces herself to the room and immediately distributes copies of the syllabus. Then Professor Vargas asks us to introduce ourselves, which I've done about fifty times this week. One of Hot Girl's friends volunteers to go first.

"Hi, everyone, I'm Mack Andrews, they/them pronouns. I'm a sophomore from Boston, and I study literature. And I'm super excited for this class!"

Hot Girl goes next, and I enjoy being able to watch her without being completely obvious.

"I'm Nat." She pauses for the tiniest moment. "Natalie Becker, I should probably say." She laughs and glances toward Professor Vargas, who writes on what must be a class roster. "She/her. I'm a sophomore...I'm from Brooklyn, and I study visual art mostly, but also a bunch of other stuff. And..." She runs a hand through her hair for the millionth time. "Yeah. That's it."

Natalie. *Nat*. It's a nice name for my first college crush.

CHAPTER TWO

Natalie

I'm ten minutes into my first class of the year and already doodling in the margins of my notebook. *Great.* Introductions are always boring, but I should probably try to focus for at least the first day. I put my pencil down and tear my gaze away from my paper even though the figure I am drawing still needs a face. A dude I know from an art history class last term is introducing himself, talking about how this class fits into his study of nineteenth-century philosophy. *What an interminable douche.* My fingers itch to draw again, but I drum them quietly on my knee instead. I'm so antsy lately, practically unable to concentrate on one thing at a time. I need to get my focus issues under control now that classes are starting up again, or I'm going to miss everything. I'm used to my ADHD affecting my focus, but it's been worse than usual since I returned to campus a couple days ago. I've had this restless energy I don't know how to quell.

Maybe it's because the summer was so utterly depressing. I missed everything here so much—my friends, the classes, even my work-study job at the campus post office. I mean, I love my family, my neighborhood in Brooklyn, and working at my mom's classic Jewish deli, Mim's. I've probably spent more time in the store, which my mom named for my grandmother, Miriam, than anywhere else in the entire world. But I spent the summer thinking about how much happier I am at school. Now that I'm here again, it's almost the opposite. Life back home is never far from my mind.

Three years of college may be a long time, but every moment feels like it's too important to waste. I have to make a promise to myself. I will forget about everything at home and enjoy my freedom while I can. I'm going to live my best damn college life.

But to do that, I need to get out of my own head already. I flip my attention back to the room around me just as Professor Vargas interrupts the philosophy douche.

"That's good, Louis…Next?" She gestures to the girl sitting directly across from me, who nods like she's been given orders from a drill sergeant. *Cute.*

"Hi, everyone." I smile at her light Southern accent. She waves at no one in particular. "I'm Ginny Holland. Uh…she/her. I'm a first-year. I'm from Virginia." *Ginny from Virginia.* I wonder if Ginny's a nickname. "I don't know what I want to study yet, but I'm really excited for this class! Um…Yeah. Thanks." She smiles and deep dimples appear in her cheeks. *Very cute.*

The next person begins their introduction, but I study Ginny from Virginia a little longer. She has long, dark brown hair and round wire-rimmed glasses. I'm such a sucker for the nerdy vibe. Normally, I wouldn't say I have a type—beyond *girls*, of course—but I reconsider as I watch Ginny push her glasses back up the bridge of her nose. I want to see her eyes up close.

She listens intently as Professor Vargas prompts the next student, who's so nervous his hands shake before he even starts speaking. He stumbles over his own name, and a smile forms on Ginny's face. She seems kind and encouraging, even though the nervous guy isn't looking at her.

Her gaze darts away from him and lands on me. Her dark eyebrows rise on her forehead, surprised, but she doesn't immediately look away, so I don't either. I smile, and she smiles back. She does a tiny wave under her desk, like she did when she introduced herself, but this time it's directed at me. I wave back and she smiles wider, showing off her dimples. *Yep. Definitely very, very cute.* She looks away, so I do too, bringing my focus back to the class.

Professor Vargas gives us an overview of the course, talking about all the books we'll be reading and explaining the essays for the term. I didn't take any literature classes last term, and I missed it more than I thought I would. I don't love writing essays, but I adore getting the chance to read books I never have time for at home. It's great for inspiration, as of course I inevitably illustrate my favorite moments.

I tap my fingers restlessly on my leg again, then I let them drift to my paper. Based on the class description, this notebook will be full of vampires and Victorian-style ghosts by the time the term is over. I'd started a figure earlier but haven't gotten past basic facial structure. I give her hair, long and dark, and pencil in delicate features and thin, circular glasses. I add one little dimple.

God, I'm such a sap, drawing a cute girl on the first day of class. There are tons of cute queer girls on this campus, and I'm determined to get to know *a lot* of them this term. Maybe Ginny from Virginia could be one of them, but there's no need to be so focused on just her. Plus, I'm sitting between my friends Lizzie and Mack, and I do not want to know the teasing I'd get from them for openly drawing a stranger in class. I think of what to draw next as I flip the page.

I haven't drawn someone in overalls in a while...Best to leave Ginny out of it, though. I sketch a pair of overalls on their own. My dream overalls. I add a tiny rainbow patch on the front pocket.

I wonder if Ginny's the type to put a rainbow patch on her overalls.

I get absorbed in my sketch, drawing patch after patch all over the imaginary overalls, and before I realize what's happened class is over. Mack immediately starts chattering about how excited they are for the first book we're studying. I take one last look at my sketch. *That turned out nice.* I flip my notebook closed.

Ginny packs her bag and stands from her desk. Yeah, I definitely have a thing for overalls. I pull my gaze away and follow my friends out the door. It's just past noon, so we head toward the dining hall for lunch.

❖

I have three texts from my brother and two from my mom. I read Noah's first.

moms upset
shes gonna text u about ur debit card
good luck

He adds a fingers-crossed emoji. Sure enough, my mom is less than pleased in her texts.

Why have you spent $86 this week?
I want you to enjoy your time at school, but
you know you can't spend money like that.

I sigh, feeling myself being pulled back into the stressful mindset I had just started to escape. I respond to my mother first.

It was all on school supplies.
My figure drawing and ceramics classes
both require a ton of materials. I bought
the cheapest options, I promise.

I go back to my texts with my brother. Noah is sixteen, three and a half years younger than me, and he should be in school right now.

Thanks but how did u know that?
Where r u?

He responds almost immediately.

mom texted me to ask if i knew if u were in
class so she could call u.i told her to text u

*and yes im in school. one mom is enough
thank u*

He punctuates that with two eyeroll emojis. I send back a shrug emoji just as a reply comes in from my mom.

Okay. Warn me next time. Love you.

I return the sentiment and shove my phone into my pocket. I hate that I have to deal with family finances even when I'm two hundred miles away. I'm on a scholarship, but college is still expensive as hell. When I got accepted here and added up all the costs, I told my mom I wouldn't attend. But she knew how much studying art in college meant to me, so she didn't entertain that idea for a second—even with the impact on her and the deli. I'm the first person in my family to go to college, and she's always wished she'd been able to attend. It's not *not* a lot of pressure, and that's just one more reason to make the most of my time here.

"Nat?" Lizzie's voice breaks me out of my anxiety spiral. I turn to see her looking at me quizzically. I've missed something. *Again.* "You okay?"

I nod, brushing off her concern. *I'm great.* "I'm *awesome.*"

Lizzie furrows her brow, but she moves on anyway. "We were talking about the party at Powell this weekend." Powell is a dorm house known for throwing some of the wilder parties on campus. A party is just what I need to forget about my shitty summer.

"You gonna go?" Mack asks.

"Of course! First party of the year? I can't wait."

It's gonna be great.

I just need to keep telling myself that and sooner or later I'll actually start believing it.

CHAPTER THREE

Ginny

God, I'm a nerd. The first big party of the year is tonight, but instead of drinking and dancing, I met a couple people from my psychology class at the student lounge for some tea and homework.

The culture here is so different than it was in high school. People think of *nerdy* as a positive trait. I don't worry about seeming uncool for loving my courses, and I don't need to feign interest in school sports. My social life isn't what I want it to be yet, but I've met a lot of nice people, and I have enough acquaintances to have people to eat with at meals. Hopefully, I'll get up the courage to go to one of the big parties one day, but I wasn't ready to push myself quite that far out of my comfort zone tonight.

I pass Powell on my way back to my room, and music from the party booms out like an earthquake, overpowering the music in my headphones. Jess tried to get me to go with her tonight, but I declined. I smile at the grass as I walk. Yeah, I'm definitely happy with my textbooks and chamomile for now.

I make my way to my own dorm, upstairs and down the hall to my room. I open my door and—

Oh my God!

The hot girl from Gothic Lit is standing just a few feet in front of me. *Natalie.* Nat. She's pulling up her jeans and not wearing a shirt.

Oh. My. God.

I tear my eyes away from her boobs to find her staring at me, eyebrows raised and an amused smile on her face. She looks only slightly surprised to see me, while I genuinely cannot process what I'm seeing.

"Hi?" She says it like it's a question, with her focus half on me and half on buttoning her pants. I snap out of my half-naked-hot-girl-in-front-of-me stupor.

"I—um—sorry." I take one huge step backward and let the door close in my face.

What the hell was that? I read the sign on the door, but it still says my and Jess's names. *Not the wrong room.* A knock comes from the other side of the door.

"You can come in," Natalie calls.

I hesitate. I mean, I wouldn't *mind* exactly if she still isn't wearing a shirt, but I'll probably act like an idiot again. But she said I could come in. And it is my room, after all.

I push the door open slowly, peering in. She wears a pastel striped short-sleeve button-up shirt now, though she's only half-finished buttoning it.

"Hey." She sends me a slightly sheepish smile. "You're Ginny. From Gothic Lit." *She remembers my name.* I blush. A girl this hot shouldn't be this nice, too.

"Yeah."

"I'm Natalie, by the—"

"I remember you."

She smiles and shrugs on her denim jacket with all its pins and patches. "Glad I made an impression." Her deep brown eyes sparkle, and I blink back at her.

I should probably clarify why I walked in on her. "Um, this is my room." I take a step in and gesture to my bed, as if that proves everything. "I'm pretty sure."

"I figured!" She laughs. "Sorry I surprised you there. I met your roommate at the Powell party, and we were hanging out."

I glance around. Maybe Jess is hiding under one of our beds or something.

Natalie must realize my confusion because she clarifies. "When we, uh, finished, she went to take a shower. I was just getting myself together before I left."

Wow. That's blunter than I'm used to, but I nod.

"Oh." It's all I can think of to say. My crush of less than one week has already hooked up with my roommate. Things move fast around here. I barely know her, but I'm still a little dismayed.

"You're from Virginia, right?" She remembers that, too.

"Yes."

"Ginny from Virginia." She hums thoughtfully. I've gotten this reaction countless times, so I know where she's going with it.

"Yeah, my parents are overly patriotic and abhorrently unoriginal."

She laughs, and I smile back at her. "So, that's your full name. Virginia? From Virginia?"

"Yep."

"Wow." She stops laughing for a moment, then seems to be hit with the ridiculousness of my name all over again. "That's— *damn.*"

"Yeah." I put my hands in the pockets of my light flannel jacket. Her laughter dies down and she looks me over. My ears go hot under her scrutiny.

"I like *Ginny*," she murmurs. "Suits you."

"Thanks." We stand in silence for a moment, but then her gaze shifts to the door. She takes a couple steps toward it, and I adjust to give her room, but she stops abruptly. I meant to get out of her way, but I somehow brought us closer together. Her hand brushes the side of my jacket as she turns to me.

"Sorry again about…" She gestures to herself.

"No, no, it's fine! No worries." Hopefully I don't sound *too* okay with it. "I'm sorry I walked in on you…" I repeat her gesture, so I don't accidentally say something about how good she looked half naked. She laughs.

"It's literally your room. No reason to be sorry. Good thing you didn't walk in ten minutes earlier."

"Oh, wow!" My brain concocts an image of walking in on

her and Jess, but I shove it away. That would be a whole other level of awkward. "Yeah, I should probably talk to Jess about protocol for…guests."

"I always forget to lock these doors."

"Yeah." Though I haven't done anything in this room worthy of locking the door.

She glances to the door, back to me, then looks at my oversized red-and-white flannel jacket. She ghosts her fingers over the bottom edge of it.

"I've been looking for something like this." Her voice is low, like her words are for my ears only. She plays with the corner of my jacket, and her knuckle brushes right above my hip. It's the quickest, tiniest touch, but my stomach muscles tense. She looks up at me from under the hair hanging over her eyes, then back to the jacket. "I have tons of flannels, but only shirts. No jackets. Gotta change that if I want to keep my reputation as a stereotypical lesbian, right?"

"Uh, right. Definitely." I laugh lightly. She cringes.

"Not to put that generalization on you. Sorry. I was just talking about me."

"It's fine." *Just say it, Ginny. It's never going to feel normal if you don't treat it like it is normal.* "I'm bi, not a lesbian, but I do get the flannel thing." I gesture to my jacket. "Obviously." She chuckles.

"Gotcha." She thumbs the fabric for a moment again. "This is a good one." She returns her hand to her side and takes a step back.

I miss the closeness more than I care to admit.

"Well, good night, Ginny from Virginia." She pulls the door open and shoots me a quick grin.

"Good night, Natalie." And then she's gone. I flop on my bed. The image of her tugging her jeans over her hips comes back to me—the unselfconscious way she held herself, even when I stared at her chest like an idiot. I have years of experience gawking at hot girls from a distance, but doing it up close is a whole new adventure.

If Nat starts dating Jess, walking in on her half-naked in my room could become a regular occurrence. That sounds like torture and heaven all at once. But last I heard, Jess still had a girlfriend. I know she'll be heartbroken if they split up, but I hope that's the answer. Or at least I hope she told Natalie about her girlfriend first. I'll have to ask Jess about that in some non-judgmental way. The door bangs open, and as if I'd summoned her, Jess comes in, wrapped in her fluffy blue robe.

"Hey, Gin."

"Hey. I met your, uh, friend, earlier. Well, I'd already met her, actually…but…yeah."

"Natasha?"

Well, not knowing her name makes it seem less likely they're going to start dating anytime soon.

"I think it's Natalie."

"Oh, damn, right." She laughs and starts to change into her pajamas.

"I don't want to pry, but—"

"Sara and I broke up yesterday."

"Oh, God, I'm sorry. That sucks."

She shrugs and turns away from me. I can't see her face, but it's clear she doesn't want to talk about it. I lie back on my bed, letting my thoughts drift back to Natalie.

She was really nice. And funny. And still super hot. And I *think* she was flirting with me. Hopefully someday I'll be brave enough to flirt back.

Chapter Four

Natalie

Usually, I avoid Monday morning classes like they're someone sneezing on the subway without covering their face, but I made an exception during registration this term since Mack and Lizzie were already planning to take the course. I thought I'd at least be tired and miserable with my friends. Surprisingly, I'm not miserable at all as we walk out of the dining hall toward the literature building. Still tired, sure, but also excited. After my awkward yet incredibly endearing encounter with Ginny in her room a couple nights ago, she's been on my mind a lot. I haven't had that much fun flirting with someone in a long time.

I love first conversations. Conversations where you first get a sense of someone. The first time you think *Hey, you seem cool. I think I'd like to get to know you better*.

I had that feeling from the moment she'd backed out the door of her own room, adorably confused and trying to be respectful even though *I* was the one in *her* space. The second I left the room I almost went right back in. I wanted to ask if she wanted to keep talking as much as I did. I wanted to keep flirting with her so I could watch her react. I wanted to keep playing with her flannel to see if she'd touch me back.

I couldn't tell if she was flirting or just being nice and meeting my energy, but she definitely seemed interested by the sight of me half-naked. If she *is* into me, I certainly wouldn't turn down the chance to hook up with her. But even if she's not interested, I'm eager just to talk to her again. So when Mack and Lizzie head toward the desks we sat at last class, I gesture to where Ginny sits.

"Let's go over there."

They shrug and follow. Ginny is rifling through her backpack, so she hasn't noticed us yet. I plop into the seat beside her, and she looks up. She smiles when she sees me, like it's an automatic reaction, and I know I must be grinning back.

"Hey," she says.

"Hey." I turn and gesture to my friends, who are settling in at the desks next to us. "Ginny, this is Mack Andrews, and this is Lizzie Moore. Mack and Lizzie, this is Ginny."

They exchange hellos and Mack immediately asks Ginny what she thought of the reading assignment for today. Mack can talk about literature endlessly, and Lizzie is incredibly friendly, so the conversation takes off quickly. I sit back for a couple minutes, listening to them chat about George Eliot books and the other classes they're taking this term. Lizzie makes a joke and I watch Ginny's dimples appear and disappear as she laughs.

My chest squeezes. I must be even more invested in friendship with Ginny than I realized if I'm this happy to see her getting along with my friends.

Professor Vargas blows in like a hurricane a few minutes later, carrying another mountain of papers that seem ridiculously precarious. I'd bet good money she's lost more than a few of those over campus today. She's the only professor I have who avoids technology in our assignments. Some students seemed annoyed when she asked us not to use laptops in class unless we needed them, but I find her aversion to the digital age charming. She distributes some academic essays on the reading, and class begins. About halfway through the class, she gives us a few questions about the reading and tells us to split into pairs for one-on-one discussion.

I turn to Ginny. "Partners?"

"Sure."

We chat about the reading for a bit, but I find myself paying way more attention to what I can learn about Ginny than the book.

She's smart, thoughtful, and clearly comfortable talking about literature. An easy confidence enters her voice and her adorable Southern-accented words become smoother and more deliberate.

"You love this," I say when we finish Vargas's questions.

Her brow furrows. "What? The book?"

"Talking like this. The questions. The analysis. All this academic shit."

"Yeah, I do." She shrugs. "Not being a nerd has never been a skill of mine."

"Aw, nerds are cool now. Smart is sexy and all that."

She glances around the room, eyes flickering over all the students eagerly engaged in discussion. "I guess it is here. I'm still getting used to that."

"It wasn't like that back home?"

"Hard no." I laugh at the way she widens her eyes at me, as if the idea is unfathomable. I grew up in a pretty liberal Brooklyn bubble, where we were all told different was special and unique was normal, so this campus full of aggressively progressive hipsters has always felt like home to me. But it's clear it is new to Ginny. "Do you like it? The academic shit, as you put it."

I tilt my head side to side a couple times, considering her question. "It doesn't always come naturally to me, to be honest. Reading eight-hundred-page books and writing tons of essays, I mean. But I enjoy it, yeah. It's not, like, my thing, but it's fun."

She laughs. "You *are* a nerd. You just called eight-hundred-page books fun."

"Hell yeah." I lean in a little closer, propping my chin on my hand. "Like I said, smart is sexy, right?"

She nods while her lips quirk with a smile. "Right." She draws the word out, her light Southern accent more pronounced than usual. *Raht.* My eyes flick from her lips to her eyes. She holds my gaze for a long moment, then looks away. "You study art, you said? That's your thing?"

"Yeah, my major is visual art. I draw and paint, mostly." She glances to the notebook on my desk, where I scribbled a couple quick sketches before the class broke into groups. I turn it around so she can see. I point to one of the more detailed sketches.

"That's my cat back home. Moose." She leans over to study the drawing.

"Moose," she repeats, smiling at the sketch. "You're very talented." She makes eye contact again—this time over the rims of her glasses. My cheeks heat.

Her eyes are so damn green.

I'm the one who looks away first this time. I'm not generally prone to embarrassment, but the intensity of her green eyes and the sincere compliment were too much for me.

"Thanks." I mean it. I flip through my notebook, searching for another drawing to show her. I think I did a couple drawings I really liked in this notebook, but it might have been another one.

There's a sketch of a tree behind the science building that's nice but nothing special.

One page has about twenty attempts to draw a mirror that all turned out weird.

There's—*Shit!*

I quickly flip back to the drawing of Moose before Ginny can see the sketch I did on the first day of this class. The one with long dark hair and glasses that might seem suspiciously familiar to her. I glance up at her, but she's looking at the floor.

I follow her gaze and realize she's taking in the flower tattoo on my ankle. I lift the cuff of my jeans so she can see all of it.

"It's a dahlia. My mom's favorite."

"It's beautiful."

"Thanks. Are you pro or con on tattoos? For yourself, I mean. If you're con for others, you can keep that opinion to yourself." She laughs.

"Pro. Generally pro. Well, pro in a very aspirational way, you know? I would love one, but I think it would take me about thirty years to work up the courage. Plus, my parents would lose their minds, so it's probably a good idea to wait a while."

"Yeah, my mom wasn't too into it. She went on and on about how I couldn't be buried in a Jewish cemetery. But she got over it. I can't wait to get another."

Ginny looks down at my ankle again. "It's very…" She tilts

her head as she thinks. "You, I guess. Not that I know you all that well. It just reminds me of your sketches."

"That's because it *is* my sketch."

Her gaze flies to mine. "Really? That's awesome."

"Yeah. I mean, I didn't do the tattoo myself, obviously, but there's a girl in the year above me who does stick-and-poke tattoos, and I gave her my sketch. She's really talented and, you know, not insanely expensive, if you're ever interested."

"Wow." She opens her mouth to say more but stops. There's a look in her eye as she studies me that I can't quite identify.

"What?"

"It's just really cool that you know yourself like that. You know what you want to put on your body and you're talented enough to make it happen."

I shrug. "It's just a flower."

"Not to you." She raises an eyebrow in challenge.

I feel the answering smirk on my face. I like that she pushes me. I like that she already sees me enough to push me. "No, not to me."

"You have a lot of drive, don't you?"

I nod. I used to think I wasn't particularly ambitious, but applying to art school changed that. I've never wanted anything more than to be able to call myself an artist, even if it won't last forever. Getting this tattoo last year was like inking a small reminder to myself on my ankle. *I am an artist. My art will always be a part of me, no matter what else I do.*

"That's amazing. I have absolutely no idea what I want to do with myself," Ginny says.

We're complete opposites. I know exactly what I want to do with myself—be an artist. But I won't be able to do that. I will have to go back home when I graduate and help my mom run the deli. Someday Noah and I will have to run the store on our own, my art will fall by the wayside, and that'll be my life.

But I don't tell Ginny any of that. I want to learn more about her, not depress her.

"You don't want to study literature?" I ask instead.

"Maybe? I don't know. I've always loved it, but I also feel like I have no idea what else I *could* do, you know?"

"I'm kinda jealous of that. That...freedom."

"Really?"

"Really."

She studies me for a moment before nodding. I think she can tell how much I mean it, even if she doesn't know exactly why I mean it. "Well, right back at you. Knowing what you want so clearly? That's...that's *everything.*"

Damn. I can barely imagine being in her shoes—no idea what to do with my life but open to all the possibilities. But despite her blissful freedom, she's jealous of me. My life can't suck *that* much if she sees something enviable in it, even if she doesn't know the whole story. I've been trying so hard to forget about my obligations back home so I can enjoy my time here, and for the first time since I got back to campus, that fantasy actually feels possible.

I lean in to ask Ginny what else she's interested in, but Professor Vargas calls our attention to resume group discussion. I turn my gaze to the professor and try to listen.

My fingers itch to flip back in my notebook and finish the sketch I'd begun last class. I want to capture the way Ginny furrows her brow when she's focused. I want to find a colored pencil that exactly matches the green of her eyes. I want to perfect her adorable dimples, making the right slightly deeper than the left, just like it is in real life. But I can't—not with the real-life Ginny barely two feet away. I have no idea how she'd react if she caught me mid-sketch. It's probably for the best, anyway. I draw cute girls all the time, but usually not the ones I actually become friends with. And after that surprisingly special conversation, I know I want to be Ginny's friend.

I draw a sandwich instead, trying to focus on how hungry I am instead of the urge to memorize her features. Maybe I can manifest mozzarella and tomato sandwiches in the dining hall if I draw them well enough.

Professor Vargas dismisses us fifteen minutes later. When

Ginny slings her packed bag over her shoulder, she turns to Mack and Lizzie.

"It was nice to meet y'all," she says, and they return the sentiment. She turns to go, but I stop her with a hand on her elbow.

"Wait, where are you headed?"

"Lunch, I guess."

"Come eat with us."

Mack and Lizzie nod. "Yeah!" Mack says. "I want to pick your brain on that Dickens book you were talking about."

Ginny's dimples make another appearance. "Sure, thanks. That sounds fun."

We all head toward the dining hall together. It occurs to me Ginny probably doesn't have many friends yet since it's only the second week of school. Maybe she can be part of our group. Given the way Mack enthusiastically echoed my invitation to lunch, it seems they like her, too.

We snag a table outside the dining hall and go inside to grab food. Lizzie and I head toward the display of sandwiches, while Ginny and Mack get in line for hot food.

"So..." Lizzie starts as I survey the sandwich options. Tragically, there is no mozzarella and tomato today.

"So?" I prompt Lizzie when she doesn't continue.

"So, what's going on? You have a crush on her, don't you?"

I forgot how easily Lizzie can tell what I'm feeling. I'm typically hard to read—or so I've been told an almost concerning number of times—but Lizzie has been an exception to that rule since the day we met.

It was only two days into orientation last year when I walked in on her crying in a bathroom in the basement of the arts building. There was a talk about clubs and activities we were supposed to attend, but instead we sat on the cold tile floor together and I comforted her while she unloaded her fears about living up to her parents' insanely high expectations. In minutes, I felt like I knew her—probably because I related to her *eldest child overwhelmed by parental pressure to excel in college* story at every turn.

After fifteen minutes, I hadn't said a word about myself, but she looked me in the eyes and said, "You know exactly what I'm talking about, don't you?" Her confidence told me it was more than a random guess. She'd seen something I had no idea I was showing.

I should have known Lizzie would notice my attraction to Ginny, but I can't pass up the opportunity to tease her a little bit.

I shrug at her knowing smirk.

"Whoever could you be talking about?"

She scoffs. "Don't pretend you don't know I mean Ginny."

"Fine. I know you mean Ginny." I hesitate to agree completely, because I know Lizzie will take me having a crush way too seriously. She loves the idea of seeing me in a serious relationship for the first time, so I need to stay nonchalant to keep her from hounding me. "I don't know if I'd say I have a *crush* on her, but…I mean, she's cute, right?"

"She's definitely cute. And…" She waits expectantly until I give in.

"And nice. And funny."

"Hmm." Lizzie raises her eyebrows at me. She is not subtle whatsoever. She may as well ask me if I *like-like* Ginny and send us all the way back to middle school.

"Oh, shut up." I shove her lightly and she almost drops the sandwich she's putting on her plate. "I want to be her friend."

"And hook up with her." Good. As long as Lizzie's staying away from the romance idea, I don't need to worry.

"Well, yeah. Have you seen her dimples?"

"I have." She sighs wistfully as we maneuver back outside. I can always trust Lizzie to drool over hot girls with me.

"But I really do want to be her friend, too."

"So, what's the order of priorities there? Hookup then friendship, or the other way around?"

"Friendship first, definitely."

We put our food on our table. Ginny and Mack haven't

arrived yet, so Lizzie continues her line of questioning. "Do you even know if she's queer?"

"She's bi."

Lizzie laughs. "How long did you wait before asking her *that*?"

"I didn't ask. That would be rude. She offered. After I not so subtly mentioned being a lesbian."

"Of course you did." She holds my gaze, a sincere smile on her face. "You know…I missed you this summer."

A twinge of guilt pricks me. I wasn't great at keeping in touch with my friends over the break, especially Lizzie. I didn't know how to respond to all the *how are you* texts when I didn't have anything remotely fun or interesting to share. We talked about her loving but deeply overbearing parents, her exhausting summer internship, and her brief interactions with her high school ex. But I froze every time she asked about me. I didn't want to wallow in self-pity or bring down her stellar summer with my shitty one. I couldn't tell her the truth. *I dissociated through a day of work with my mom, tried to draw but didn't feel inspired, then binge-watched TV on my laptop alone in my room.* So instead, I gave her bland, diluted updates, and our conversations got shorter and more sporadic as the break went on.

"I missed you too, Liz. And I…I know I'm not the best at keeping up with texts and everything. I'm sorry about that."

She blinks at me, sandwich halfway into her mouth, then puts it back down and reaches out to squeeze my arm. "It's okay. I know you were busy. Working at your mom's store and… everything." I nod, but she's left an unspoken question between us. I wasn't too busy to talk about her life, and yet she doesn't know anything I did this summer beyond work.

Our friendship lives in this awkward, undefined limbo sometimes. There's a line I haven't crossed yet—a line I haven't wanted to cross. She's the closest person I have to a best friend, though I know I can't really call her that. Your best friend knows you, the good and the bad, and I still hate the idea of Lizzie seeing all the bad. I want to fix anything I damaged between us over the summer, but I'm not ready for that level of vulnerability.

I'll have to find another way to get our friendship back to where it was last year.

Whatever the hell that might be.

We eat in silence for a moment before she spots something over my shoulder and whispers, "Try not to stare too much."

I glance behind me to see Ginny and Mack approaching. Mack gestures animatedly as they discuss a book I've never heard of. I'm grateful for the reprieve from my conversation with Lizzie, especially when Ginny sits next to me. I can focus on how the tiny table means her leg keeps grazing mine instead of what a shitty friend I've been.

As we eat, our friends Beth and Rafael join us. I introduce them to Ginny and have that same feeling of sudden relief when they seem to get along. All my closest friends are here now—plus Ginny. Maybe she'll become one of my closest friends, too. I like that idea a lot.

Rafael says something that makes the rest of the table laugh, but I don't catch it.

Ginny catches my eye and gives me a *wasn't that so funny?* look. I laugh with her even though I have no idea what he said. She leans toward me and whispers, "Thanks for inviting me to have lunch with you and your friends."

"Of course." I match her intimate volume. "I'm really glad you came." She smiles, and I do my best to not stare at her dimples.

I wonder if that stereotype about lesbians staying friends with their exes is true. So many things like that are stupid generalizations, and yet I'm a lesbian who loves flannel. Lizzie's a lesbian who hates flannel but owns a Subaru Outback. I know some queer people who had crazy dramatic breakups and can't stand to be in the same room with their exes now. But my best friend from high school still video chats once a week with a girl she dated for our entire sophomore year. I'm sure Ginny and I could hook up once or twice and still be friends. Now I just have to find out if she'd be interested.

Laughter resounds around the table and pulls me back into the conversation.

"—and he just keeps talking and talking and talking, so we're all looking around at each other like, is this guy for real. Even the professor—"

Everyone is captivated by Mack's story, but I've missed too much to understand.

My friends are bound to notice if I keep spacing out. Lizzie probably already has. Ginny helped me get out of my head for a moment earlier. I need to hold on to that feeling and not get trapped in anxiety about what each interaction with her might mean. Whatever happens with Ginny, it's supposed to be fun. Casual. Easy.

"It's only been two classes, and I already want to explode every time he talks. He is the most annoying literature bro I've ever encountered, and that's saying a lot at this school."

I can only assume they are talking about the philosophy-obsessed guy in our lit class.

I lean forward and catch Mack's eye. "What about that guy who wouldn't stop talking about Hemingway in your feminist lit class last year? I wasn't even there, and I remember every insufferable thing he said."

Mack throws their head back and groans. "Oh, God, Nat, Hemingway dude! I can't believe I forgot about Hemingway dude. You're right. No one could be worse than him." They recount some anecdotes about their least favorite classmate to Ginny. We all listen, rapt despite the fact that the rest of us have heard these stories multiple times before.

Ginny's shoulder shakes with laughter against mine, and I feel luckier than I have in months. I want to bottle the rush I get from the simple melody of her laugh.

CHAPTER FIVE

Ginny

Vermont in October is unbelievably beautiful. The endless rows of trees display their multicolored leaves like autumn's coat of arms. The backdrop of mountains in every direction paints such an idyllic pastoral picture, it's hard to believe it's real. Living here is like being inside a postcard, but everything is even more vibrant than you would imagine. Today—my first time in an apple orchard—takes my comprehension of Vermont's spectrum of beauty to new heights.

Nat texted me yesterday morning just as I was getting out of my final class for the week.

> *U up for apple picking w everyone tomorrow?*
> *Gotta take advantage of the weekends before*
> *it gets freezing*

I read the message about five times in a row before I confirmed.

I think it was the *with everyone* that made me nervous. That's something you say assuming the other person will know who you mean. Like I know all her friends. Like maybe I'm one of them.

As casual as this outing may be for Nat and her friends, the stakes feel impossibly high to me. This is the first time I've hung out with the whole group outside of the dining hall, where we all have to go anyway. Nat's invitation was a purposeful effort to include me, not just an offer of salvation for a first-year eating dinner alone.

I didn't have a ton of friends in high school. The friendships I did have were supportive and reliable, but not especially close. We were all quiet, reserved nerds. Good kids who listened to their parents and didn't ask too many questions. There was solidarity between us, but also an impermeable layer of restraint stopping us from forming genuine connections.

If I could have a real friend group here—not to mention a *queer* friend group—that would mean the world to me.

Today is like a friend group interview. They liked my resume, but now I have to impress if I really want to get in. I need to be interesting and funny. I need to be likeable, but not the restrained, demure, ultrafeminine type of likable I was raised to be. I need to be a young, artsy, queer genre of likable. I've been asking myself how to do that for twenty-four hours now, and I still have no idea.

We drove out this morning in two cars—Lizzie's and Mack's. I was squished in beside Nat, hyperaware of the heat of her body next to mine. Overwhelmed, I stayed quiet the whole ride. But now that we're here, walking toward the orchard of apple trees and appreciating the absurd amount of natural beauty in front of us, it's time to push myself and engage.

Nat wouldn't have asked me to come if she didn't want me here. Her friends have been nothing but nice and welcoming. None of them is insincere. I just need to remember that, and I'll be great.

We head into a cabin-like building that serves as a check-in and pick up little plastic bags for the apples.

"Ever done this before?" Beth asks as we go out into the orchard. She's the quietest of the group, excepting me. I want to know more about her.

"No. You?"

She shakes her head. "Lizzie, Nat, and Rafael met at orientation last year and went together their first weekend, but Mack and I didn't know them then."

I learned a few days ago that Beth and Mack are a couple. "How long have you and Mack been together?"

"Mack met everybody early on, but I didn't until I had a class with Rafael last term. Mack and I got together a couple months after that. So…it's been about six months, I guess."

"Y'all seem really close."

"Yeah, we are. *Now.* It was weird to enter a group like this once they already knew each other."

I cough out a laugh. "Yeah, I—I do get that, as shocking as that may be."

She smiles. "I thought you might. When I first met everyone, I was a sophomore and I had some friends, but I didn't feel like I'd found my people yet. I was so nervous. I mean, everyone was welcoming, of course, but also kinda intimidating."

"Yeah." I backtrack immediately. "Sorry, I—I don't mean that you are—"

She puts a hand on my arm. "It's okay, Ginny. I was just saying that the intimidation thing, you know, fades." She smiles gently.

"Thanks." I squeeze the hand on my arm. She asks me about my classes as we roam through the trees, sometimes as a pack, sometimes breaking apart into smaller groups. We find a section of the orchard that's far enough away from the main cabin to be deserted, and Lizzie gets a blanket from her tote bag. Most of us settle in, watching Mack try to climb a tree that's way too big for climbing. Nat runs over to a slightly smaller one and scales it like a graceful cat. She sits in the fork between two big branches and lets her feet dangle below her.

"See?" she yells over to them. "It's all about picking the right tree."

"But you're tall, Nat!"

"I am not that tall, Mack. I'm five-seven."

I'm a lowly five-three, so that sounds pretty tall to me.

Mack looks shocked. "Seriously? What the hell? I'm five-eight. Why do I think of you as taller than me?"

"Uh…I don't have a polite answer to that question."

Mack laughs. They abandon their tree-climbing endeavor and turn toward the rest of us. "Well, you can enjoy your tree, Nat. I'll be over here with the doughnuts."

Nat's head snaps over to Beth, who is indeed opening a giant bag of apple cider doughnuts. "You wait for me to climb a tree before you pull those out? Rude." She looks at the ground and slowly scooches forward. "How the hell did I get up here?"

Mack snorts and Lizzie groans. I send her a questioning look and she leans toward me.

"Nat isn't a big fan of heights. I knew she was gonna regret going up there sooner or later."

Natalie inches her way toward the edge of the branch she's on. She's not up high enough that she could hurt herself by jumping off, but I can see the fear on her face even from far away.

I hop up and jog over to her. "You okay up there?"

She catches my eye and smiles tremulously. "Uh, mostly."

"Can I help?"

"No, no. I know it'll be fine, I just need to psych myself up." I nod. *I get that.* "I like going up high places, but I don't love getting down."

"Now *that* sounds like a metaphor for something."

She laughs. "It probably is." She moves a little further toward the edge. "Fuck, I did not think this through."

I try to think of something reassuring that isn't too clichéd. "Well, I'm sure—Jesus!"

Nat lands on the ground, suddenly inches in front of me. She reaches for my shoulders to steady herself and I put a hand on each of her arms. My breath catches at her proximity.

"Wow." Her voice is shaky. She takes a deep breath in, then lets it out. I breathe with her and try not to seem too flustered by her closeness. "Well, that was a trip." She relaxes her arms, letting her hands skim down my arms before they drop to her sides.

"You okay?" I feel a little more in control as I push my glasses back up my nose.

"Yeah. Thanks."

"I wouldn't have guessed you don't like heights. You scaled that tree like it was nothing."

"I'm a girl of much confidence and weirdly common fears.

Heights, small spaces, spiders, needles." She squints. "Skunks…
bad Wi-Fi…end of list."

"Can skunks climb trees?"

"I sure as hell hope not. They definitely don't spring for
good Wi-Fi, though."

We laugh. I see her eyes dart over to the blanket where
everyone else sits. They're just far enough away it feels like
we're alone. I want to get to know everyone better, but now I
wish it was just the two of us. *Say something. Be flirty or friendly.
Just say something.*

She holds my gaze. My palms go clammy. *Say* anything,
Ginny.

Nat turns toward her friends. "We should head back."

Great. I was awkward instead of charming or funny or
anything remotely appealing.

"Thank you for coming to help me. Very gallant," Nat says.

"I did literally nothing but scream in your face when you
jumped down."

Nat laughs, shaking her head. "You provided moral support.
I appreciated it." She reaches out and squeezes my hand. I can't
think of anything to say, so I just nod.

We arrive back at the blanket and settle down for doughnuts.
Beth and Lizzie are telling a story about their science professor
mixing them up since they're both Elizabeth on class rosters.

"Thank fuck we both already used different nicknames,"
Lizzie says. "I refuse to go back to middle school and be Elizabeth
M again."

"I'm Elizabeth M, too, though," Beth says.

"Well, thank fuck for a lot of reasons, then."

I laugh. Lizzie and Beth share a look, then turn to me in
tandem.

"If you were Elizabeth, what nickname would you choose?"
Lizzie asks, and everybody looks at me expectantly.

"Why do I get the feeling this is a whole thing?"

"Because it is!" Beth laughs. "Currently the vote is one for
Beth, one for Lizzie, and one for no comment because Rafael is

too conflict averse to answer." She sends him a playful glare, and Lizzie boos loudly right in his ear.

"Oh, shut up," he says, shoving her away. "Or I'm gonna say Beth just to get back at you."

"I'm tempted to say Lizzie," I admit. "But ninety-nine percent because of Lizzie Bennet."

"That's a damn good reason," Mack says. "I don't care if it's unoriginal. She's one of the greatest literary characters of all time, and she deserves our recognition."

"It better be a good reason," Beth grumbles. "Otherwise, it would be your duty as my partner to vote for me."

"Of course." Mack kisses her cheek.

Mack and Beth are so damn cute. Wait. *Oh my God!* Mack and Beth. Mack-Beth. Macbeth.

"What are you thinking about over there?"

I look up to find Nat studying me, then turn to Mack and Beth. "You two have the best ship name ever."

Mack groans while everyone else laughs.

"Macbeth! Macbeth! Macbeth!" Nat, Rafael, and Lizzie chant in unison.

Mack shakes their head. "You're all idiots."

The chanting devolves into laughter.

"Mack thinks it's asking to be cursed," Beth says. "And *I'm* the drama student."

"Why would we want to align ourselves with a couple who killed a bunch of people, then died tragically?" Mack shudders. "Bad karma."

Beth just laughs and lays her head on their shoulder.

The conversation turns to debate about whether karma exists, then fate, then astrology. A lot of people at school seem to take astrology seriously. It's not something I've ever really understood. My aunt loves astrology, and I can't count the number of times I've heard my dad laugh at her when she talks about it.

"Virgo," I say, when Rafael asks my sign. Everyone nods like that means something they all understand. "I don't know much about this stuff, to be honest."

"Me neither," Nat assures me. "I know just enough to make the occasional unjustified judgment about someone." I laugh. "But they are right a weird amount of the time."

"That's exactly how I feel about the whole thing," Rafael says. "People identify with their signs just enough I feel like it must be real, but then someone will be the exact opposite of their sign and it's all just a big coincidence."

"You seem like a total Virgo, though, Ginny." Mack tilts their head as they study me.

Beth and Lizzie agree immediately.

"Thanks?" I can't tell if that's a good thing. "I think."

"Virgos are awesome," Nat says. "Creative. Loyal."

"Responsible and logical." Mack counts off the traits on their fingers.

"Hardworking too, I think," Lizzie adds. "Perfectionists."

Wow. I *am* all those things. Or that's how I see myself, at least. "Well, yeah. That all makes a weird amount of sense."

"See!" Rafael points at me. "That's exactly what I mean."

I'm caught off-guard—not only by how accurate that all was, but by how confident they were. They listed those traits like they knew I would identify with them. Like they know me. Today is less like an interview than I thought. Maybe I'm already in and all that's left to do is…be myself.

Mack pulls out a small portable speaker and selects a playlist on their phone. A MUNA song I love starts playing. I have this song saved on YouTube, since my parents pay for my Spotify account and my mom looks at my library periodically. I don't know if it's to bond with me or to check up on me, but I'm irrationally afraid she'll be able to tell how gay my taste in music is. That story would probably be an awkward overshare at this point. But I want to say something. I lean toward Mack and tap them on the shoulder.

"I love this song."

They grin and raise a hand for me to high-five. "Hell yeah! I could tell you have good taste." They ask me what music I listen to, and I tell them. It's a question I've never answered honestly before. The others join us, and everyone trades concert stories, but no one blinks an eye when I say I haven't been to one.

Something loosens inside me from nothing more than this simple conversation. I haven't felt this calm since I got here… since long before I got here.

Huh. So, this is what I've been missing.

CHAPTER SIX

Natalie

I remind myself that today has just been a fun time with my friends, like I've had a million times before, but the utter specialness of it all stops me in my tracks.

This is what I've been wanting my time here to be. I want to have fun, make some kick-ass friends, and learn as much as I can before I have to go back to my reality at home. I have to take in and enjoy these days with my friends while I have them. The pressure of that sits on my chest and forces the air out of my body. It's like every two minutes someone kicks me square in the heart with *Have the best time ever right now or else!*

And I had a great time. Today was amazing. But now that we're driving back to campus together, the euphoria is quickly being replaced with dread.

This perfect day is about to end. Everything I look forward to ends up passing in the blink of an eye, and I never know how to keep the joy with me when it's over. I don't want to blink my way through days like these and be left back home in Brooklyn, eyes wide open but looking at nothing.

I hate that I'm obsessing about my life back home. I shouldn't feel this way when I'm here—in the place I spent the whole summer dying to see again.

Lizzie and Mack park right next to each other in the lot behind our dorms. As we walk back toward our rooms, I picture myself lying on my bed, staring at the ceiling, trying and failing to relive every good moment of the day. Then, next week, all I'll remember of today is being alone and feeling like shit, all the good stuff lost under a mountain of bad.

I want to cry.

No.

Just no.

Absolutely no goddamn way.

If I go back to my room alone, I'm going to break down completely. Plus, I probably won't be alone. My roommate Payton will be there and then I'll have cried in front of her, which I've flawlessly avoided doing since we were placed together last year. Whenever I've had a bad day, I've always been able to hold it in until I'm completely alone. But even though I haven't had a bad day, I don't think I can hold it in today. If I say good-bye to these wonderful people—even if it's only until dinner later tonight—I'm gonna lose it.

I sling an arm over Lizzie's shoulder and force a smile to my face.

"So, what are we doing now? Whose room are we going to?" I ask the group, but Lizzie checks her watch and shakes her head immediately. My heart sinks.

"I can't. I have so much work." Her gaze moves from her watch to me, and she frowns. "Are you okay?"

"What? Yeah, of course." The only thing worse than being alone would be guilting my friends into spending time with me. If Lizzie needs to work, I don't want to bother her with all my bullshit.

"You just seem…I don't know." She hesitates, and I brace myself, frightened by what she sees in my expression. "Sad."

Sad.

It's such a small word, but something about it disturbs me. I've never thought of myself as particularly sad before this summer, and the person I was then is the last person I want to be.

There's no reason for me to be sad today, and I don't want to dwell in it. I just want to move on already.

"I'm really okay." It's a lie, and I doubt Lizzie believes it, but it's all I've got. *Please don't push me, Liz. Not right now.*

"Okay, well…dinner at six thirty in the dining hall?"

A sigh of relief rushes from me before I can contain it. "Sure, sounds good." I find my phone. It's barely four. That's two and a half hours of alone time too many.

Thankfully, Lizzie's dorm is the first one we pass, so I only have to endure a minute or so of awkward silence between us. Once she says her good-byes to the group, I look around at the rest of my friends. I need to find someone who wants to hang out, or even just study together. Beth and Rafael are discussing an assignment for a class they're both in, Mack is on their phone, probably looking through their to-do list. Ginny is strolling a few feet ahead of me, her hands in the pockets of little red shorts I've been staring at all day.

I'm hesitant to ask her if she's free because the urge to cry is still pressing at the backs of my eyes. I don't want to cry in front of any of my friends, but if I break down in front of the girl I have a crush on, I'll never forget the embarrassment.

But then her green eyes lock with mine, and she smiles. Damn, those dimples are just unfair.

I take a few steps closer so we can walk in tandem.

"What are you up to now?" I hope I don't sound too desperate.

She shrugs and pushes her glasses up the bridge of her nose. "Not sure if this is still embarrassing here, but I'm kinda super ahead on my work for next week."

I laugh. I can already feel the pressure of tears subside. I lean into the release and joke with her. "It's not embarrassing. I mean, I'm incredibly jealous and I hate you just the tiniest bit, but it's definitely not embarrassing."

"It so would have been back home." Her voice is quiet, as if she's still embarrassed despite my assurances. "Still getting used to that."

"I'm getting that we grew up in very different situations."

She gives me a look and chuckles under her breath. "Definitely."

There's so much in that one word. I want to ask her about her home life, learn everything I can about what the little comments she's made about her family really mean. Maybe I can.

"So…wanna hang out?"

"Sure." I love when her accent comes out. "If you don't have too much work." She frowns, shaking her head. "God, that sounded super rude. I didn't mean to be, like, mom-ing you or something. I just mean if you feel like you have the time."

"I get what you mean, Ginny. And yes, I have the time." I absolutely have too much work, but I don't think I'd be able to get any of it done now anyway. That's tomorrow-Nat's problem, as it has been on just about every Sunday I've had in college, even though I have a shift for my work-study job for half of tomorrow.

"Your room?" I'm ninety percent sure I won't cry if we go there instead of my own room.

We say good-bye to everyone else outside Ginny's dorm. I relay the dinner plans Lizzie and I made, and we all hug way too much for people who will see each other again in a couple hours.

As she leads me up a flight of stairs and through the halls, I remember that I've been to her room before. Her roommate isn't there when we arrive, thankfully. That might be a bit strange. I'm not embarrassed—I've hooked up with too many girls on this campus to find running into one of them uncomfortable. But I'd like to be able to flirt with Ginny without any kind of awkwardness.

"This is a nice room." It really is. It's on the larger side for a dorm room, and two big windows let in tons of light. She seems a bit nervous to have me in her space, and I catch her glance at the pile of clothing on her roommate's unmade bed. I walk around, taking in the room and trying to think of a joke to put her at ease. "Much nicer in the daylight, too."

She snorts out a laugh. "Right. You've only seen it in the dead of night."

"The witching hour. The ideal time of day to hook up with someone you just met." She smiles but doesn't laugh. Maybe she's put off by the fact I slept with her roommate. "I hope that's not awkward for you. Your roommate seemed pretty chill, so I don't think she'd be too weirded out to see me here." She swiftly shakes her head and leans back to sit on her bed.

"Jess would be fine." I was hoping she'd mention her roommate's name so I wouldn't have to admit I don't remember it. "She's the definition of chill most of the time." She gestures to a cute purple armchair in the corner and to her desk chair. "You can sit wherever." She turns to look at the bed next to her. "Or here."

I choose next to her, obviously. I kick off my shoes so I can sit cross-legged on her bed, and she mirrors my position. She leans against the wall where it meets her bed, so I lean against it too, my knee bumping hers.

One of the posters hanging behind her head catches my eye. "Hey, you like *Wynonna Earp*?"

Her eyes light up. "Oh, yeah." She starts to say something more, stops, shrugs, and tries again. Her voice is quiet when she answers. "I love that show."

"Me too."

"Really?" She sounds surprised.

"Yeah, of course." I gesture to myself and pop an eyebrow at her. "What about my vibe makes you think I wouldn't love a super queer sci-fi show?" She laughs and I see her shoulders drop as the tension leaves her body.

"Sorry, just a reflex, I guess." I don't want to push, so I stay quiet, just watching her, and wait to see if she wants to say more on her own.

"I'm not really used to being around other queer people, to be honest. And I've gotten enough weird looks for mentioning some queer thing I like to be prepared for a bad reaction."

"That sucks." I lean over and give her hand the quickest squeeze. "I'm sorry."

She shrugs. "It's not too bad. So many people have it worse. This one guy in my grade came out sophomore year and his parents kicked him out. After that happened it was all just rumors. No one else came out the rest of my time there, and it was *not* a small school. Maybe there just weren't any other queer people in the entire place, but that seems unlikely."

"I bet it was rife with secret queers. Someday you'll go to

a reunion and the prom king will have a husband and the queen will have an undercut, two cats, tons of tragic stories about her ex-girlfriends, and...I've run out of stereotypes."

Ginny's eyes crinkle, she shakes her head, and she pushes her lips together like she's holding something in. "Forgiving the stereotype, I will not take that bet, but only because it feels like stealing." She lets out a small laugh, but it tapers off and leaves her frowning at her lap. She seems sad, which makes sense, I guess, given we're talking about all the homophobes she grew up around.

"I'm sorry, Ginny." I catch her eye for a moment before she stares at her hands in her lap. "I can't imagine living somewhere like that."

She just shrugs again. "It's fine. Like I said, I had it okay. I dated a guy for half of junior year, so there weren't any rumors about me. Or at least any I ever found out about, I guess. I..." She trails off, a contemplative look in her eye I wish I could understand. She glances at me, then away again. Her eyes settle on the tattoo on my ankle for a moment, then shift to a poster on the wall.

I don't want to push her, but I can't help myself this time. "What?"

She laughs lightly, still not looking me in the eye. It sounds hollow.

"It sounds totally stupid and awful, but...I was really just hoping it wouldn't come up. Maybe I'd fall in love with a guy, and we'd be together forever, and I'd just never have to deal with it." She closes her eyes. "Not that being queer is all about who you're with. I don't mean it like that. I just mean...that always felt easier. And I'm bi, not a lesbian, so it felt possible." She squeezes her eyes tighter and laughs self-deprecatingly. "God, that sounded even worse. I feel like I'm getting dangerously close to accidentally saying some bullshit that my parents have put in my head, but I totally don't mean. Who I like has never been a choice for me, obviously, but I hoped maybe it would never have to be a real part of my life."

Her eyes pop open and she makes a sound somewhere

between a groan and a laugh. "Jesus. I'm just getting worse. I just mean maybe I'd never actually have to come out there, because it's definitely not a place where it would go over well." She squeezes her eyes shut again. "I really hope that makes some kind of sense because I'm barely understanding myself."

I get what she means. I've had to unlearn my fair share of hetero bullshit and not let it take over the way I look at myself.

"It totally makes sense, Ginny."

She opens her eyes to squint at me. "Yeah?"

I smile and bump my knee into hers playfully. "Yeah, of course. I get what you mean. There are advantages to being able to blend in, but I also can't think of anything more soul-killing than having to hide yourself like that."

She nods now, and I can tell it's something she understands deep down in her bones. Now that we're talking about this in depth, I'm hoping she won't mind me asking some more personal questions.

"How long have you known you're bi?"

She holds my gaze this time. "Since I was thirteen."

"Does anyone back home know?"

She shakes her head. "No."

"Well…that sounds like a really long time to be hiding. And just because other people have it worse doesn't mean your shit isn't some serious shit."

She smiles shakily at me and nods. I lean in and lower my voice. "Blending in isn't easy just because no one notices."

"No. It's not."

I smile. She smiles. I watch the tiniest bit of a dimple appear and disappear on her cheek. I shift my eyes to the left to study the curve of her lips when she smiles. I want to capture that curve in a drawing later. I move my gaze back to her bright, magnetic eyes.

"I'm so happy I'm here now." Her low tone gives me goose bumps. I nod, though I'm not sure exactly what *here* she means. I'm happy to be here with her—my knee brushing hers, and her face barely a foot away from mine. "I never thought I'd get to live somewhere where being queer is so…normal, I guess."

"I've always lived around relatively queer spaces, but I get what you mean. It's special here." Sometimes I forget how rare places like this are, where you can be as obviously gay as you want, and no one bats an eye. I am unbelievably lucky to have never worried about finding queer safe places.

"Yeah, exactly. I get, like, queer imposter syndrome or something here sometimes. Like I'm not queer enough to be somewhere as rainbow filled as this."

An understanding hum slips from me. "I get that."

Her eyebrows tick up on her forehead, rising high above the rims of her glasses. "Really?"

I burst out laughing at the incredulity in her voice.

"Sorry, I—"

"No, no, it's okay. I know I'm practically a walking lesbian stereotype now. But my vibe was not always this obviously queer. I felt that imposter thing all the time in high school."

She smiles softly, her green eyes crinkling at the sides. "Good to know that that's something you can talk about in the past tense."

"It totally is."

Her eyes look back and forth between mine for a moment. "How long have you been out?"

"Since I was ten."

"Wow. Young."

I study her wide eyes. "Yeah. I feel like I basically always knew."

"And your family? How were they about it?"

"Fine. My mom's cool." I don't say how uncool the other side of my family has been. I don't want to talk about myself, and especially not about my dad. I like talking about Ginny. I like feeling this close with her, and that's going just fine so far without me having to share myself. That's hypocritical, given everything she's shared with me in the last few minutes, but this moment is too nice to ruin.

"That's awesome." She smiles. She opens her mouth to say something else, but I jump in first and push the conversation back to her.

"I'm sure you'll be able to talk about the imposter stuff in the past tense someday. At least mostly." I don't know how deep her issues about this go, but I do know some of it is too deep to ever go away fully. Her smile fades a bit.

"I think I'd have to change a lot about myself to feel that way."

"Like things you want to change, or things you feel like you *should* change?"

She shrugs. "Both, probably."

"What's something you've always wanted to change?"

She hums while she considers. "Hmm…My hair, I guess? I like the idea of shorter hair, but it's always kinda freaked me out. Not super short. Just like…" She demonstrates, putting her hand just above her shoulder. "Like here."

"Classic bisexual bob."

She bursts out laughing. "Yes! Exactly! God, why are so many clichés kinda true?"

"No idea, but they definitely kinda are." We laugh, and I lean in a little closer, soaking up the euphoria of sharing a joke with her. "You should totally go for it, Ginny. The haircut, I mean."

She shakes her head immediately. "No, I don't think so. I really shouldn't pay to get a haircut right now. I'll have to explain the money to my parents, and my mom will be all *come home and I'll cut it for you*, then she'll cut an inch off and call it a day."

"Get one from someone on campus, then. I know a few people who cut other students' hair for like twenty bucks or something." Ginny makes a small sound of acknowledgment, but I can tell she doesn't really mean to follow through. "Why not? What's holding you back?"

"I just…I mean, I know it will grow back, but cutting it feels so serious. Plus, I have no idea what I'd even say. *Cut my hair a little shorter and also a little queerer please*? I don't know."

"Find some looks online. Something you like."

"Yeah, maybe. That just feels so…"

"Imposter-y?"

She nods, giving me a half smile, half grimace. "Exactly."

"I don't think people just make up the haircut they want out of thin air. They see things they like, and they find something that works for them." She doesn't seem convinced, so I tap her knee with two knuckles, bringing her gaze to mine again. "Ginny, if you think I didn't google *how to Kristen Stewart Charlie's Angels hair*, then you're giving me way too much credit."

She bursts out laughing again and I laugh with her. The sound of her laugh is addictive. All I want to do is make her laugh and share a blissful moment with her.

"I'll have to find someone even half as hot to google, then." She studies my hair. I fight the urge to adjust it in some way. "Your hair really works for you, you know."

Hell yeah, it does. And she's exactly the person I want it to be working on.

Emboldened by her compliment, I brush a strand of her long brown hair behind her ear. "I really do like your hair, too, but, for what it's worth I think you'd look really hot with a bisexual bob."

She blushes but holds my gaze. "Well, then I'll definitely have to consider it."

She's flirting. We both are. There's no mistaking what's happening between us—chemistry. I could lean forward just a few inches and kiss her. It's probably the perfect moment. We're here alone on her bed talking about our queerness and complimenting each other's hair. I've never experienced a more obvious moment to make a move.

But my pulse pounds in my throat. I'm nervous—not an eager kind of nervous, but genuinely afraid. *Hell no.* I am never this nervous about kissing someone. Usually hooking up with a girl is a way to shut off my stress. I get lost in her and forget about the rest of the world.

But now the idea of kissing Ginny is like opening Pandora's box. She could reject me. She could want more than I can give her. I could ruin this fledgling friendship completely. I have no idea what will happen, but whatever it is, I'm not prepared for it. This is way, way too complicated. I'm looking for something fun and simple, not this tangled mess of feelings.

I just need to wait and try again another day. Sometime when we haven't just been discussing the kind of deep personal stuff that makes me feel soft inside. Sometime when I'm in full control of myself, confident, and sure of what we both want. Then I'll take her beautiful face in my hands, kiss her, and revel in that perfect moment without it feeling complicated.

CHAPTER SEVEN

Ginny

Crushes are not a new experience for me. I've had my fair share, usually on hot people I only knew from afar. Most of them didn't even know my name, and *none* of the girls were openly queer.

This thing with Nat is different, and I need a new word for it. I'm getting to know her, and now the feelings are deeper and more complex than a crush. I don't just have a crush on the way she looks, or the way she talks, or the way she messes with her hair. It's not based on quick observations and assumptions about who she might be. I have a crush on the way she looks at me, the way she talks to me, and all the little things about her that I didn't see at first. It's based on the real person I get to talk to every day. Crushes are simple, and this isn't simple anymore.

Which also means I can't idealize her so completely, like I tend to when I have a crush on someone. On that first day of Gothic Lit, I saw her in an easy, simple way. She was confident, happy, and settled in her own skin. That was it. But it was a two-dimensional point of view. I hadn't yet seen the way she dons that layer of bravado like armor, or the tireless effort she puts into her ever-positive aura.

It's clear to me now that she doesn't like to talk about herself in a serious way. I'm pretty sure I could bring up just about anything about myself and she'd listen intently, offering heartfelt advice. But sometimes it hits me how little I know about her inner life. She avoids questions about her family so easily I've basically stopped asking, and I don't think I've ever heard her admit to experiencing an emotion more negative than *fine*. There's always a point when I notice the distance between us. I sense her pull away from me or hold back somehow, and I question whether our connection is real.

So, I suppose a crush is all it is after all. I don't know what other feelings I could have for someone who refuses to be vulnerable with me. And yet it still seems like more than that. I know her in some indescribable yet important way...but also maybe not at all. I don't understand it.

One thing I know for sure. I'm kind of desperate for her to make a move on me. I'm fairly confident she likes me back, but for whatever reason, she hasn't acted on it. Over the last few weeks since that afternoon in my room, I've had multiple moments where I thought she was going to go for it—maybe kiss me, maybe ask me out—but she never has.

Theoretically, I could be the one to make the first move, but I'm too nervous to actually do it. I'm still afraid to discover I've completely misinterpreted the situation. It's possible that flirting is just one of her default modes. Plus, I've never kissed a girl, and I don't think I can muster the courage to dive in headfirst. Waiting for her to initiate may be cowardly, but for now it's the best I can do.

Our conversation about haircuts is stuck in my mind. I made an appointment at a salon in town but canceled it the next day. My mom would find out sooner or later, and I'd get endless questions from her about why I decided to cut off half my hair. She'd probably accept some kind of *because I wanted to* excuse, but I'm not sure I can make one without confessing more.

Yesterday I chatted with a girl in my psychology lecture who said she cuts hair for cheap prices and showed me some really cool photos of haircuts she's given. She gave me her phone number and told me to text her if I wanted. I'm sure she'd do a good job, but I'm still nervous.

But now I'm sitting on my bed, doing absolutely nothing on a Friday night, thinking about how much I've come to hate my super-long hair. I should just go for it.

I grab my phone off my desk but stop short at the sight of texts from my mom.

Missing you sweetheart!
Call me this weekend. I feel like
we haven't talked in ages!

She always manages to text me right as I'm about to do something she'd hate. And the text is so…nice. Actual conversations with my mom are rarely that nice. They're usually eighty percent gossip from her friends at church, fifteen percent criticisms veiled as suggestions, and five percent genuinely nice conversation. Her *just checking in* texts are not as innocent as they seem.

A lump forms in my throat. I hate how one unremarkable message from my mom makes me feel like I'm doing something wrong, even when she has no idea what I'm doing. I picture her disappointed face—brows scrunched, and lips pressed together. I hear her aggrieved huff that comes right before a lecture. I've spent so much of my life trying to avoid my mom's dissatisfaction.

I wasn't popular in high school, like she was.

"You spend too much time on your own, Virginia."

I broke up with Paul, my decent junior year boyfriend who she loved so much.

"He's such a nice boy, Virginia."

My taste in clothes isn't feminine enough for her.

"If you're going to wear overalls so often, you could at least let me teach you how to garden, Virginia."

Somehow, I'm none of the things she wants me to be. She disapproved of my decision to go to school here instead of her alma mater, University of Virginia, barely an hour from home. I'll disappoint her again if I cut my hair. She loves my hair—it looks just like hers. We share the same dark brown shade, and she's kept hers below her shoulders since she was a teenager.

But it's not her hair. It doesn't belong to her. *I* don't belong to her, despite the fact she and my dad pay for everything in my life.

Screw it. I'm not home. I'm never going to learn how to be myself if I don't try. I find my text chain with Nat and shoot her a quick message.

> *Seriously considering going*
> *for that bisexual bob.*

She responds in less than a minute.

YES!!! DO IT!!!! Can I come??

I anchor myself to Nat's encouragement. I can do this. I *want* to do this.

I text Abby, the haircut girl from my psych class, exchange a few messages with Nat about my haircut goals, and within five minutes it's all scheduled. For half an hour from now.

Wow. Well, it's probably better that I don't have too much time to get nervous and back out.

I text Abby some photos of cuts I like and head to Nat's room to pick her up.

She greets me with a tight hug and a loud whoop right in my ear. "I'm so excited for you!"

Nat warned me Mack and Beth were studying in her room when I texted and they asked to tag along, so they greet me with excitement as well. Even Nat's roommate, Payton, waves and sends me an encouraging smile. We walk to Abby's dorm as Mack talks about all the different haircuts they had when they were first figuring out their gender identity and expression.

"I've had so many hairstyles." They marvel as if they've surprised themself. "When I list them all out like this, it's like *damn*. I'm not old enough to have had so many. I've probably had more hairstyles than…I don't know…" They glance at themself, looking for an end to that comparison. "All the jackets I've ever owned."

"Is that possible?" Nat asks.

"Well, that's because you don't wear enough jackets," Beth says.

Mack nods.

"That's true. Damn, I really need to buy a good winter coat before it gets too cold."

"Like I've been telling you for months now. I don't know how you survived a Vermont winter last year."

"Ugh, I'm getting cold just thinking about it." Beth rolls her eyes as she laughs.

I turn to Mack. "Did you like them all, Mack? All your hairstyles, I mean."

"I swear I thought each one was my favorite when I had it."

I laugh, but I can tell they're serious. "Do you think you'll change this one soon?" I point to their closely cropped dark green hair.

"Probably. I dunno, though. I like it like this." They eye me for a moment. "You know hair grows back, right? 'Cause you look nervous."

"*Hair grows back* is the mantra today." Nat bumps her shoulder into mine.

"I get it, Ginny," Beth says. "There's always a moment right when I'm in the middle of getting a haircut where I'm like *What the fuck am I doing? I hate change.* But then it turns out fine."

"It will be fine." I'm trying to convince myself more than anyone else.

When we arrive at her room, Abby laughs at the excitement on my friends' faces.

"Ready to pack into a ridiculously tiny bathroom?"

She isn't kidding about how small the bathroom is, but no one seems to mind. She sets me up in a chair in front of the sink and drapes a garbage bag over me as if it were one of those silky salon capes. Abby apologizes for the less-than-fancy beauty shop.

"I'll try not to let it make me feel like garbage."

"You're *hot* garbage!" Nat is already laughing at her own joke.

"Thanks?"

"It was definitely a compliment."

I sit back so Abby can wash my hair in the sink. She asks me to remove my glasses, and Nat quickly steps toward me and offers to hold them. I slip them off and the world blurs. My friends become fuzzy blobs. I'm half-blind with my head at the mercy of a girl I've talked to twice. My mother would be horrified.

"Can I ask you a question about undercut upkeep?" Blurry Beth lifts her hair to show Abby the closely shaved section of the back of her head.

Between pieces of undercut advice, Abby asks me to sit up so she can begin cutting. I flinch at the first snip of the scissors. I listen to Mack's jokes and Nat's comments about how great it will look, but the sound of my mom's voice in my head is louder. Mom would hate Beth's undercut. She would hate Nat and Mack's dyed hair. If I come home with hair like any of my friends' styles, my mom will never get over it.

Abby cuts and cuts. She tells me I'm getting rid of about a foot of hair, and I laugh like that isn't the scariest thing ever. This decision feels more cataclysmic by the second. My hair is at stake. I know hair isn't everything, but it's *something*. It makes a statement. It's a choice you make about who you are and who you're trying to be. I know that on some level, that's all bullshit and it's not nearly as important as people—especially women—are told it is. But right now, mid-haircut, it's absolutely everything.

Abby stops cutting and starts blow-drying. She stops and picks up the scissors again to cut a bit more. I stew in my anxiety, regretting this choice completely. Abby brushes and blow-dries, and then she's done. It's been either fifteen minutes or two hours, too long and too short and altogether too frightening. She tells me to check it out as my friends chatter about how good it looks. Nat returns my glasses. I slip them back on and immediately find her comforting brown eyes.

"You look amazing."

She would probably say that even if it was the worst thing she'd ever seen. I turn to look in the mirror.

Wow. It's…*short.*

I run a hand through it. Reality crashes in when I feel how little hair there is to run through. I barely believe I'm looking at

my own reflection and not some kind of funhouse mirror. It is…
really short.

"Do you like it?" Abby asks.

"Yeah!" I respond immediately, my innate politeness over-
riding my dread. "It—Wow, it's…" *So short.* "It's great. Thank
you."

"Of course! I'm so happy you like it."

I look back in the mirror, running my hand through it again,
shifting it. It *is* a lot easier to move around than it used to be, and
it has a lot more volume. People in hair commercials are always
talking about volume. I pay Abby and thank her profusely, and
we leave.

The moment we step outside the building, Nat turns to me.
"So, do you really like it?"

"I—Yeah. I think so. It's just so different. I don't know. I'm
not used to it enough to know if I like it yet."

"Well, I know it's not about what I think, but I love it." She
smiles.

It shouldn't be about what she thinks, but I cling to her good
opinion since I'm not yet sure what mine is.

Mack and Beth assure me they feel the same, reiterating how
much better I'll like it after I have some time to get used to it. We
drop them at Beth's dorm, then Nat offers to walk me home.

"Do I look like I'm gonna pass out or something?"

She laughs, shaking her head. "No, you just look a little
overwhelmed." She pauses, looking me over again. "You also
look great, but I can stop repeating that now."

I smile at her, hoping so hard that she means everything she
says. "There are worse things you could be repeating."

"Oh, I can definitely keep repeating. You look—"

"No, no." I laugh, waving her off. "No need for that."

"If there is a need, you can just let me know."

"Will do."

Her eyes crinkle as she smiles at me. She then looks toward
her feet, and we walk in silence for a moment. I match my pace
to hers.

"You don't have to like it, you know," she says abruptly.

"I know," I reply, though not liking it doesn't feel like a great option right now.

"I mean, just because me and Mack and Beth like it doesn't mean you couldn't hate it. You know that, obviously, but it's worth saying."

It definitely is. I know I have to focus more on my own opinion, but it's hard not to care more about hers...or my mom's.

"Thanks." We walk in silence for another minute. "What do I do if I don't like it?"

She shrugs, wincing. "Give it some time? It may grow on you, and it's going to grow back eventually anyway. Or you could make another change and cut it all off or something? There's a lot you could do."

I nod as we reach my building. "Well...thanks for coming with me."

"Of course. Thank you for letting me come with you." She hesitates, then brushes some of my hair behind my ear. "Do me a favor?" She looks into my eyes, waiting for permission.

"Sure. I mean, probably. If it's not crazy."

"Different is good, I think. But I also get feeling like different just totally sucks. So just give yourself a moment before you look in the mirror. Try to forget how different it is and see if you like it for what it is." She shrugs. "Maybe you'll hate it, I don't know." She ghosts her fingers over a strand of my hair. "Either way, I hope you know you can find something you like, Ginny."

I nod but I'm at a loss for words. *Kiss me. Please just kiss me.*

She drops her hand back to her side.

"Okay. Well...Good night."

"Good night, Nat."

She turns away and heads in the direction of her building. A pull in my chest tells me to follow, like it always does when I see her walk away. I go up to my room instead. Jess isn't here, which is typical for any night there's a party on campus, so I flop onto my bed and groan loudly at the universe. I've been assuming

Nat will make a move on me for a while now, but given how many times she's had the chance, I'm starting to think she's not planning to. Ever.

The obvious answer to this problem is to talk to her about it. I could walk up to her and ask "Hey, do you want to kiss me as much as I want to kiss you?" That sounds easy enough in theory. I know her enough to know she wouldn't laugh at me for being a dork. I trust her enough to believe our friendship would not be ruined if her answer was *no*.

Maybe I should just go for it. I know what Nat's looking for—a hookup, maybe a few. She's not looking for a relationship, and I think I could be okay with that. After all, I don't think I'm ready for a serious relationship yet. I barely have the confidence to flirt with Nat. So, a hookup or two makes more sense than a relationship. All I really know is I'd do pretty much anything to kiss her, to feel her mouth on mine, to hold her face in my hands and run my fingers through the softness of her hair— *Oh.*

Hair. I totally forgot. I laugh aloud to no one at all. Nat probably didn't mean that I should forget about my hair by lusting over her, but it did the trick.

I take a deep breath and approach the mirror. My hair is still short. Still surprising. I mess it around, moving it back and forth. I put it up in a little ponytail. I try it half up, half down. I turn away from the mirror, overwhelmed. I survey the posters I've hung on my walls and the knickknacks I've put on display. I've given my room more character in the weeks since I first arrived, making the space mine. My eyes settle on a tiny bisexual flag Nat drew on one of my notebooks with her fancy colored pencils.

Right. I'm here. I'm in Vermont, at this school with these people who don't look twice at someone with more piercings than I can count. I'm not at home, and my parents aren't going to pop out of my closet to question all the posters I never would have hung at home—or to judge my hair. I look back into the mirror and hold my own gaze. No one's in the closet here. My parents aren't going to jump out of a literal one, and I'm not in a metaphorical one. I tilt my head back and forth, watching my hair flop around. I watch myself start to smile. *Huh.* I've been obsessing over my mother's opinions, but if I forget about her for a moment, I can start to see my own.

My forehead thuds on the mirror and I close my eyes. What if I love it? What if it makes me feel more like myself than I've ever felt before? I have spent so much time trying to be someone my mother would approve of, but the only thing I have to show for it is a voice in my head telling me to reject the person I really am. I want to be myself. I do not want to be a faux replica of my mother, even if that means I'll disappoint her. There is a theoretical version of me where I feel purely like myself, and she probably looks a lot queerer than my mom can handle. I lift my head and open my eyes, staring right back at my reflection.

I don't want to be afraid to like myself anymore.

I flop back onto my bed, feeling like I'm about to laugh or cry or explode or something else I can't quite explain. I run my hands through my hair, feeling it for the first time without staring at it, without judging it. The door bangs and I bolt upright. Jess notices my hair.

"Hey, nice haircut."

"Thanks. It's, um…" I run my hand through it again and try to find a word for how different I feel. "A lot lighter, you know?"

She nods. "Yeah, totally."

I fall back on my bed with a sigh.

Everything feels lighter.

CHAPTER EIGHT

Natalie

I fucking love Halloween. It's been a crazy, awful, endlessly stressful Tuesday, but I still fucking love Halloween.

One of the dorms always holds a huge party on Halloween, no matter what day of the week it is, so we're all getting ready to head over there for some arguably irresponsible midweek partying. We're in Beth's room, since she's the only junior in our group and doesn't have a roommate.

I've been looking forward to this for weeks. On a trip to Goodwill in early September, I found an amazing faux fur coat, if you can look past a few questionable stains. I immediately decided to go for a classic 1950s ensemble for my Halloween costume, mostly due to my never-ending love for the movie *Carol*. I borrowed a dress from Lizzie, and Beth helped me find an adorable vintage hat in the drama department's costume room. She checked it out, saying it was for an acting class, and she assured me we won't get in any trouble as long as I keep it clean.

I loop a soft pink scarf around my neck, shrug into the fur coat, and fasten the hat to my hair. I put on some lipstick and check myself out in the mirror. I look exactly like I hoped I would: not as good as Cate Blanchett—because that's blasphemy—but classy, glamorous, and pretty damn hot for a mere mortal.

And yet I'm still thinking about the conversation I had with my favorite professor earlier today. Andre is extremely casual, so I don't think I've ever heard anyone call him Mr. Thompson.

He approached me after class to ask about my application for this term's Student Gallery. The visual arts department hosts a gallery of student work in the last week of every semester, and applications are due in less than two weeks. First-years can't submit, but it's already one of my favorite events on campus, even just as a viewer. At the end of Andre's life drawing course last term, he told me he was excited to see my first submission and encouraged me to start over the summer.

Now the summer is long over, and I don't have anything to submit. I tried to work while I was home, but I was hopelessly uninspired. I asked Andre about submitting a piece I finished last year, and he said it had to be something I've spent time on since the last Gallery. I have some half-done pieces from my classes this term, of course, but nothing I love enough to submit.

So, I had to tell him I don't have anything, and I don't know if I can pull something together in time. Andre is way too professional to show disappointment in me, but I know it must have been there. He still acted encouraging, of course, trying to give me ideas and assuring me that my submission can be a work in progress, but I know I let him down.

I let myself down, really. Working with Andre last term, I started to feel confident in my art for the first time in my life. He saw something special in my pieces and I started to believe I could be a real artist, but now I've proved us both wrong. I've had months to work on this and here I am, just ten days before the deadline, with absolutely nothing. I don't have it in me.

Maybe it doesn't even matter. It's not like my art is going to take me anywhere. The only place I'm going is right back home, so there's no point in trying to excel here.

No. I can't think like that. Not today. It's Halloween and I'm going to have a great time no matter what. I can't change the past, but I can have an awesome night and forget about all the depressing shit in my head today.

Tonight, I just need to dance with my friends and ignore the rest.

Rafael ties an intense orange scarf around his neck. It's atrocious yet perfect. I flash my biggest smile.

"Ready to have the best night ever?"

"Hell yeah." He returns my grin. He checks himself out in the mirror, then turns to me for inspection. "What do you think?" He strikes a couple poses and I pretend to consider his ensemble, but we both know he looks great. He and Lizzie are going as Fred and Velma from *Scooby-Doo* as if they were, to quote Rafael's own explanation, "Sexier, not white, and finally out of the closet." I couldn't have said it better myself.

"You look amazing. Hot without sacrificing accuracy."

"Yesss. You get me." He holds up a hand and I high-five him. He goes to pose for photos with Lizzie, and I look around the room, taking in everyone's costumes. Rafael and Lizzie look weirdly sexy for cartoon characters who were a beloved part of my childhood. Mack and Beth have cat ears and drawn-on whiskers, which Beth said was because they want to get a cat together, but I think is because neither of them is really that into dressing up. Ginny has paired denim overalls with a flowy white shirt to emulate Donna from *Mamma Mia!* A few nights ago, she told me and Lizzie she had no ideas for a costume, so we went through her closet. Lizzie came up with the winning idea after discovering Ginny owned overalls practically identical to Meryl Streep's in the movie.

Ginny sits on the window ledge, watching everyone take pictures of each other. I let myself stare. She seems happy. She's seemed that way more and more recently. She laughs at something I don't catch, shaking her head at our friends playfully and letting her hair fall into her eyes. *Beautiful.*

She catches me staring, then smiles and waves me over.

"You look so, so good," she says.

"So do you."

She rolls her eyes. "This was all in my closet anyway. It's a half-assed costume at best."

"Doesn't mean you don't look good."

"Well, then thanks." She holds my gaze for a moment, and I feel that pull between us that I've felt so many times before.

Maybe tonight we will finally hook up. I have been stalling for weeks, unsettled by how scared I was to kiss her in her room.

The timing wasn't right then. That's the only explanation that makes any sense. We were becoming friends, and everything was too new.

Tonight is completely different. Now our friendship is solid. We can dance together, get out of our heads, and then I can pull her aside and tell her what I want: *You know I'm not looking for a relationship, but I can't ignore our chemistry anymore. I don't want to do this if we can't stay friends, but I think we can.* That's simple enough. She'll either be interested or not, but I believe our friendship can survive it. Maybe tonight is our night.

"Everybody ready to go?" Lizzie gathers everyone's attention. We take a few group photos, then embark on the five-minute walk to the dorm that's hosting the party. The blaring music is audible five buildings away—loud enough to drown all the worries and regrets I don't know how to clear from my head. I've been waiting all day for this chance to release my stifled, restless energy. I'm going to dance, have a drink, and maybe at the end of the night I'll see if Ginny wants to go somewhere we can be alone.

I have my whole night planned. Now I just need to enjoy it.

The inside is so packed I'm almost surprised, even though these things are always dangerously crowded. Lizzie and Beth find a corner of a couch where they can people-watch and rate costumes until they want to dance. Ginny joins them. I shove my coat behind the couch—I really don't want someone to steal it, but there's no way I can dance in it—and pull Mack and Rafael into the middle of the throngs of people with me. They're always ready to dance, and that's what I need right now. We jump around like crazy, scream-singing along when we know the lyrics. I lose myself in the music.

Yes. This. This is what I needed.

I close my eyes and move with abandon. I'm not a dancer in the least, but I love this. There's no right or wrong or pressure to dance well. The only thing you have to do is surrender to the music and forget who's watching.

The song changes to one I don't know. I slow down a bit to catch my breath. I open my eyes. All around me there's the beautiful, stupid chaos of flailing limbs and grinding that maybe shouldn't be done in public. I spot Ginny, Lizzie, and Beth in the corner. They're chatting, laughing together, and watching everyone dance.

Ginny catches my gaze as she scans the dance floor. She smiles and waves, just like she did the day we met. Well, now I care a little how I look. I could try to pull out my sexiest dance moves, but I'm not really sure what those are. So, I just keep hopping around like an idiot, holding eye contact. She laughs. I beckon her out to the dance floor, but she shakes her head. I pout and she gives me a skeptical look. I keep pouting. *Yes, come dance with me, Ginny.* A couple dressed as Ross and Rachel who are ten percent dancing, ninety percent making out block my view.

Damn. I'm not going to push her if she really doesn't want to dance, but I'm disappointed. I turn away from the PDA couple and back toward Mack and Raf. I need to rethink my plan. We were supposed to dance and then I would pull her aside, but I'm off course already.

"Hey!" I look behind me. Ginny. She changed her mind. *Thank God.* I grab her hand before I can overthink. She holds on to mine tightly, without hesitation.

"Hey! You came!"

She smiles and nods, but I can tell she's nervous. She says something just a little too quietly for me to hear over the pounding music. I shake my head and take the excuse to lean in closer.

"I'm not much of a dancer," she repeat-shouts.

"Look around!" I yell back, gesturing around the room. "Pretty much everyone looks like an idiot."

She moves with me, but she's still hesitant. She mentioned on the way over that she never went to parties like this in high school, so I'm not surprised she seems unsure. I use our clasped hands to twirl her around, and she laughs but spins smoothly under my arm. I take her other hand as well, and she laces her fingers through mine easily.

The song changes again, this time to a Maggie Rogers song I love. Ginny relaxes even more as she bops along to the music.

She knows the song, too. We shout a few lyrics together. I keep a tight grip on both her hands and hope she won't let go. She doesn't.

I am so lucky every time I get to see her up close like this. I'm near enough to distinguish the striations in her eyes and spot the tiniest beauty mark next to her left eyebrow.

A slightly slower song starts, and our energetic hopping shifts into swaying.

This is the moment I've been waiting for since September. Her hands are in mine and her eyes are trained on me. I am loose, relaxed, and happy, and I bet she feels the same. I have to tell her now.

"You're—" Wait. I can't improvise here. I prepared what I was going to say for a reason. I don't want there to be any confusion between us.

"I want to be friends, but I can't stop thinking about how beautiful you are."

That's not it.

"I don't want anything to change between us, but please, please, please let me kiss you."

That is definitely not it.

"I…" Fuck. I can't remember. I have no idea what to say. I swallow, my throat dry and tight. I cannot believe I'm still nervous to do this.

"What were you saying?" Her brow is furrowed, head cocked to the side. Her swaying slows to a halt.

"I…" I've fucked this up completely. I found the perfect, heady moment, and wrecked it immediately. My palms are sweaty. She's holding my hands. She must know how terrified I am. I pull my hands out of hers and she frowns. *Shit.* Everything I do makes this worse. I have to cover somehow.

"I'm gonna go get a drink." I need to get away from this moment. "Do you want something?"

She shakes her head. "Uh, no, I'm fine." She speaks just quietly enough that I have to read her lips. I point over to where Mack and Rafael are dancing together.

"Go join them and I'll be right back!"

She nods, but the furrow between her brows doesn't disappear. I push through the crowd as fast as I can and get in line for drinks.

I shouldn't be anxious anymore, and yet my nerves are even stronger than they were a month ago. I haven't been scared to make a move on a girl since I was fifteen. But tonight, I practically wrote myself a script and I was still fumbling around without a clue.

I check my phone to distract myself. There are two texts from my mom from about an hour ago. I texted her this afternoon to ask if she could spare some money so I could get more supplies to work on my Student Gallery submission.

I'm sorry, but no.

Damn it. I knew it was a long shot, but I'm still disappointed. The second text just makes my heart sink further.

Call me tomorrow. What days are you back for Thanksgiving? Elliot just gave me 2 weeks' notice and I need to know what days you can cover if I haven't found someone new by then.

Great. My project is screwed because I was so exhausted from constantly working at the deli this summer, and now I have to work more hours over a barely four-day break. I guess that's always how it's going to be. Art will go on the back burner so I can focus on the store, until someday I've given up on it altogether. Might as well be today.

I can't do anything I want to do, even when there's nothing in my way.

I return to see Ginny, Mack, and Rafael all dancing together. Ginny looks like she's enjoying herself. Good. I'm not prepared to handle her questions about my haphazard behavior.

We all jump around in a group, and I try to lose myself in

the music like I did before, but it's not happening. I force myself to keep dancing. Maybe if I pretend to be having a great time for long enough, I'll start to believe it.

I still fucking love Halloween. I always will, and I'm not going to lose that.

But I fucking *hate* today.

CHAPTER NINE

Ginny

The student lounge hosts karaoke every other Saturday night. Lizzie and Mack are both completely obsessed with it, so we've been twice. Both times I've regretted not getting in on the fun with my friends, so I promised myself I'd at least consider it tonight. My karaoke aspirations are a good distraction. I'm going to focus on that tonight, not whatever's going on with Nat.

She seems off recently. Her smiles are a little more forced and her jokes flow a little less easily. I've asked her about it a few times, but she always reassures me so confidently I let it drop. Still, I know something's wrong.

I did not fully understand the term *mixed signals* until this last week. It's like she's here with me one minute and somewhere else the next. When she's here, she's *really* here. It's like nothing else is as important; like I'm the most interesting thing in the room. The intensity of her attention is exciting and overwhelming and intoxicating. Then it's gone so quickly I question whether it was really there in the first place. She smiles and nods if I ask her a question, and she'll laugh if I make a joke, but more than anything she seems detached.

I've been overly preoccupied worrying about her, and I need a night off. I need to have fun watching my friends make idiots of themselves and try to be in the moment with them.

The student lounge has a selection of snacks and appetizers for decent prices. After we find a table, Lizzie says she's going to get a couple orders of mozzarella sticks—the student lounge mozzarella sticks are truly unparalleled—and anyone who eats can pay her back. I offer to help carry them and we head to the counter together.

"Hey…" We're waiting for our food. I want to ask her if she knows what's going on with Nat. Everyone knows each other pretty well in the group, but it's clear that Nat's closer to Lizzie than anyone else. Lizzie raises an eyebrow in question when I don't immediately continue. "Can I ask you something? About Nat?"

"I mean, sure." She seems hesitant. "If it's not, like…I don't know. What's up?"

"Is everything okay with her? She seems a little off recently. Or maybe it's just me."

Lizzie shakes her head immediately. "No, no, it's not just you. She's definitely been kind of, um, withdrawn lately. I know she's been having some stuff with her mom, and she's not looking forward to Thanksgiving break."

I haven't heard Nat talk about any of that.

"I know she seems like the most carefree person on the planet a lot of the time, but Nat can be very existential. She takes everything so much more seriously than she says she does. For every word out of her mouth, there are fifty others being overanalyzed in her head. If that makes sense."

Wow. That actually makes a lot of sense. "Yeah, it does…I just…I haven't been sure if there's a good way to help. She never seems to want to talk about it."

"I wish I could tell you more about what's going on with her, but…"

Part of me wants to wait and see if she says more, but I worry I've asked for too much already. "Of course, Lizzie, I'm not trying to get you to, um, speak out of turn or—"

"No, I mean I don't know more. I've tried to talk to her about it, but I just get vague surface-level comments about her mom. The other night we talked for an hour about all this bullshit with my parents, then I asked her one question about her mom, and she completely shut down. Honestly, I really wish I knew more, too."

Poor Lizzie. We're in the same situation even though she's known Nat an entire year longer than I have.

"I'm sorry, Lizzie."

She waves off the apology. "Don't get me wrong, Nat's a good friend, she's just…she's kind of a fortress, you know?"

"Yeah, I do." The student working the register hands us our food, and we thank him. "Also, I hope the, um, stuff with your parents is okay."

She smiles at me as we weave through the busy room together. "Thanks. Everything's fine, they're just really intense about my grades. They have high expectations."

"Oh, well, I get that."

She chuckles. "I thought you might."

Rafael grabs Lizzie when we return to our table and tells her they're up next for karaoke.

I glance at Nat, who sits next to me. She watches Lizzie and Rafael move toward the stage, but her brown eyes seem dull and distracted. When she glances away, her hair falls into her eyes and she doesn't fiddle with it. She pulls a foot up onto her chair and plays with one of the cuffs of her jeans, right next to her tattoo. She looks so…sad.

I should say something, even if it's completely mundane, just to try to bring her back into the conversation. I'm concerned by how quiet she is tonight—not even trying to engage. I bump her shoulder, and her gaze flies to mine. I hold up a mozzarella stick.

"Want one?"

"No thanks."

I try to think of something else to say, something that'll bring a smile to her face and light to her eyes, but my head is strangely empty. Usually we're all talking over each other, so much to say there's never enough time. The quiet is eerie.

I'm saved by Mack's and Beth's cheering when our friends take the stage. Rafael and Lizzie totally kill a Queen song the entire crowd of thirty or so students seems to know. It's kind of amazing to see all these people singing along with my friends. Lizzie has a great voice and Rafael absolutely doesn't, but everyone cheers along like it's a real concert.

This place really is a community. Home was a community, too, but one I never felt welcome in.

We clap and scream when they finish, and Rafael bows repeatedly like a dork. We congratulate them when they return to the table, then listen to them debate what they should sing next time. I glance at Nat. She's watching them with half a smile on her face, but she doesn't join the discussion.

Mack taps my wrist, and I look into their intense blue eyes.

"Beth refuses to help me choose between these songs," they tell me.

Beth snorts. "Because I don't know them! You'll ask me why I chose what, and I won't have a good answer."

Mack just shrugs. "Okay, I have a few options. I really wanna do 'Dancing Queen' but I did that two weeks ago. But, then again, it's kinda always the best choice. But I was thinking maybe some other ABBA? Or maybe 'What's Up?' but I'm not sure how many people know that, and I live to hear people sing along. Or—"

"4 Non Blondes?"

They nod so enthusiastically I worry for their neck. *That must hurt.*

"Yes! You know it?"

"Completely from *Sense8*, but yes, I love that song."

They grab my wrist. "You have to come sing with me! Seriously!"

I hesitate. I know karaoke isn't a competition, but I've never sung in front of people before, other than singing along to the hymns at church.

Nat's shoulder bumps into mine and I turn to her. "You should do it." She smiles encouragingly.

"No pressure, but yes, c'mon, let's do it!" Mack is practically jumping up and down in their seat. "If you want to. But also, pleeeeaaasssee!"

"It doesn't need to be amazing or anything, Ginny," Beth says. "We're all gonna scream our heads off for you no matter what."

"Wait, who's gonna sing?" Rafael tunes back in from his discussion with Lizzie.

Mack turns to me, waiting for my answer. "Me and Mack."

"Oh my God, yes!" Lizzie exclaims. "You're gonna kill it, I'm so excited."

Mack pulls me toward the stage before I can question the impulse. We sign up with the student running the karaoke machine. We're up next.

"Are you nervous?" Mack asks me quietly as we listen to the person on stage belt a Cher song in an uncanny impression.

"Uh, yes? Are you?"

"I feel like I should say yes, but no."

"No, no, knowing you're confident makes me feel better. If both of us were terrified, that would not be good."

They nod, looking back to the current singer, who's nearing the end of the song. When they finish, we cheer loudly along with the rest of the room.

"Any advice?" I ask Mack as we head over to grab mics.

They shrug. "Just have fun."

We take our places on the stage, waiting as the sound of guitar begins wafting from the speakers. I see a few people cheer, recognizing the song. I look to our table, where they're all standing and screaming, encouraging us. I lock eyes with Nat, and she smiles. She puts her hands on either side of her mouth and whoops loudly.

Mack is bopping their head along to the beat, so I follow their example, trying to get into the music. I turn to the screen displaying the lyrics, just in time for the first words to appear. We sing the first line together, and I keep my eyes on Mack, trying to sing at a normal volume. Mack sounds good and I'm pretty sure I'm doing okay, too.

I'm so glad Mack picked this song. It's so brilliant yet kind of ridiculous, easy to get lost in and sing with attitude without having to sound that good.

Mack and I scream-sing together when the chorus comes, and I hear people in the crowd singing along. I laugh, totally missing a line, but I don't care. Mack starts to jump around on the stage, and I jump with them, happy to just act like an idiot for a few minutes. We sway to the verse, *oohing* at the wrong moments half the time, but always getting in as much feeling as possible. We truly scream the last chorus, completely lost in it. Then we laugh our way through the ending. Mack pulls me into a hug as the song ends, and we rock back and forth there for a moment, laughing together.

"That was amazing!" They pull me offstage. "We should totally sing together again next time."

I nod, meaning it way more than I thought I would have. I wanted to push myself to do it, but I didn't think I'd love it as much as I did. Our friends clap when we arrive back at our table, whooping way too loudly, even for karaoke night.

I take in all of their smiling faces and— *Wait. Where's Nat?*

Rafael hugs me, and I glance over his shoulder, checking again. It's still true. Nat's not here. Lizzie tugs me into a hug as well, and I ask her where Nat went.

"She got a call from her mom just as your song started." Lizzie frowns. "She said she'd be back, but she took her stuff, so I'm not sure."

"Oh." I try not to let that bring me down from the joyful moment I'm in.

Lizzie squeezes my arm, a sympathetic half-smile on her face. Mack tugs on my arm and I turn to listen to them tell the group how they and I are going to be the next big karaoke duo, as if that's a real thing.

I wish I wasn't so disappointed Nat left. I wasn't singing for her. I was singing for me. I was singing for this moment— this moment of friendship, community, and disinhibition. I don't know if I've ever had a feeling like that before. But I also don't know if anyone's ever made my heart beat the way it does when Nat is nearby.

Mack asks a question I miss, so I ask them to repeat it. *No.* I'm not going quiet and losing the feeling of tonight just because

Nat's not here. I tune back into the conversation and find myself comforted by everyone's upbeat energy. Right. These are my friends. I may have found them through Nat, but they've become my friends. Her being gone doesn't make me an imposter.

And it's more than just them. Jess comes over to tell me how great Mack and I were. She's with a group of friends, a few I recognize, and they enthuse about our performance, too. A guy from my psychology lecture stops me to say he loved the song choice, even though we've never spoken before. I'm so happy to be here for so many reasons that go way beyond Nat. With or without her, these are my friends. This is my community.

I may finally be exactly where I'm supposed to be.

CHAPTER TEN

Natalie

I'm not a morning person, but I like to get up early once a week or so and eat breakfast alone when the dining hall isn't too busy. It's never that crowded before nine, mostly occupied by exhausted-looking students grabbing coffee before a morning class. I use the quiet time to find a table by a window and sketch in relative silence for a while.

Payton has class at eight thirty, so we walk to the dining hall together, but we have an unspoken agreement to split up once we get there. We get along well as roommates, though we owe a lot of that to the fact we know when to leave each other alone.

We get there at eight, two and a half hours before my class. I eat and stare out the window at one of the last trees on campus that still has leaves. I sketch it, then draw a few more trees at different stages, enjoying what I love without the pressure of an assignment or a time limit. When I finish, I check the time. It's nine thirty. I still have an hour. I would do anything for this peaceful sketching time.

I've been drawing so much the last week, but I'm not fulfilled or encouraged like I normally would be. Instead, I'm bitter because the sudden burst of inspiration came right after the Student Gallery deadline passed. I'm finally producing work I like, but I have no use for it. It'll live in my sketchbook forever, which I'm sure is some kind of overly clichéd metaphor for the rest of my life.

I am such an idiot. I neglected my art for months, even though there's nothing more important to me. I'm supposed to be using this time to do all the things I won't be able to do once school ends. Instead, I've been wasting time, brooding, and overthinking—just about the only things I know for a fact I can do back home.

A knock on the other side of the table startles me, and I look up into curious green eyes. Ginny.

"Hey." Her tone is quiet and hesitant. She holds a plate of scrambled eggs and toast.

"Hey."

"I—You seem busy. Sorry." She turns just as I realize she was probably waiting to see if I'd invite her to sit down.

"Wait!" I move some of my stuff off the table to make room. "Sit with me." She smiles tentatively and sits across from me. I came here to be alone, but I can't imagine turning down time with Ginny, even when she's offering to leave. We've seen each other tons recently, as always, but I can't remember the last time we were alone together.

She asks what I thought about *Dracula*, which we finished reading for today, and we talk for a minute. But it's stilted. It's my fault. I'm just not very talkative.

"You..." She pauses. "Is everything all right? You seem a little down." Her brow is so furrowed my fingers itch to smooth it. I hate that I'm the reason for her concern.

"Yeah, everything's fine." The lie feels unbearably wrong. "I—I mean, mostly."

"What's up?" She tilts her head.

"Just—do you know about the Student Gallery thing?" She nods. "I wanted to submit, but I couldn't, and I'm pissed about it." Now that I've begun, the words flow from my mouth. "Well, *couldn't* isn't the right word. I could have. But I didn't start early enough. You can only submit something if you've worked on it over the summer or during this term, and my summer was insane—or normal, I guess, but it *felt* insane, and I just let it fall by the wayside and then the term began, and I was so busy, and I kinda forgot all about it somehow and then the deadline passed, and it all felt like it happened really quickly, you know?" She nods again, but I'm already barreling on. "I'm just pissed at myself. So stupid, right? Like it didn't actually happen quickly. I had months. I don't understand how shit happens so slowly like that and you don't even notice, but I feel like that happens to me all the time. Like I only ever notice stuff once it's already happened, and then I'm stuck with it, you know?"

"I—I think so." She watches me with wide eyes.

Stop talking, Nat. I'm usually much better at keeping a lid on my stupid thoughts. "Sorry."

"No! No, don't be sorry. I do get it. It just took me a moment. I think you're being a little hard on yourself. Stuff like that—"

"Yeah." I don't agree. I just want to stop talking about this. She frowns and opens her mouth to say something else, but I keep going.

"So. *Dracula.* Where are you on vampires? Yes, or no? Despite my love for Kristen Stewart, she did not sell me on it. Maybe if she had been the vampire from the beginning. *Buffy,* though. That's my kind of vampire content. Have you seen *Buffy*?" She nods but seems dazed by the deluge of words coming from my mouth. "You're kind of a Willow, aren't you? She had the whole cute overalls thing going on, too." The comment lands weirdly. Ginny doesn't laugh or do her I'm-trying-not-to-blush smile.

Fuck. This is completely wrong. I'm forcing the kind of conversation that usually comes naturally to us. I panic and turn to my backpack. Maybe I'll notice I've forgotten something I need for class. I haven't, but the lie comes out anyway.

"Shit, I completely forgot my book. I should go grab it before class."

She knows I'm lying. She must know. We still have an hour before class, anyway, and my dorm is only five minutes away. But she nods as I pack and doesn't question me.

"See you soon," she says as I sling my bag over my shoulder.

"Yeah. See you soon." I rush out like the place is on fire. Tears push at the backs of my eyes, but I don't let them come.

Maybe I've fucked this up too, just like my Gallery

submission. I waited too long and now I've dug myself into a hole. I could have made a move a month ago and had exactly what I wanted. Now flirting with her isn't some light, easy thing. There's too much emotion there. I care about her too much.

I cannot believe I said all that to her. I didn't expect those honest words to flow so readily. Once I started, it was shockingly easy to keep going. And it actually felt *good*. I shouldn't have left so quickly. I should have given Ginny a chance to respond. Maybe it could have been better than good.

I stop short. I'm light-headed and nauseous. I sit at one of the outdoor tables next to a dorm. I close my eyes and try to take a deep breath, but my chest is too tight. I'm on the verge of a panic attack. My heart thumps as if I'm in danger. I'm not in a scary situation—or even a bad one—I just care about someone. I want to talk to her, share myself with her. That shouldn't be so terrifying that my fight-or-flight instincts kick in.

The bench across from me squeaks. I look up to see Rafael sitting across from me.

"Hey, I…" I don't know how to ask him to leave. I'm not sure I can say anything without crying.

"Take a deep breath, Nat." His voice is low and calm.

"I—What?"

"Just take a deep breath, okay?" His tone is quiet but sharp and leaves no room for argument. He inhales slowly and I follow.

In…Hold…Out…And again.

My pulse slows to a semi-normal speed. Rafael watches me and breathes with me.

"I, um, thanks. I…" I have no idea what to say. I'm not sure I understand why I panicked, so I definitely don't have the words to explain it to someone else.

Raf just smiles. "You seemed like you needed to take a breath."

"Yeah. I did."

"Cool. Me too, honestly."

Of course, I jump on the opportunity to not talk about myself. "What's up with you?"

"Uh…Isaiah and I hooked up last night."

"What? Seriously?" He and his ex have generally been on good terms since they split up, but I wouldn't have guessed that.

"Yeah."

"Wow. Are you happy about that?"

"I genuinely have no idea."

I nod. Raf and Isaiah were totally crazy about each other, but then their breakup was somewhat tumultuous. I don't really know why, exactly—just that Isaiah wasn't a great communicator. We all spent weeks helping Raf through the heartbreak, but I never talked to him about their breakup in detail. Rafael can be pretty private, so I didn't want to push him, but now I regret not asking him more about it.

"Want to talk about it?" I want to listen, and I'm decent at giving advice, as long as it's not to myself.

Rafael shakes his head. "I'm not really ready to process it yet."

I want to tell him he can talk to me about anything—because he totally can. But that's hypocritical since I don't feel like sharing with him right now. I don't feel like sharing, full stop.

It has to mean something that just ten minutes ago I did share—with Ginny. That must mean something.

"What about you?" Raf pulls me from my thoughts.

"What about me?"

"You want to talk about something?"

"I—" *Yes.* "No. Not right now. Thanks, though."

He nods, checks his watch, and then gets to his feet. He says he needs breakfast before his class, and I thank him again for sitting with me before we say our good-byes.

He was so...calm. Normal. He saw me panicking, but he didn't ask a million questions or stare at me like he'd never seen me before. I barely understand my own behavior, but he wasn't surprised at all. I think I'm good at pretending, but lately it seems like the only person I know how to fool is myself.

And I don't want to lie to myself. It doesn't help me. I never escape my problems. I just avoid them until they become too big and overwhelming to ignore. I can't keep doing this to myself.

Okay. So. *Truth.*

Being honest with Ginny was bliss and hell all at once. I was horrified and relieved by every word out of my mouth. I don't fully understand why vulnerability is so hard for me, but I know why I want to try with Ginny. Because it's not some little infatuation. I have to be able to admit that to myself, even if it terrifies me. *I'm crazy about Ginny.*

But that doesn't change the fact my emotions are completely uncontrollable lately. I have no idea what to do with all the anxiety and dread I've been trying to ignore. If I decide to dive headfirst into this thing with Ginny, I'll have to be okay with welcoming more out-of-control feelings into my life. I'll have to be completely honest with her and not lose my mind over how scared I am.

I don't know if I can do that. Even if it *is* what Ginny wants, I don't know if I can handle it.

CHAPTER ELEVEN

Ginny

I was kind of excited to come home at first. I'd never been away from Virginia for longer than a week before college. But the second I saw my parents at the airport, reality hit. *I won't be the person I am at school while I'm here. I won't be myself. I can't do it—maybe I'll never be able to.* I kept my sexuality to myself for years here for a reason. Still, even though I knew I wouldn't be able to be me, I didn't expect to feel quite so out of place.

My mother woke me up at eight thirty this morning, exuding frustration from every inch of her body, and asked me why I wasn't ready to leave. It took me a minute to realize what she was talking about. Sunday. Mass. At the same time and the same place it was for my entire life before college. I hadn't skipped it for anything less than a fever before Vermont. I'd forgotten, not only to set an alarm, but that Mass was a part of my life at all.

Religion has always been an obligation to me. The only connection I've had to it has been for my parents' sake. At school, I didn't miss church for a moment—the hymns, the dissociating, the endless concern about whether I seemed interested enough for my parents to believe I wanted to be there. I told my mom I had woken up earlier, thought it was Saturday, and went back to sleep.

She seemed to accept the lie, even though it barely made any sense. I'm not used to being a liar. I've always thought of myself as private, and perhaps a bit secretive, but not like I was purposefully deceptive. Now every move I make seems disingenuous, and every moment I spend here I feel more and more like an imposter. I forgot how much I worry here. How much I watch the things I say, how much I monitor the way I move, how much I temper the reactions I have to everything around me. I never realized how unhappy I am here, and I'm not sure how I missed it.

My parents have been so excited to see me, asking endless questions about school. I told them all about my classes and the campus, but quickly ran out of topics that felt safe. Luckily my extended family have been at the house a lot, so I've survived on the same few stories about my courses. I usually love Thanksgiving, but now I'm glad the break is almost over. Tonight, I'll be back in Vermont, and I can feel like myself again.

My phone buzzes with a text. It's a picture of Moose. Nat's cat sits on a case of her favorite colored pencils.

He REFUSES to let me draw

I smile and grab my phone, but another text comes through before I can respond.

How are you?

I've talked to Nat a couple times these last few days, and there's something different in her energy. She was more withdrawn than ever for the last week of school before the break. She's stopped flirting with me altogether. Maybe she's not into me like that anymore. Maybe she never was. She's different over text, though. Just a little more open. Her heart is nowhere near her sleeve, but she drops hints about how much she misses school and we've bonded over that. She still hasn't shared what makes her time at home so unpleasant, but I've learned more about how much she loves campus.

Just finished packing.
Flight isn't for hours but I hope to
manifest it coming sooner

She responds almost immediately.

An anti-delay. i will manifest with you

Thanks

I add a smiling emoji and she sends a heart one back.

A heart. People text those all the time, but it still affects me coming from Nat. I brush off the butterflies and ask her what she's up to. Two messages come through in quick succession.

Train leaves in a couple hours. I should pack
like u but also im trying to sketch
What time r u gonna get to campus? Theres
gonna be a back-from-vacation party in my
dorm starting at 10

I lie back on my bed.

Wow people really will throw a party
for any occasion, won't they?

Hell yeah

I check the timing on my flight.

Plane lands at 8ish
then have to take a bus to school
so not sure but prob 10-10:30

Awesome!! You should come by!! I would love
to see u

I've missed her more than I thought I would, but now I am almost nervous to see her. She asked me to come to the party, but I don't know what to expect from her tonight. Maybe Nat will be animated and flirty and we'll find our easy chemistry again. Or maybe she will stay subdued and distant, and I'll spend the party wondering if she ever liked me at all.

I tell her I'll be there, of course, because no matter what else I'm feeling, I'm always dying to see her.

Sure! Excited to see you too

Great

She punctuates that with another heart emoji. *Stupid heart emoji.* As much as I tell myself it's just friendly, I can't help reading it as something more.

My fingers tremble over the keyboard for a moment. Sending one back feels like admitting something. But it's normal. I have to remind myself it's normal. Beth ended our text conversation with one yesterday when we were talking about how much we hate going home. I responded to that one immediately, without hesitation. I push send.

Right. Normal.

Will she write back? She doesn't have to, I guess. That seemed like a natural end to the conversation. And yet, here I am, staring at my phone, waiting to see if typing bubbles will appear.

I'm startled by a knock on my door. I recognize the quick, sharp sound. It's my mom.

"Come in!" I sit up in my bed. She comes in smiling and closes the door behind her. She sits next to me and looks straight into my eyes. Oh God, I can already tell I'm going to hate this conversation.

"So, you're leaving tonight."

"Yes."

"We're going to miss you here, you know."

"I miss y'all, too." That's not a lie, exactly. I love my parents.

I miss them when I'm gone. Sometimes. But also, a once-a-week phone call is more than enough for me right now.

"I know I keep saying this…" She touches my hair, and I brace myself for her comment. "But I'm surprised every time I see your hair like this." She tucks some of it behind my ear with a frown.

"I like it like this, Mom." That's already way more assertive than I usually am with my mother, so I'm not surprised to see her eyes widen as if I've offended her.

"Of course, Virginia. I'm not saying I don't like it. I'm just surprised." I nod, as if saying she's surprised for the tenth time isn't basically the same as saying she doesn't like it. She must see something in my eyes because she continues. "I do like it. It's just an adjustment, you can understand that. But I promise, I like it. You look very pretty."

I cringe internally, but I'm sure the practiced façade I keep around my mom doesn't let it show. I usually don't mind feminine compliments, but coming from my mother I always feel boxed in.

"You had it up at the airport, and I was afraid it was much shorter, but it's nice like this." She was *afraid*—as if the idea of me with a bob is a sign of the apocalypse. I just nod because I don't have the energy to engage with her further.

"So…you've told us so much about school and your classes, but you haven't said much about your friends. I thought maybe you could use some girl talk."

"I'm fine," I assure her. "I mean I—I have friends. Good friends."

"Oh, I'm sure! Who wouldn't want to be friends with you?" She glances at my phone where it sits on the bedspread next to me. She reaches for it, and I have the urge to grab it before she can, but I stop myself. It's not like she knows my passcode.

She clicks the button once and my lock screen displays. It's a picture of me and my friends at the apple orchard. I see the picture through my mom's eyes for a moment. Mack and Nat's dyed hair and Beth's undercut are fifty times queerer than my medium-length bob. Lizzie and Rafael, both not white, when there were only six people of color in my entire high school class. Nat's arm around my shoulder in a way that could be completely friendly—or could be a sign of something else. For her, every aspect must be like a giant flashing sign that says *Danger.*

"I saw this yesterday after dinner. I just…" I hold my breath as I wait to hear what she says. "I don't know these people, Virginia. And I've always known the people in your life. I suppose that's just you getting older, but I'm still getting used to it. I just hope your new friends are good to you. Good people, good influences, who are worthy of being friends with someone as special as you."

Every supposed compliment makes me want to cry. She sees them as *the other* and me as *her.* She's never really learned that whole my-child-is-not-me thing that parents are supposed to learn. Maybe she never will. I just nod.

"They are. They're good people."

She taps my phone again and studies the photo in silence for a long moment. Then she looks toward my suitcase. It's fully packed, but still open.

"I should leave you to your packing, I suppose." She walks to the door but stops on the threshold. "I love you, Virginia."

"Love you too, Mom." My reply is automatic. She closes the door behind her, and I flop back on my bed. I'm both relieved and upset she didn't say something more clearly depreciative about my friends. If she had, then I might have stood up to her. I might have been honest.

I might have come out.

I don't have any more messages from Nat, but I do have a gif of running corgis from Jess. She doesn't go two days without texting me a cute animal-related meme or Instagram post, sometimes even when we're both in our room. There's also a text from Rafael inviting me to the party at Nat's dorm, since he lives there, too. These last few days have reminded me how grateful I am to have made such awesome friends. I've exchanged a few messages here and there with all of them, and it's been the only thing keeping me grounded while I've been here.

I'll be back soon. Back with people who get me and who I don't have to tiptoe around. Back to being myself again. Even though I haven't known them all that long, they probably know me better than anyone.

Especially Nat. In a way, she's my best friend. If there wasn't this whole other thing between us, fraught with chemistry and tension I don't know what to do with, it would be a pretty amazing friendship. Well, there would still be the fact that she doesn't open up to me, but it would be the *beginning* of an amazing friendship.

At this point, I think friendship is all it will ever be. Nat has given me so many mixed signals recently, she must not be interested in an actual romantic relationship. And despite what I've been telling myself, I don't want to just hook up with her. I thought maybe this new version of me—out and at least attempting to be proud—would be open to hooking up with someone without strings, but I was fooling myself. I'm a relationship person, no matter my sexuality.

And even if I was open to just a hookup, it's not worth it. Our friendship is too important. Having a close-knit group of friends means the world to me. I'm finally able to be myself, and I'm not going to risk that over something that could turn out to be nothing. Between our friendship and Nat's mercurial tendencies, there are more than enough reasons we are never going to happen.

On top of all that, I'm not really ready for a relationship, either. All the attention and perceptions that would come with having a girlfriend...I don't know if I could handle it. I'm not ready to come out to my parents or anyone here in Virginia. And as much as I hate to admit it, I'm still not quite used to being out to *myself*. Could I get over my own insecurities enough to really commit myself to a girl? Could I jump into a relationship without being completely consumed with fear about what other people think? Could I walk around outside, hold her hand, and not feel overwhelmingly self-conscious? I hope so, but I don't know.

It's time for me to be happy with what Nat and I have now and give up on our relationship growing into anything else.

CHAPTER TWELVE

Natalie

I'm so glad to be back. My dorm common room is full of people dancing, drinking, and catching up, and it is exactly what I need. Well, maybe it would be better to actually be doing some of the dancing and catching up, but I haven't gotten there yet. I'm still in a corner, watching everyone else and trying to force myself to act like I'm at a party. I guess it's less like *glad to be back* and more like *can't wait to finally feel like I'm back*. When I close my eyes, I'm still in my bedroom at home, depressed and lonely.

It was a strange break. I'd missed my mom and brother, and it was great to see them again, but only really on Thanksgiving itself. I had that one day of busting Noah's chops and teasing my mom about her dating life. But then I spent the next two days working long hours at the store and spent my nights alone in my bedroom, exhausted and numb.

I don't usually find my work at the deli so draining. It's an obligation, certainly, but also a second home, filled with employees and customers who have known me since I was born. Both my grandparents died when my mom was twenty-five, and she used the money they left her to start the deli. It was her first baby, before me and Noah, and I loved growing up amidst the blintzes and pastrami.

We were never particularly religious Jews—I rarely went to synagogue, other than for Hebrew school or my bat mitzvah. But Mom ensured that Noah and I were immersed in Jewish culture and didn't feel like outsiders because of it. The deli was our family, our community, and our temple.

My mom would love nothing more than for me and my brother to take over the store when she's older. I don't have to, technically, but I don't know how I could refuse. Mom has always been a superhero to me. She raised me and Noah with little help and made endless sacrifices. I owe everything I have and everything I am to my mother and that store.

And yet this morning I told my mom I was sick and couldn't work, just because another day behind the register felt interminable. I sat at my desk alone instead, trying and failing to draw until it was time to leave. On the train ride back to school, I thought about all the things I could have done with my time instead of wallowing in my room—sketch in Prospect Park or browse at the Brooklyn Flea—and tried desperately not to cry in public. I'm still there, in that doing-anything-I-can-not-to-cry place.

Then the front door opens, and I see Ginny.

Ginny, in her adorable puffy jacket and a beanie, pushing her glasses up the bridge of her nose as she looks around. I've been sipping a beer over the last hour, so I'm not nearly drunk enough for these tingles to be from the alcohol. It's just her. I missed her.

I push through the crowd of dancers and hug her. The force of it knocks her back a little and she laughs.

"Whoa! Hey there." She hugs me back. Beth and Mack are just behind her and I pull them into tight hugs as well. Mack laughs as we embrace.

"Wow, are you drunk already, or did you just miss us all that much?" Mack jokes. "You're a hugger when you're wasted."

Rafael and Lizzie come over, which saves me from having to answer Mack. *Yes.* I'm wired and overemotional from the alcohol, but mostly I missed them so much I'm falling apart.

There are hugs all around, and everyone chats about their trips home. My chest tightens as I look around at my friends. We're all together again. I'm so relieved. Tears prick at the back of my eyes.

No, no, no. Please no. Not now. I shouldn't be sad now. I'm exactly where I want to be, but the tears aren't going away. I try to choke them back, but it doesn't matter. I'm going to cry, and now all that matters is not doing it in the middle of a fucking party.

I run from the room, shoving my way through the crowded dance floor. I hear my friends calling behind me, but I just run faster. I can't have them see me like this. I just can't. I go down the hall to my room and shove the door open.

Payton isn't here. The second that sinks in, I let the tears flow—no matter how much I hate them. I lean against the wall, sink to the ground, and the empty beer can clatters to the floor.

There's a knock at my door. *Shit*. It's probably Lizzie.

"Not the bathroom!" I call out as clearly as I can. Hopefully she'll take the hint and leave me alone. But the door creaks open, and Ginny peers in. Her face falls. I try my best to wipe the tears from my face, even though I know she's already seen them.

"Hey…" She comes into the room and lets the door close behind her. I want to tell her to go away, but I can't manage the words. She sits next to me and places a soft, comforting hand on my back. "Come here." She pulls me into her arms. I rest my head on her shoulder, letting myself cry against her. She's so warm. Her arms are tight around me, but she strokes my back with a gentle touch.

I can't believe she's seeing me like this. I pull away, dashing the tears from my eyes again and trying to find anything to look at but her.

"I'm sorry. I shouldn't—"

"Don't be sorry."

I snap my mouth shut at the vehemence of her tone. I stare at the sliver of tattoo visible between my boot and the cuff of my jeans, just to focus on something other than how much I hate that she's seeing me cry.

"I—I just want to be here for you." Her tone softens, no longer harsh, but still insistent. "What's going on?"

A tear trickles down my cheek and lands on my knee—a tiny, darkened spot marring my jeans. More tears flood my eyes, and this time, words pour out with them.

"I hate going home. And I can't leave it behind. It's like I'm still there, still in my room, feeling so stuck I can't move. And I—I love home! Or I used to, I don't know. But I don't know how to accept that home is all I'll ever have. I don't want to work at the deli. I know I need to—my mom needs me to—and I was fine with that before I came to college. But now it's like I've seen this whole big world I could have if my life wasn't already planned for me. And when did that happen? Why didn't *I* ever get to say okay to it? Why had I already agreed to it before I even thought about it? And whatever, if that's my life, then that's my life, but then I just need to stop acting like an idiot and get over it already. I'm not gonna be an artist, I'm not gonna—"

"Nat—"

"I'm not! It's not gonna happen. But I'm here now. Doing everything I've always wanted to do with my life: going to art school, meeting all these awesome people, living in this perfect place that's everything I know I should love…and I'm still just thinking about the future. Thinking about what it'll be like when this is all over. Why can't I just live in the moment? Why is that so hard?"

"Hey, it's okay." Ginny tugs me into her arms again, and I hug her back tightly this time. "It is hard." Her voice is soft in my ear. "When you find somewhere that makes you feel safe and happy, the idea of losing that is terrifying." She eases me back and looks me in the eye. "I don't know much about the situation with your mom and the store, but you don't have to work there if you don't want to. From what you've told me about your mom, I can't imagine she would want that for you if it isn't what you want. I'm sure she wants you to be happy." The eye contact overwhelms me and I look away, but she ducks to keep my gaze on hers. "I'm sorry you've been feeling like that, Natalie." She moves some of my hair out of my face. "I'm sorry you've been feeling so alone. I'm here for you, you know. I've dumped my emotions on you more than once. I can't tell you how much I want to be able to do that for you when you need it."

I nod at her, words beyond me. This is amazing. She's amazing. I don't know what I feared she would say, but I'm still surprised by how wonderful she is when my walls are down. Retreating when I feel like shit may protect my friends, but it doesn't give them a chance to really be there for me.

"I mean, we're friends, right?" I nod immediately. "We don't have to pretend around each other."

The truth of that hits me square in the chest.

She's right. We don't. *I* don't. I've known that on some level for a while now, but feeling it is entirely different. I've been terrified that I wouldn't be able to be open, and that would mean the chance of a real relationship with her was unattainable. But maybe everything I want is right here in front of me.

She smiles at me softly and brushes my hair from my face. She's just inches away.

I close the distance and kiss her. I cradle her face in my hands like I've wanted to since I met her. *Finally.*

Then, she kisses me back. I feel her hands on me, one on my knee, the other on my shoulder. Something deep in me eases with relief. *She's kissing me back.*

I should say something. I should tell her I'm crazy about her. But the idea of pulling away seems impossible. I tug her closer, our legs tangling between us. I want to kneel, stand, bring her to the bed—anything that allows me to be even closer with her. I want to feel her against me from head to toe. I try to bring her even closer, but suddenly she pulls away. Her hands shoot off me and she darts out of reach.

The look on her face shocks me. She swallows, the muscles in her jaw tense, and the affectionate smile from moments ago is nowhere to be found. She blinks rapidly, eyes wide and dazed. She looks...terrified.

"Ginny..." I have no idea how to soothe her. She jumps up and slips out the door before I can say another word. I run down the hall after her. "Ginny!" She doesn't stop. I reach her just before the door to the common room. "Wait!"

She stops with her hand on the door but doesn't turn around. "I can't...I don't know how to deal with this, Nat." She opens the door, pushes her way through the dance floor, and leaves.

I stare after her and my eyes sting with tears again.

She can't...I mean...She must feel something. There's no way I've been reading everything wrong and she doesn't even like me. Or maybe I invented everything between us to make myself feel better.

Lizzie approaches, brow furrowed. I paste on a smile.

"Everything okay?"

I nod and laugh like the question is crazy. "Yeah, of course. Everything's fine." *There's absolutely no chance I'm in the middle of getting my heart broken for the first time.*

"Nat...Come on. You're not okay. What happened with you and Ginny?"

"Nothing."

"It wasn't—"

"It was nothing, Lizzie. Can you please just leave it alone?"

Her concerned scrutiny shifts into a glare. "Fine. Have it your way. The next time you look absolutely miserable I'll just keep my concern to myself."

"Wait, Liz—"

She walks away without another word. *Fuck.* Everyone is walking out on me tonight.

A girl from my sculpture class approaches me, and I force another smile. *Just smile. The hurricane of shit swirling in your head doesn't matter. You can smile through anything.*

"Hey, Nat."

"Hey, Carly, how are you?" I nod along intently as she talks about her break, but I barely hear a word she says.

"Do you want to dance?" She looks at me expectantly while I struggle for an answer. This is an awful idea. I'm in no state to dance with this girl.

But the alternative is so much worse. I don't want to go back to my room and sob over Ginny. If I stay out here, the pressure to seem normal will keep me from crying. I can dance, flirt, and pretend for just a little bit longer that I'm not torn to shreds inside.

Carly smiles at me. There's not a single sign on her face that she can tell how I really feel. If I can convince her I'm okay, maybe I can force myself to believe it, too.

CHAPTER THIRTEEN

Ginny

I run out to the lawn. I have no idea why. Instinct, maybe. I was so overwhelmed I could barely process what was happening.

That is how she kisses me? Really? I've been dying for her to kiss me for months now, and she finally does when she's messed up, drunk, and crying on the floor.

I walk toward my dorm. What am I supposed to think after all the mixed signals she's sent me? For all I know, she was so wasted she didn't know what she was doing. I only saw her with one beer, but the party had been going on for a while before I got there. Or maybe she just needed some comfort and would've kissed anyone who offered her sympathy.

I have never seen her like that before. Was that the realest version of her, or a whim she'll never act on again? I have no idea what's real.

Wait. I stop. I do know some of what's real. I know we had chemistry long before tonight. I know I like her so much it scares me. I know kissing me couldn't possibly mean nothing to her.

I've wanted her to kiss me for months, and I run away when she finally goes for it. I still don't know what the kiss means, or if I think we could have a relationship, but I'm not going to be the idiot who runs out because she was too scared to have a real conversation.

I turn back toward the door I ran out of just a couple minutes ago. I'm going to talk to Nat. I can be an adult about this.

I go inside and search the crowd. She probably went back to her room. I maneuver through the crowd in that direction.

Then I spot her.

She's…dancing. Practically grinding with some girl I don't know. She spins the girl around like she did with me when we danced together on Halloween. The girl falls into her, laughing, and Nat laughs with her. The girl leans in. The girl kisses Nat.

Nat smiles.

Are you fucking kidding me?

How? How could she experience the same moment I just experienced—that special, intimate, emotional moment—and move on from it in less than five minutes? I guess it wasn't very special for her.

The girl loops her arms around Nat's neck and whispers something in her ear. Then Nat's eyes lock on mine over the girl's shoulder. The smile falls from her face immediately.

Okay, now I'm going to let myself be too overwhelmed and run away. Screw being an adult. I rush out the door and onto the lawn just like before, but this time I hear the door open just moments after it closes behind me.

"Ginny!" I can hear her behind me.

What do I do? Make her chase me halfway across campus? We'll still have to have this conversation. I need to tell her to leave me alone. I turn to face her.

"I don't want to talk to you right now."

She stops just a few feet away from me. Her dark, sad eyes look nothing like they did when they were glittering at that girl less than a minute ago.

"You came back." Her voice is ragged and shaky. "Why did you come back?"

"What? I—I'm not doing this, Nat. I don't want to talk about this right now." I walk away from her quickly. *Please don't follow me again.*

"I'm crazy about you, Ginny. Totally, completely crazy about you." Her words stop me in my tracks. I have to turn around. I have to see if she's sincere. Her eyes are pleading, and she holds my gaze without hesitation. "I've liked you since we met. Since you introduced yourself as Ginny from Virginia and you waved at me and smiled your adorable, dimpled smile."

"That's not liking me, that's thinking I'm cute." It's not my best comeback, but it's all I can muster. She isn't deterred.

"I've had *feelings* for you since then. And every day I've spent with you, getting to know you, they've gotten stronger. I'm crazy about you. I'm—I've never felt this way before." It's the first time she's struggled to get out these amazing, impossible words, yet I still don't see hesitation in her eyes.

"You're drunk." She seems steadier with each passing moment, but I sling the excuse at her anyway. She shakes her head.

"No. I had one beer, that's it."

"You—" My voice breaks. My eyes mist. "You were dancing with that girl. You kissed her."

"I'm so sorry, Ginny. I never should have done that. I didn't really want to. I just didn't know what else to do with myself."

"It's not even about that! I don't care about you kissing her. Or—Well—No. Of course I care. But that's not what I'm angry about. Not really." I refocus on what's upsetting me more than anything else. "We had that conversation. That moment. You were open with me—really, truly open with me, like I've never seen you before. And then we kissed. You kissed me. That happened. That happened, and then you kissed her, too. Then you went off and enjoyed the party." I see her throat work as she swallows. "I don't understand that. I can't understand that. How could we share that moment and then you just forget about it and—"

She takes a step closer. "I didn't forget about it! It was all I was thinking about!"

"Then why were you acting like it didn't happen?"

She shakes her head and looks away from me for the first time since she followed me out here.

"I just..." She shoves her hands into her hair, and her knuckles turn white with the force of her grip. "I was overwhelmed, and I didn't understand why you ran away, and I'd had a drink, and I felt kind of fuzzy and—"

"You just said you're not drunk."

"I'm not! I swear. And I shouldn't make excuses, I'm sorry. Dancing with her—kissing her—I shouldn't have done that. I know how it must feel for you. It's just…" She squeezes her eyes shut and shakes her head.

Is that it? Is that all the honesty she can handle and now she's going to retreat again?

But then she takes a deep breath and opens her eyes.

"It's so easy for me to slip into pretending like that—so easy I don't even understand it. I hate it, honestly. It's not how I feel. But it's so much easier to pretend I'm having a great time. Does—does that make sense?"

I nod, picturing the I'm-having-the-best-time-ever look I've seen on her face so often, trying to count the number of times it seemed genuine.

"I've seen you do that before, I think. A lot."

"I know it's completely idiotic, but—"

"No, Nat, it's not. I mean, it makes sense in a weird way. I…I think I understand." I have made countless guesses about what could be going on in her head, but I don't think I realized how much she has been struggling.

A tentative smile forms on her face. She seems relieved.

I look away. I want to be relieved with her. And I am, in a way. I'm glad she wasn't able to forget about the moment we'd shared as if it was nothing. But her capriciousness tonight is hard to reconcile. She kissed me with so much emotion I could barely believe it, then two minutes later it was as if she was someone else entirely. Even if I understand some of her mixed signals better now, I'm not sure how to get past them. I'm not sure I trust her.

"Nat, I don't want to lie to you—"

"Me neither! I want us to be honest with each other, completely honest, finally." She moves closer as she speaks, but I step back and regain the distance.

"Wait. I don't want to lie to you, so I'm not gonna say I don't have feelings for you. I—I do. But this is an awful idea." I can't look at her. I don't want to see the effect I can have on her right now. "I've known you for months, and today is the first time you've actually been open with me about something important."

"I know, but—"

"I want to trust you, I do. But I can't open myself up to you like that. These last few weeks, you've been here one minute and gone the next. You're going through some shit right now, and I want to be there for you as a friend, but I can't do anything more than that."

"Please tell me you don't mean that."

"I do. Honestly, I don't think I'd be a good girlfriend right now anyway. I ran out on you, remember? I'm not ready for this. Neither of us are."

"Okay, well, couldn't we be not ready for it together?" Her mouth quirks in a tremulous half-smile, at odds with the fear in her eyes. "We don't have everything figured out, but who does? Isn't a relationship supposed to be work?"

I shake my head and force myself to keep eye contact with her while I speak.

"I'm sorry, Nat, but I just can't do it. I don't trust it." I look away again, unable to bear the disappointment on her face. Which just proves my point—I can barely make myself look her in the eye right now. She deserves honesty, even about the reasons I'm afraid to trust her. I owe it to her to voice my fears when she's being so open with me. "What if tomorrow you pull away from me again?"

"I won't." Her voice is clear and full of conviction, but I've heard that tone before. She may be resolved now, but who knows how she'll act in ten minutes.

"I wish I believed that." I stare at my feet, and we stand in silence for a long moment.

"Okay. I understand."

What did she say? I meet her gaze. "You do?" It's selfish and strange, but I'm disappointed she's backing down already.

She chokes out a sad little laugh and shrugs. "I guess? I mean, I don't agree with you, but yes, I think I understand where you're coming from. I don't know, honestly. I'm just trying to be an adult here." She sniffles and wipes away a tear. I fight the urge to comfort her. It's probably not fair to console her when I'm the reason she's crying. Then she nods abruptly. Her features harden, and she looks me directly in the eyes.

"I have to say one thing before you go. If you…If that—If you're okay with that."

"Okay…" I'm kind of afraid to hear whatever is turning the sadness in her eyes to determination.

"I don't want to pretend anymore. I *won't* pretend anymore, at least not with you." She takes a deep breath and lets it out slowly before she continues. "You can't do this right now. Okay. *Okay*. I can deal with that. And yes, I probably would be a shitty girlfriend. I constantly pretend I'm fine when I'm not, and I can basically only express my emotions in an emergency. But you… you feel like an emergency. How I feel about you feels like an emergency. I want to learn how to be a good girlfriend. I'd do anything to be yours."

A lump forms in my throat. A few weeks ago, I would have died to hear her say all that. Now I am entirely lost and uncertain.

"I—" I choke on my words, clear my throat, and try again. "I don't know what to say to all that."

"That's okay. I get it. I just couldn't let you leave this conversation with any ridiculous rom-com misunderstanding bullshit, where you think I don't really like you that much or I wouldn't be willing to try." She's just near enough I have to tilt my head to meet her eyes. "I want to make things work. I want us to be shitty girlfriends for a while until we figure out how to be good ones. And if you ever want that too, you can just let me know." She holds eye contact, dares me to break it first. "Okay?"

"Okay." It's the only possible answer. I've never adored someone as much as I adore her right now. Her resolve in this moment, even though it's so difficult for her, means everything to me. But I can't shake this feeling, like maybe I'll see her tomorrow and she'll pretend this conversation never happened. Like this moment—this beautiful, perfect moment—is just a blip of honesty before she puts all her walls right back up again. We stare at each other for another moment, then she nods one more time.

"Okay. Um...maybe I should leave it at that."

"I—Yeah." A startled laugh escapes me. "Definitely."

"Okay. Well, good night, Ginny."

"Good night." I turn in the direction of my dorm.

"See you in class tomorrow!" Her voice echoes after me.

Oh. Right. I'll see her in less than twelve hours, in a room full of people. I will have to act like a normal person—listen to the professor, make interesting comments, take notes—as if Natalie didn't just tell me the most beautiful things I've ever heard in my life.

This is why you don't fall for someone in your friend group. I'm not sure if I know how to be her friend after this. But our friend group means everything to me—her friendship in particular. One conversation can't change that. The fact that she means everything to me in a different way doesn't have to change that. I glance back and find her right where I left her, watching me.

Damn it. Well, friendship is what I just told her I want, so I better find a way to make this work. I can learn to live with the knowledge of her feelings for me. And the memory of the way she kissed me. The feeling of her hands in my hair...

Oh God. Why did that kiss have to be even better than I imagined?

CHAPTER FOURTEEN

Natalie

I woke this morning half lost in a dream I can't remember now. Memories of last night flooded in. Images of Ginny's eyes formed a collage in my head—narrowed and icy, wide and unblinking, red-rimmed and ablaze with emotion.

In a way, last night went horribly. I had this terrible, nightmarish moment—where I was as sad and defeated as I can ever remember feeling—when I saw all the pain and anger on Ginny's face after she spotted me with that girl. I felt like I'd fucked up everything forever.

I came out of that darkness quickly because I was desperate to know why she returned. I followed her, and she said the words I'd been terrified to hear. She doesn't want a relationship with me. But she doesn't hate me, like I feared she would. She has feelings for me, she said. She was hurt and angry, but the feelings are there. She still wants to know the real me.

She doesn't trust me. I can relate to that more than anyone. Sometimes I believe my own bullshit so much that I don't know what's real. But I want to change. I want to leave the pretenses behind so that we can both trust me. I want a relationship with her. Last night, that dream started to seem possible. So, despite the sting of rejection, hope blooms inside me. Ginny likes me back. I can choose to focus on that. We want the same things, and it's time for me to be brave enough to give them to her.

Payton took one look at me from her bed when I was packing

my bag for class earlier, and asked why I was so happy to be going to class on a Monday morning. I'm deciding to lean into that joy. I'm happy I have class with Ginny first thing this morning. I need to keep my intentions clear. I'm not going anywhere, and neither is the honesty I showed her last night.

I arrive in the classroom a few minutes early, instead of my usual barely on time, but Ginny's there first, as always. When I flop into the seat next to hers, she looks up with surprise in her wide green eyes.

"Hi." I smile at her.

"Hi." She stares at me, practically unblinking. I don't think she could look more startled if she tried. I lean in so I can whisper to her, and her eyes widen even further at my approach.

"You know we're still friends, right?"

She blinks and a frown forms on her face. "What?" I'm comforted by the fact that she seems genuinely confused by the question. "Of course."

"Just checking." I raise my palms briefly in surrender. "You could not look more shocked to see me sitting next to you, like I do every class, so I thought I'd check in and make sure we're on the same page."

"No, I'm not—No. Of course we are."

I nod, enjoying how flustered she is more than I should. She's so cute.

"Great. This is my new thing, you know. Being up-front and straightforward and all that fun stuff."

She finally laughs. "Good to know."

I grab my notebook and flip it open to a blank page. The urge to lose myself in a sketch is strong, but I don't want to waste any of this time with Ginny.

"So…" I can't think of anything to say that doesn't feel charged. "How was your night?"

The sound she makes in response is half surprised laugh and half groan.

"You realize that's an entirely crazy question to ask me, right?"

"You don't have to answer if you don't want to. Do you

mind if I do?" She shakes her head but narrows her eyes at me. "I had a super weird night, personally. It kind of sucked, because I acted like an idiot for half of it, but it ended up being really good. I was honest with you, and you didn't, like, laugh in my face or say you never wanted to talk to me again." Her eyebrows shoot up, but I bulldoze on. "Not that I really thought you would, but I still sort of did, you know? Basically, it was just really nice to be honest with you."

"That's…a lot of honesty when I've been awake for less than an hour."

I'm conflicted. I don't want to push, but I also need Ginny to know that last night's sincerity wasn't a one-time thing.

"Sorry…" I don't know what else to say.

Her face falls, and she sighs. She reaches out and I will her hand to grab mine, but it lands between us on my desk instead.

"Nat. You don't have to be sorry. I'm happy you're being honest with me, really. I just didn't realize we were gonna, like, actually talk about this. And I—I feel like I'm…" She lowers her voice. "Like I'm leading you on, or something." She takes a deep breath, and I brace myself for more rejection. "I like you, but I just don't…"

"Trust me." She nods, and her eyes stay trained on her desk. "And that's totally fine." Her brows knit together. Shit. "Not that I'm, like, happy about that. I realize that's how it just sounded, but I'm not." She seems even more confused by my attempt at clarification. I try again.

"I'm not happy that you don't trust me, but I get it, and I'm happy we're being honest with each other." She nods slowly, her eyes flicking back and forth between mine like I'm a puzzle she can't quite piece together. "And you're not leading me on. I'd like to think we understand each other now. You want to be friends, I want to be friends, and I also want the other stuff, if you do." I roll my eyes at myself. "And I'm gonna get better at not saying things like *the other stuff*. I mean the feelings stuff. The—"

"Yeah, I—I understand what you mean."

I nod and she nods back. The tension between us has returned in full force.

"So…how was your night?" I make a face, so she knows I'm joking. She laughs and shakes her head at me.

"Also weird. Super weird."

Ginny's gaze catches on something behind me. Mack approaches with a big smile on their face. They sit and immediately ask for details about our breaks. I listen as they and Ginny exchange stories about spending too much time with their parents, but I don't say much. I don't know how to talk about my break without ruining the vibe. I don't even want to think about my break, really. My fingers drift to my pencil. Maybe I should finish one of my sketches of Moose. Or— *No. Stop it.* I'm not going to disappear into my head. I need to be present and listen, even if I can't push myself to talk. I tune back in as Lizzie arrives.

She sits next to Mack, even though the open chair next to me was closer. *Shit.*

Lizzie recounts her chaotic family Thanksgiving. She avoids eye contact with me while she speaks. I was harsh with her last night, but she's angrier than I expected. Mack turns to me when Lizzie finishes her story.

"How about you, Nat? You didn't say much. Is NYC still awesome?" They lived in the city for a few years as a kid and never miss an opportunity to tell people how much they can't wait to move back. I'm tempted to just agree with Mack and push the topic to something else. It would be so, so easy—but Ginny is watching me.

"Uh, yeah…" I don't have a clue what's going to come out of my mouth next. "Um…Being in the city's always great. Being home was kinda um, overwhelming, though. A lot of work, and…I don't know…I missed it here."

Mack nods. Lizzie's eyebrows scrunch together as she studies me. Ginny smiles and I can sense her support.

"Yeah, me too. I missed it here a lot," she says.

"Same," Mack says.

Professor Vargas's arrival saves me from saying any more. I rub my sweaty palms on my jeans. I'm not used to hesitating and fumbling over my words like that. I'm usually pretty self-assured, but I guess that's only because I never put anything too deep on display. Now that I'm trying to be honest about my feelings, my confidence has evaporated.

❖

When class ends, we all walk toward the dining hall.

Ginny asks Mack what book they're writing their final essay about, so I take the opportunity to talk to Lizzie.

"Hey, I need to apologize to you—"

"Are you gonna tell me what happened with Ginny?"

I glance at Ginny, who walks just a few feet ahead of us with Mack. "I—What?"

"Are you going to tell me or not? Because I don't feel like talking to you if you're gonna tell me it was nothing again."

"She…" I lower my voice. "She's right there."

"Fine. Then I don't want to talk to you right now." She speeds up to join Mack and Ginny's conversation.

Fuck. She's really mad at me. It takes a lot to make Lizzie angry, but apparently, I've done more than enough. I'll have to talk to her later, in private.

I check my phone and find a missed call from my brother about ten minutes ago. I missed a call from him last night too, but I was too drained to return it. We text a decent amount, but he doesn't call very often, so a kernel of worry forms in my stomach. I stop my friends just as we're arriving at the dining hall and tell them to go ahead without me so I can call Noah. There's a grassy patch next to the building where there are a few tables. No one eats outside in the winter, so it's relatively private. The phone rings twice.

"Nat?" I can barely hear him over the din of talking and laughing in the background. He must be at lunch right now, too.

"Hey! I just saw I missed your call. Everything okay?"

"Yeah, I—One sec." He says something indistinct to whomever he's with, then the background noise slowly dies. "Sorry, just heading somewhere a little quieter."

"No worries." I hear movement on his end, then a sigh. I picture him on one of the benches just outside our high school's cafeteria.

"Okay, so, how are you, Nat?"

I narrow my eyes, even though I know he can't see me. There is no way that's the reason he called me in the middle of his school day. "I'm all right." I wait for him to say more, but he doesn't. "How are you?"

"Good, good. You know, realizing how much work I didn't do over the weekend." I laugh, but I'm still cautious about my little brother's intentions. "So, are you feeling any better?"

"Better?"

"Yeah." When I don't say anything, he clarifies. "Better than yesterday."

Right. I faked sick so I wouldn't have to work.

"Oh, oh, yeah. Much better."

He laughs, and I envision his dark hair swishing back and forth as he shakes his head at me, like he always does when I do something stupid. "Didn't you used to be a good liar? Or was that just all my younger sibling hero worship?"

"Is that what I taught you? Proficiency in the art of lying? I am an awful sister." He makes a noncommittal noise, and we laugh. "But yeah, you caught me. Mom is a sucker for the stomachache routine."

"I love that you think I don't know that." He clears his throat, and then his voice turns earnest. "So, that was all made up? Because you seemed a little…"

"What? Pale and vomity? Offense taken."

"No. I don't know. Kinda out of it." He pauses. "Sad," he adds in a soft voice.

My stomach drops. Well, of course he noticed. I was quiet and withdrawn all weekend, and Noah's always been observant. It wouldn't have taken a genius to realize I wasn't at my best.

"Yeah." My voice is hoarse and choked. I clear my throat. "Yeah. It's been a tough couple of weeks, I guess. I've been pretty out of it, like you said."

"That sucks."

An awkward half laugh trips out of me. I'm not used to receiving his...empathy, I guess.

"Yeah." I'm at a loss for anything more substantive to say.

"Anything you want to talk about?"

"Um..." Talking about how suffocated and sad I felt being home isn't fair to him. I don't yet have the words to fully explain why I felt that way, and I don't want him to think it had anything to do with him. I have the instinct to just say no, but then memories of last night return to me.

Maybe I can talk to Noah about Ginny.

"It's a lot of stuff, really." I don't want to lie, even if I'm not ready to talk to him about my issues with being home. "But, um...there's this girl."

"Ooh..." He reminds me of a middle schooler, teasing me about *like-liking* someone. "Do you have a *giiiirlfrieeend?*"

I laugh and shake my head at him. I bet he can picture it the same way I'm picturing him wiggle his eyebrows.

"I wish."

"What's her name?"

"Ginny."

"Wow. I don't think I've ever heard you talk about having a crush. I thought you were kind of a...what's the female version of a player?"

"Nothing not super sexist. Can't player be genderless?"

"Fine. I thought you were a player. Casanova. Lothario. Heartbreaker—"

"That's enough, thank you."

"You're very welcome."

"Well..." He's essentially right, despite how stupid all those terms are. "Yeah. I haven't had real feelings for someone in a while. Or ever, really. At least not like this."

"Does she like you back?"

"Yeah, she does. But we're friends, so it's complicated. She doesn't want to risk our friendship or make things weird in our friend group. And I..." I falter again on how much to share.

"And I've been kind of big on the mixed signals, so she's a little hesitant. Or more than a little."

"Hmm...is she hot?"

"That's really your first question?"

"It's like my third or fourth question."

"You're such a classic straight dude."

He scoffs. "Like you wouldn't ask the same thing if I was dating someone."

"We're not dating. And yes, she's hot."

"What does she look like?"

"Noah, I can't believe I'm saying this, but can we talk less about hot girls and more about feelings?"

"Wow, that would be a first for us, I think."

"I know." I'm self-conscious now. He's right that the only talking about girls we've ever done was to express mutual admiration for someone's hotness. "We don't have to talk about this at all, you know. I mean, I just—"

"No, of course I want to talk about this. I asked, didn't I?"

"I guess."

"Tell me more about her."

I tell him a little about how we met, though I omit the fact our first conversation was just after me having sex with her roommate. I talk about how funny she is, about how she makes the subtlest faces at me in class when someone makes a pretentious point and I have to force myself not to laugh too loudly. I tell him how safe and comfortable I feel with her. I give him a vague description of last night since I'm not ready to tell him all my shit. And yes, I mention her dimples and all-around nerdy-hot vibe.

"She's way too good for me, basically." I chuckle but I don't hear his laughter mix with mine.

"You know, Nat..." I brace myself. I'm much more used to my brother's teasing than his sincerity. "I bet you'll be a really great girlfriend."

I swallow, my throat suddenly tight. We may not be the closest siblings in the world, but Noah knows me as well as anyone.

"Really?"

"Totally. When you're serious about something, you commit yourself a hundred percent."

"Yeah, well…" My voice is gruff. "I hope you're right."

"I definitely am. You're ridiculously stubborn. If you commit to showing this girl you're serious, she'll get it eventually."

I smile at his confidence. "I can do eventually."

"Good." He huffs in my ear.

"What are you laughing about?"

"I'm not laughing, but yeah, you in this player-falls-head-over-heels-for-a-girl situation is pretty hilarious."

"Well, I'm glad you're enjoying yourself."

"Hell, yeah." He sighs. "I should go."

"Of course. Go eat lunch. I should too, actually."

"I'm really glad we talked about this, though."

"Me too." I'm surprised by how much I mean it, given how nervous I was at first. "I—thank you for asking, by the way. I really appreciate you calling to check up on me."

He scoffs again. "Of course. And keep me updated. I need to know about all your wooing."

"You're joking, but honestly, if you have any wooing ideas, let me know."

"Uh…I have no clue."

"Me neither. Damn. Do I really have the romantic maturity of a sixteen-year-old boy?"

"Is that news to you?" We laugh, and I suddenly wish I was home just to hug him for being such a good brother.

"Okay, well, I'll talk to you soon, Noah."

"Yeah. Bye, Nat."

"Bye." I hang up, the smile on my face so big it almost hurts.

CHAPTER FIFTEEN

Ginny

No matter how dedicated and prepared I am, college finals are a formidable amount of work. In the next week, I have to finish two essays and a creative writing assignment, plus prepare and give a twenty-minute presentation. Every student on campus seems to be in the same incredibly stressed-out position.

Rafael suggested we spend our entire Saturday, minus meals, in the library, so we can incentivize each other to focus and not procrastinate. His plan has mostly worked, though I can't count the number of times Beth has shushed Mack or Rafael has sent Nat a dirty look for sighing dramatically at her computer.

My biggest distraction is, of course, Nat. Not because of her giant sighs or the way she bops her head to the music playing in her earbuds, but simply the fact we're all in the same room together. Since her confession on the lawn, I've managed to regain some sense of normalcy when we're alone, but I can't seem to shake an awareness of her when we're with our friends. I worry if any of them have noticed the tension between us, or if they talk about us when we're absent.

On one hand, they'd be pretty obtuse to have gone all this time without noticing anything. We've never been that subtle about our flirting, and the way Nat looks at me sometimes is unmistakable. On the other hand, we still feel like a secret. I haven't told anyone what happened between us, and I don't think she has either.

Our connection is like a transient concept to me—just real enough I know it exists, but not real enough to be spoken aloud to anyone besides her. Occasionally, Nat pushes her feelings further into reality with an offhand comment about her newfound commitment to honesty, but mostly it seems like all these feelings only live inside our own heads.

The clock on my laptop reads 9:47 p.m., and a quick look around confirms we're all losing our drive. Mack is on their phone, Beth stares into space, and Nat now has her eyes closed as she moves her head to the music in her ears. Rafael is still working, but he's visibly frustrated. Lizzie heads back toward our group with papers she's just printed in her hand and a determined look on her face.

"Okay, we're done." Her tone leaves no space for argument. "We've been working all day, and the sanity levels in here are dangerously low." Everyone but Rafael agrees, since he has an essay due by midnight. We wish Raf good luck and head toward the door.

A girl near one of the printers waves as we pass. Nat and Lizzie wave back. Lizzie turns to Nat.

"She has such a crush on you, Nat."

Nat shoots Lizzie a look with her brows drawn low. I would love to say that the idea doesn't affect me, but I feel jealousy niggling in my brain all the same.

I glance back over my shoulder to see if I recognize the girl. She looks vaguely familiar, but maybe I've just seen her around campus. She could be a girl from my psych lecture, but—

Oof. I walk right into a desk, inducing the unbearably loud screech of wood scraping against wood.

"You okay there?" Concern and amusement mix in Nat's voice. Mack and Beth watch me from the door with confusion. I'd wonder too if one of them didn't turn left toward the exit, but instead walked straight into a piece of furniture.

"Yeah, sorry, just tired." Nat hums and nods with a half-restrained smile. We follow Mack, Beth, and Lizzie to the door, and Nat holds it open for me. My cheeks heat as I thank her. I love it when she does that.

"No problem," she murmurs, watching me walk just inches in front of her.

Once we're safely outside, Lizzie turns to Nat again. "Seriously, I think she's crazy about you."

I trip over my own feet, but Nat catches me by the shoulders.

"Whoa, there." She laughs and steadies me.

Mack squints at me. "Are you usually this clumsy and I've just never noticed?"

"Definitely, Mack. That's on you. I haven't tried to be subtle about it."

Everyone laughs but Lizzie.

"Honestly though, Nat. She's always looking at you." Nat stares at Lizzie with her mouth half-open, like she has no idea what to say. *What on earth is going on with them?*

"Are we still talking about this?" Beth asks.

"And who are we talking about?" I should probably ignore my curiosity, but I have to know who this girl is.

"Just a girl who lives in Lizzie's dorm," Nat explains. "Lizzie tried to set me up with her last term, but I thought she was done with that by now." Nat cuts her eyes in Lizzie's direction.

"I'm just saying, maybe you should go out with her. It's not like you're interested in anyone else." They stare at each other. Lizzie raises her eyebrows, like she's waiting for something. Nat's jaw clenches.

Beth deftly changes the subject, starting a debate about the merits of the vegan chicken tenders that the cafeteria served today. Mack and I follow her lead.

We pass Lizzie's dorm first, then Nat's, and soon it's just me, Mack, and Beth. They basically live together in Beth's room, which is in the building just past mine. We walk in silence for a minute, which is unusual for us.

"I was—"

"Hey, Ginny—"

Beth and I speak in unison, then insist the other goes first.

"No, you can—" She cuts herself off and shakes her head. "Actually, yes, I want to go first, because *what* is up with you and Nat?"

My mouth snaps shut. I was afraid this would happen. I open my mouth again, but I can't seem to find any words.

"We won't talk to her about it," Mack says.

Beth nods. "Of course not," she says.

"That's sweet, but…I don't know. Y'all have been friends for so long, I don't want to put anyone in a weird place or anything."

"You're not!" Beth seems almost offended. "We're your friends just as much as we are hers."

"Plus, we're dying for the gossip. C'mon, we can't keep living with all these questions."

I shake my head at Mack, unsure. I don't want to say anything that could cause awkwardness in our group, but I don't have anyone else to talk to about it.

"Well…how much do you know?" I keep my eyes trained on my feet as we walk.

"Know? Nothing. Guessed? Like six different universes worth of scenarios." Beth and I laugh at Mack's enthusiasm, and I try to let some of the tension slip from my shoulders.

"Honestly, there's kind of a lot going on, and also kind of nothing. We're not together or anything, but we do…like each other." I chuckle at the lack of surprise on either of their faces. "But you knew that, apparently."

"No offense if you're trying to be, like, really sneaky or something, but it's not that hard to figure out," Mack says.

Beth frowns at her partner. "Well, it was easy to figure out how Nat felt, because we know her so well, but it took longer with you."

"But you did figure it out." They both nod. I nod back. I'm not sure what to say now that it's clear they've given this a lot of thought already.

"Soooo…" Mack clicks their tongue. "Should we bet on when you're going to get together, or should Beth and I get a new hobby?"

"Mack!" Beth slaps their shoulder. "We haven't been betting. Just…guessing."

"Well, you may want to look for a new hobby either way,

I'm afraid. I don't think either of us is ready for a committed relationship, and..." It doesn't feel right telling them everything Nat said to me that night on the lawn, but they must know how shut down she can be. "It can be hard to trust she means what she says sometimes, you know?"

Mack frowns, shaking their head. "I know she's done a lot of hooking up or whatever, but Nat's basically the most loyal person I know. If she tells you she—"

"No, no, I don't mean it like that. I mean, she's so upbeat and positive and carefree all the time, sometimes I don't know if she's being honest. With herself or with me."

They both nod.

"Yeah," Mack says. "Wow. Huh. I get that more than I thought I would."

"So, is that...I mean..." Beth stammers. "Did you—"

"Are you the one who said you didn't want to go for it?" Mack looks to Beth. "That's what you're asking, right?"

Beth nods, affection practically palpable in the air as she looks at her partner.

"Are y'all gonna be pissed at me if I say yes?"

"No," Beth answers immediately.

"We may tell you you're a dope, but of course we won't be pissed."

Beth sighs. "We're not gonna call you a dope either, Ginny."

"Probably," Mack adds. Beth rolls her eyes.

"Well, at the risk of being called a dope—weird choice of insult, by the way—"

"It's loving," Mack explains.

"Yes. I'm the one who said no. Not just because of the honesty thing, though. I don't think either of us is ready to be someone's girlfriend." They both nod, but Mack squints at me in a curious way. "You're totally judging me."

"No! It makes sense."

"It definitely makes sense." Beth smiles at me. "But you're kinda regretting it a little bit, aren't you?"

"I—I mean, yeah, I guess. How could I not be? I think it's the right choice, but...I don't know."

"That makes even more sense, I think." Beth speaks softly. "Not knowing."

We've been in front of my dorm for a bit now, but they don't seem eager to leave.

"Is it weird being a couple within the group? I mean, were you ever worried it would make things weird?"

"Sure, when we first got together." Beth looks at Mack, and they nod. "I was nervous I'd always be more Mack's girlfriend than anyone's friend, but that faded."

Mack shrugs. "I didn't worry about that. At first, I was so freaked Beth might change her mind about wanting to be my girlfriend, I didn't have the space to be worried about anything else." Beth lays her head on Mack's shoulder, and Mack smiles at the top of her head.

The love between them is so clear—obvious as any visible thing. Nat and I must have some tiny version of that if other people have noticed us. Could I ever be at peace with it, like Mack and Beth so clearly are? I look back and forth between them—at the curiosity in Mack's blue eyes and the knowing smile on Beth's face—and my heart lurches with anxiety. It's been nice to talk, but their awareness of me and my feelings is suddenly oppressive.

"You can talk to us about whatever, you know," Beth says.

I nod again. I'm too in my own head to find the right words to say. They say good night without asking any more questions, and we part ways. When I get to my room, Jess asks if everything's okay. I must look as spacey as I feel. I assure her I'm fine but can't seem to convince myself of the same thing. My heart is beating abnormally fast from a short conversation with barely any detail.

I talked about my feelings for Nat. *We* talked about them. They're big enough that Beth and Mack noticed. They're noticeable enough that they're not just in my head. My feelings are real—concrete and perceptible.

What am I doing? In the back of my head, a voice—the one I know is more my mother's than my own, but still can't ignore—tells me I'm crazy for talking about my feelings for a girl, and stupid for having those feelings in the first place. I know it's wrong, but it's there.

Coming out gave me access to so much love and confidence I haven't felt before, but also to all the shame and self-loathing I have never wanted to face. I hope it will all be worth it—that I'll reach a place where the good outweighs the bad—but looking between the shame that's dwelled inside me for years and the pride I've developed over the last few months, I worry my pride doesn't have a very good chance of prevailing.

I want to be past all of this, finally at the part where I'm just out and I don't have complicated feelings about it anymore, but that's a myth—a fantasy I conceived to give myself the courage to come out in the first place.

Even if Nat can deliver all the openness and honesty she's promised me, I don't know if I will deserve it.

CHAPTER SIXTEEN

Natalie

The theme of the day is *doing shit I know I need to do but would really rather not be doing*. I already cannot wait for today to be over, and it's barely ten in the morning.

I'm on my way to Lizzie's room. It's been a week since our tense exchange at the post-Thanksgiving party. I thought she wanted space, but after all the weirdness last night—where she prodded me about that girl in her dorm I've met once—it's time to talk. Maybe I should have texted her first, but I'm here now. I knock on her door and try to ignore the knot in my stomach.

"Come in!" I step inside. Lizzie sits at her desk. At least her roommate isn't here. "Oh. Nat." She stands but doesn't approach me. I thought she would glare at me the moment I came in, but instead she seems quiet and uncertain.

"You look…way less angry than I was expecting."

She shrugs. "I was hoping I'd see you today. We should talk."

"Yeah. Or—well—really, I need to apologize about last weekend. I'm sorry, Lizzie. You were just trying to talk to me, and I was such an asshole. You were right. I had a bad moment with Ginny, and I didn't want to talk about it, but I should have just said so instead of being mean and dismissive. I really am sorry." She starts nodding before I've even finished speaking.

"I need to apologize, too. I provoked you in front of Ginny

yesterday, and that wasn't cool. I just…I know you like her, and it sucks to watch you do nothing about it and not be able to help because you refuse to talk to me about it. So, I don't know—I guess I wanted to push you and see what you'd do. It was childish. I'm sorry."

I shake my head. "You really don't have to apologize. Mostly you just made Ginny walk into a desk." She smiles, but it's easy to see she's still upset. "Liz, I'm really here to talk, okay? You can say whatever you need to. I want to understand why you're so angry with me."

Her brows shoot up in surprise. "Okay. Well…" She frowns. I don't know exactly what she wants to say, but I doubt I'm going to like it.

She studies me for a moment before she gives me a single, sharp nod.

"Nat, this term it's like you're half here and half on some other planet. You're a great friend when I need to talk about something. You listen, and you give advice, and you're supportive, but you completely disappear when I ask you anything even remotely personal. Sometimes it feels like you don't want me to be your friend at all. If you don't want to talk to me about a crush, then what the hell kind of friendship is this?"

Well, shit. I know I've kept walls between us, but when she puts it like that, I can see how much damage they've done. I can't keep holding back from her.

"I'm sorry, Lizzie. I know I haven't been open with you, but I never meant to hurt your feelings."

"I know you didn't."

"I want to tell you everything that's going on with Ginny. That is the kind of friendship I want this to be."

She smiles but shakes her head. "You say you want that, but are you actually gonna talk to me?"

"Yes, I promise. Right now, if you want."

"Seriously?"

"Seriously." I glance at her laptop and the stack of note cards on her desk. "Unless you need to work?"

"I have an essay due at midnight, an exam tomorrow

afternoon, and if you leave this room right now without telling me everything, I may kill you."

We laugh and I pull her into a hug. I've been missing so much by keeping Lizzie at arm's length. I want to salvage our friendship and finally let it grow. So I do what I should have done from the start, and I talk. The tension between us lessens with every word.

She teases me about sleeping with Ginny's roommate. She swoons over my retelling of my confession on the lawn. She hugs me when I tear up as I tell her about Ginny's rejection. I don't tell her every single thought I've had, but I tell her as much as I can manage, and it's a good start.

❖

The Student Gallery is held in a cavernous room that manages to feel both open and packed at the same time. It was built for student art shows and galleries, so it has distinct museum-like vibes. I've always found it grand and impressive, but I've never felt intimidated by it before today.

The Student Gallery is the second part of my day of doing shit I don't want to deal with. Both times I went last year, everyone's work filled me with inspiration and hope. I still feel that, but I'm also poisoned by guilt and disappointment in myself. I spent those last two Student Galleries thinking about how exciting it would be next year, when I could have my work displayed. Now it *is* next year, and I'm still just an observer. *Last-year-me* would be so pissed at *today-me*. She wouldn't understand how I got here, how I failed to do something she wanted so badly for no good reason. She'd think I was an idiot.

Ginny's hand lands on my shoulder. I turn to see her supportive smile.

Ginny is the only positive in this situation. I told her how terrified I am—how the only thing I want less than to come here and be filled with guilt is to miss it and add to my pile of regrets. She offered to come along for moral support.

"You okay?" She tilts her head in question. I nod, because

it's hard not to nod when she looks at me with so much concern. Then I shrug, because that's closer to the truth.

"Mostly." I don't have access to much more honesty than that at the moment. Not while we're in public at this event I've been dreading all week. Ginny doesn't push me on my weak half-answer to her question.

We stroll for a while, only trading the occasional comment about a piece. There's so much creativity and beauty around me, I don't possess the words to do it all justice. Maybe it's better to stay quiet.

Ginny compliments a stunning set of colorful oil paintings, and fear settles like a rock in my stomach. She asks what I think, and I agree they're beautiful, but don't say anything else. I could never create something as amazing as these paintings.

I'm struck by the inventiveness of a multimedia piece by a friend of mine, Emily. I would never think to do something so out-of-the-box. My cheeks heat with jealousy. Emily comes over when she sees us looking at her art. I smile, hug her, and pour out a litany of compliments, slipping into that eternally positive and enthusiastic version of myself. She asks if I have anything here, and I spout some lie about not having anything that worked with the time constraints. I sound like a self-important asshole, but she nods like my excuse makes perfect sense. I congratulate her again, laugh at a joke she makes that I don't really take in, and we walk away. I keep my I'm-having-the-time-of-my-life smile. The falseness of it is weirdly comforting.

Ginny is quieter as we make our way through the rest of the Gallery. She's probably disappointed in me after seeing me pretend like that. I'm disappointed in me.

"Hey, Nat! Ginny!" Raf calls us over. When we approach, he gestures to the small sculpture he's standing next to with a flourish. I look at the title card next to it.

Rafael Silva.

I cannot believe Rafael has a sculpture in the Student Gallery. I've never heard him say a word about art before.

"You—I didn't know you took art classes." I hope I sound surprised in a good way.

"I don't!" He laughs. "Well, I'm in a ceramics class this term, but it's my first one. I totally didn't expect this either, but I got really into this piece and then my professor said I should submit it." He shrugs like it's no big deal. I break eye contact so I don't glare at him.

It's not fair to him, but I'm not happy for him. I am pissed and jealous and unbelievably angry at myself. I'm a jerk. Rafael, who took one art class for fun, had the time and talent to get a piece in the Gallery. Visual art is my major, and I haven't done shit.

"Nat?" Raf and Ginny watch me. I've missed their conversation.

"Sorry, just looking at your piece…It's beautiful, Raf." It's all I have in me right now.

"Thanks!" He doesn't look upset, but I should have said more. I've taken classes on how to analyze and describe art. I am such a shitty friend.

"Where's yours?" He smiles at me expectantly, while Ginny's smile drops from her face.

"Oh, um—" *I'm an idiot and a failure and I didn't get myself together in time.* "I don't have anything this term." *Or any term, obviously, because this was my first chance and I wasted it.* "I didn't have a piece from this term I liked enough to submit."

"Gotcha." He nods, but he looks unsure, like he doesn't know what the appropriate reaction is. Ginny asks him a question about his piece, and I use the opportunity to take a deep, centering breath.

It may have been a bad idea to come here after all. I feel too shitty about myself to enjoy the art, and now I'm forcing myself to be nice about my friends' works. That's not the person I want to be.

I give Raf a hug, congratulate him again, and hope I've made up for my lack of glowing comments about his piece. He either doesn't notice my struggle to be nice and normal, or he lets me pretend.

And really, why would he notice? I'm doing everything I can to keep up the façade, and he knows nothing about how stupid I feel not having a piece in the show. I've never been open enough with him for him to notice something like that. We tell Rafael we're going to finish our route around the Gallery, and I glance at Ginny as we walk away.

She smiles at me, but she seems subdued. Of course she noticed how I was acting with Raf. I hope she isn't mad at me. I didn't know how to get through that conversation honestly. I would have been a much worse friend to Rafael if I looked at his piece and told him how sad I was about my own problems. But I committed to being honest with Ginny, and I don't know how she'll react to watching me put up a front again. And this time, she saw everything. She knows how anxious and sad I was coming here today, and she watched me slip a mask over my emotions. I feel uncomfortably exposed.

As we turn a corner into the final section of the Gallery, I see Andre chatting with an older art student I know by reputation only. She's practically famous among underclassmen for having two paintings hung in the entrance of the art building. I wonder if Andre saw something like that in me, something special and new, or if his support is just part of his job as a teacher.

He spots me and waves. I wave back. He says something to the art student, then walks toward me.

Oh, please no. I don't want to talk to him right now. I don't need any more reasons to feel guilty about not submitting to the Gallery.

"Who's that?" Ginny asks quietly.

"One of my professors."

"Natalie!" Andre gestures at the grandeur of the room around us with wide open arms. "Isn't this amazing?"

"Yeah, totally." I put everything I have into sounding positive. It is amazing, even if I don't feel it today. He asks me what I've been enjoying, and we trade a couple opinions on pieces that stood out to us. As we talk, Ginny looks at a painting just far enough away to not to be part of our conversation.

"I..." Andre hesitates. "I just wanted to say, I know you're disappointed you didn't have anything in time for the Gallery this term, so if you want any support or advice next term, I'm always happy to help. We have so many talented art students here, people sometimes make it out to be easy, but it's not. Everybody here got their project in with a ton of help."

I look away, embarrassed. I'm not good at asking for help, and I was not expecting such an earnest offer after I failed to take his advice for this term. I force myself to look him in the eye as I speak.

"Thanks, that's…Thanks. I don't think I'm taking any of your classes next term, though. I wish I was, but my schedule is—"

"The offer isn't conditional on you being in my class, Natalie. I'm your teacher. Helping isn't extra, it's part of the whole school deal. Though if you're ever looking to switch advisors, let me know."

My eyes widen at the suggestion. Every student here has a professor as their academic advisor. Mine is a graphic design teacher, who I get along with well enough, but we don't have a particularly strong artistic connection.

"Really? I mean, I like my advisor, but my work isn't that similar to hers."

"I'd be happy to talk to you about your work either way, but I would love to have you as an advisee."

My heart clenches in my chest. *He still wants to help me.* "Wow, I…wow. Thank you."

He shrugs again, like the offer is no big deal. "The more advisees I have, the fewer helpless first-years I'll get next year."

"Oh, okay." I laugh. "So, that's your motive."

"My motive is having advisees committed to developing their art. I know you've had a tough time producing stuff you're happy with this term, but don't think I haven't noticed how hardworking you are."

I look away again, overwhelmed by his praise. I search for the right words to tell him how much his compliment means to me. "That's the kind of artist I'd like to be, I think."

He smiles. "Well, let me know if you decide you want to switch advisors, then. No pressure, I'll gladly help you either way."

"I will. Thank you." We say good-bye, and he strolls away, probably to make another student's day.

"Wow." Ginny voices my own thoughts as she appears by my side again. "He seems cool. Super supportive."

"Yeah, he's the best."

"I hope you don't mind that I was totally eavesdropping. It probably would have been more normal to pretend I hadn't heard that whole conversation. Or I could have just not listened in the first place."

I laugh and shake my head. "I don't mind."

"Are you going to take him up on the advisor offer?"

"I mean, I should, right?"

She frowns. "Uh, if you want to? You sounded like you wanted to, but if you don't—"

"No, I totally want to."

She looks confused, brows furrowed as she tilts her head. "Then…yeah, why wouldn't you?"

I shrug and start walking through the Gallery again. I'm not ready to look her in the eye.

"I don't know."

She doesn't say anything. She probably wants more of an answer. I would, too. We walk in silence for a minute before we arrive back at the entrance. I think I got as much out of the Gallery as possible in my current headspace.

"You ready to go?"

She nods. "Yeah, sure, if you are."

We go out into the lobby of the art building, then outside, pulling on our jackets and winter accessories. The tension within me eases as we walk away.

It's easier to consider her question away from all the happy people who were competent and well-adjusted enough to submit their work. The idea of accepting Andre's offer feels like… pressure. If I accept his help, then it will be so much worse if I fail again.

"I think I just don't want to disappoint him."

The confession tumbles out of me abruptly. The last few moments of silence certainly mean I could have moved on, but I don't want to. "Andre. My professor, I mean…It's easier if there's no one to disappoint but myself. Not that I didn't disappoint him this term."

Ginny frowns. I consider my words and hear how they must sound to her—negative and self-critical.

"He didn't sound disappointed to me."

I hesitate. She's right, he didn't, but it's not like he would have conveyed it if he was. But I also know I'm liable to think everyone is disappointed in me because it's how I feel about myself. "No, I guess not."

Ginny sighs and raises an eyebrow at me. "And yet you think he probably was."

"I…Yeah."

"Even though you're aware you're probably just projecting your feelings onto him?"

I laugh at her accurate picture of me. "Yeah."

She shakes her head at me with a small smile on her face. "Okay."

"Okay?" I was expecting a don't-be-so-negative speech, but she just shrugs.

"Yeah, I'd feel the same way. As long as you know on some level that you're probably projecting."

I smile at Ginny. She called me out, but she didn't lecture me about it. She wants to make sure I'm aware of my negativity, but she doesn't feel the need to force me out of it. I squeeze her hand.

"Thanks."

"For what?"

"Saying that. Reminding me not to be so negative. Being supportive. Coming here with me. All of the above."

She smiles and her eyes crinkle at the corners behind her glasses. "Of course. Thanks for asking me to come along."

I nod, grateful but still overwhelmed. And embarrassed over my behavior with Rafael and Emily.

Right. I should apologize for that.

"And I, um, I know I wasn't at my best in there." Her brow furrows at my words. "With Rafael in particular. I'm sorry about that."

She tilts her head, confusion written all over her face. "You don't have to apologize to me. I mean, you asked me to come because this was going to be hard, right?"

"Right."

She nods, like that resolves everything. "You told me it wasn't going to be an easy day. I'm just glad I could be there for you."

"Oh."

She really doesn't seem mad. I examine her face for traces of disappointment, but I can't find any. I guess I'm the only one who's disappointed in me.

"Can we talk about you now?" She looks surprised, so I backtrack. "Or not. I don't want to be avoidant. This was just a lot for one day. But we can—"

"No, no. We can talk about something else. I don't want you to feel, I don't know, pressured."

I nod, even though I don't really mind the pressure. I'm hoping it will force me to be honest until it feels natural.

"Thanks. So…what's up with you?"

"Uh, finals? It's so much work, but I'm weirdly loving it. I kinda don't want it to end, but that's mostly because I don't want to go home." She groans. "I did something stupid a couple days ago."

"What?"

"I got my plane ticket home for the twenty-third because I want to spend as little time at home as possible, but now I keep asking people when they're leaving for the holidays and everyone's going home as soon as break starts. I should have guessed that, probably, but now I'm gonna be alone here for two days. When are you leaving?"

"The twenty-first, probably." Classes end on the twentieth, so I'm leaving pretty much as soon as possible, like Ginny said. "It's the last night of Hanukkah, so I don't want to miss it." An idea pops into my head. "You should come stay with me! Where's your flight from?"

"Uh, Albany, but I couldn't—"

"That's perfect! You can come home with me for a couple days, then take the train back to Albany to catch your flight."

"No, Nat, I couldn't. I don't want to impose on your holiday."

"I cannot even tell you how little you would be imposing." She laughs, but her eyebrows pull together, unsure. "I'm serious! We always have a big dinner together on the last night of Hanukkah, but it's mostly not that big a deal. We're pretty lax Jews."

"Are you sure? I'd love to go to New York, but I really don't want to bother your family."

"My mom works almost constantly and my brother is the chillest guy ever. They would be fine with it. You can stay in my room." Her startled gaze flies to mine, and I laugh at how shocked she looks. "Or in the living room. The couch is super comfy. You wouldn't be a bother at all, I promise." She glances away. "It's up to you, of course. I'd love to hang out for a couple days, show you around my home and everything, but I get it if you don't want to make that whole trip for just a couple days in the city." I stay quiet while she mulls it over.

"Okay," she agrees, finally.

"Really? You're sure?"

"Yeah, I'm sure." She laughs at my expression, which I'm sure is a mix of delight and surprise. "What, you're gonna try to talk me out of it now?"

"No, no! Definitely not. This is awesome."

We share a smile, and I have to hold myself back from kissing her. I'm excited to bring her home with me. She'll get to know me in a way almost nobody else does, and that's as thrilling as it is terrifying.

CHAPTER SEVENTEEN

Ginny

That's a wrap on my first college semester!

Well, almost. I just had my last class, but I do still have one paper left to finish before tomorrow afternoon.

I'm more emotional than I expected, walking out of Gothic Lit for the final time. I don't think I was worried about being able to do it, but I'm still surprised I'm here—one college semester done. This term hasn't been perfect, but I don't think I have ever been this happy in my own skin before.

My friends talk and laugh as we walk to the front door of the literature building, and gratitude washes over me. It's amazing I found these wonderful people so quickly. I'm incredibly lucky to be at this place in my life. Nat pushes the door open and holds it for me, Lizzie, and Mack. I gasp at the sight that awaits us outdoors. There's white, fluffy, beautiful snow. So much of it, almost completely untouched by people, covers everything around us in a thick blanket. We've gotten little bursts of snow here and there so far this winter, but I've been waiting for my first real Vermont snow. This morning when I walked to class, snow fell so hard I could barely see, and I couldn't appreciate the beauty of it. But now—

"Wow." The word falls unbidden from my mouth. There are no words that can do justice to the wonder in front of me. Lizzie lets out a breath, and her eyes glide over everything with appreciation. Mack tugs their beanie over their ears and grumbles about the cold, but then marvels at some gigantic icicles hanging from the side of the building. Nat runs right into the middle of it. She stomps around in her snow boots and laughs.

"I fucking love snow! You really don't get it like this in the city."

"Yeah," Lizzie agrees. "No pee, no dirty slush."

"It's beautiful," I say. Lizzie and I exchange smiles, then jump out of the way as a snowball whizzes by us.

"Holy shit, no." Mack shakes their head emphatically at Nat. "I like the snow just fine, but I am not dressed for this right now."

"And whose fault is that?" Nat raises an eyebrow at them.

"Definitely mine, I know, but I had a last-class outfit I really wanted to wear." Mack gestures to the color-block jacket they're wearing. Stylish, but not super snow appropriate.

"Fine, fine, no snowballs." Nat pouts, but she's already skipping through the snow toward the dining hall.

When we get there, Beth and Rafael are outside talking animatedly. Raf holds three colorful, plastic sleds. He whoops when he sees us approaching.

"We're going sledding!"

Mack groans. "What about lunch?"

"It's the perfect time! The caf is unbelievably crowded right now, and the snow is still pristine and untouched. Lunch will still be there in an hour." Mack surveys everyone else's excited faces, then sighs when they take in Beth's ear-to-ear grin.

"All right, I'm down." They loop an arm around Beth's shoulders.

Rafael has a favorite sledding hill, apparently, because he leads us to it with authority. It's tall and suitably steep but ends dangerously close to a walking path.

"Is this a good idea?" I ask, as we trek up the hill. "Won't we go over the path down there?"

"People sled here all the time," Beth explains. "It's probably a bad idea, objectively, but everyone knows to expect it when it snows like this." I note a couple other people coming our way with sleds and I nod. If they're all confident, I can be, too.

We all take turns. Rafael has two small circular sleds and a longer two-person one. I haven't been sledding since I was little, and my memories of it are relatively mediocre, but everyone else's enthusiasm is infectious. I try one of the round ones on my first ride, and it's just as exhilarating as my friends make it out to be.

When I get to the top again, I choose to watch for a while and just enjoy these wonderful, silly weirdos I'm so grateful to call my friends. I laugh at the way Rafael absolutely screams every second of the way down. I watch Lizzie use the biggest sled on her own so she can lie back peacefully with her eyes closed as she goes. I listen to Beth and Mack argue good-naturedly about how Mack needs to buy new gloves.

After Nat goes for the second time, she walks uphill in comically gigantic steps, like she's willing her legs to elongate so she can get back to the top sooner. She passes her sled to Lizzie, then sidles next to me.

"Having fun?"

"Yeah! This is amazing." My cheeks hurt from smiling.

She grins back at me. Her breath comes in little white puffs. The light reflects off the snow and accentuates a bright sparkle in her brown eyes. Her blue beanie pulls her hair back and draws my gaze to her widow's peak, and the shift from brown roots to blond hair. The sight of her overwhelms me. *God, she's stunning.*

I look away to watch Mack give Beth a shove, so she careens down the hill at top speed. When I turn back, Nat still watches me.

"What?"

She shrugs, nonchalance emanating off her in waves. "Just thinking about the purple sled." Her gaze darts between me and the purple two-person sled on the ground in front of us.

"What about it?"

"It's the fastest one, you know."

"Really? Even with two people?"

Nat nods decisively, as if it's of the utmost importance. "Especially with two people. It's longer, so it's more aerodynamic, and two people fall faster than one. It's physics. Have you ever used one?"

"No? I don't think so."

"Oh, you have to. It's the ultimate experience, really. I wasn't planning on it, but, you know, if you're looking for someone to go with…" She smiles at me, a teasing curve to her lips, and I laugh, realization dawning.

"Ah, okay, got it. Wow, I really believed you knew all about physics for a moment there."

Her grin kicks up a few notches. "I know nothing about physics. But I'd love to go with you if you're interested." She holds my gaze and waits for an answer, but I hesitate, unsure if accepting would constitute leading her on. Her smile drops after a moment, and she looks away. She half smiles and shrugs. "It's cool, no hard feelings or anything if—"

"Sure." I cannot bear the rejection on her face when I can stop it so easily. "Let's do it."

Her smile returns full force, and she nods eagerly, like she can't contain herself. "Great! Awesome. Let's—yeah. Sounds great."

I turn away to grab the sled, so she doesn't see me smile at her bumbling enthusiasm.

Lizzie goes, then we position the two-person sled at the top of the hill. We both gesture for the other to go first, so she laughs and sits at the back of the sled, making room for me in front of her. This doesn't have to be awkward.

As I settle in, she wraps her arms around me tightly, and I realize it's not awkwardness I should have been worried about. Even through puffy jackets and winter clothing, I feel the curl of her legs around mine and her breasts against my back. I'm totally turned on by being this close to her. But more than anything, I'm struck by how not weird it is. Being this close to her isn't awkward. It's natural and thrilling in equal measure. We fit together—her long limbs around my shorter ones—in a way I've never felt I fit with anyone before. I just want to close my eyes and revel in the warm familiarity of her.

"Ready?" Her breath is hot against my ear.

Yes. No. I don't know…*Sledding. Her question was about sledding, Ginny.*

"Ready."

And off we go, speeding down the hill so fast it's like flying. I squeal when we go over a bump, and she tightens her arms around me, laughing the whole time. I laugh with her—not because it's funny, but because it's all so much that the feelings have to come out somehow. Her heart beats against my back, just as fast as my own, and I close my eyes for the briefest moment. So, *this* is how it feels to be completely in sync with another person.

We're laughing so hard it hurts by the time we drift to a slow stop at the bottom of the hill.

"That was awesome!" She's breathless, her arms still around me tightly, even though we're not moving anymore.

"Yeah. Wow. You were right about…aerodynamics." This sends us into peals of laughter again, and she moves her hands to mine, her gloved fingers squeezing mine.

"Hello there." Professor Vargas stands a few feet away with a bemused expression on her face.

Oh no. We stopped right in the middle of the walking path and in the professor's way. I bolt upright, out of Nat's arms, and the force of the movement turns the sled on its side. Nat laughs harder, but all sense of humor has drained from my body, replaced by an acute feeling of mortification.

"Natalie, Ginny." Vargas chuckles at our state of disarray.

"Hi," Nat says through her laughter, as she shoves the sled back to a horizontal position. I untangle myself from her immediately and push to the front of the sled so I can stand.

"Hi, Professor." My already windblown cheeks grow hotter with embarrassment. Something about this situation just feels off—like I've done something wrong.

Nat reaches to brush snow from my arm.

"You good?" She's still unable to speak a single word without laughing.

"I'm fine." My voice is sharp as I brush off the snow myself, and her hand along with it.

I see confusion crinkle her eyes and bring her laughter to a halt, but I look back toward the professor and apologize.

"Don't worry about it," Vargas says. "Looks like you're having fun."

Nat launches into a speech about how much she enjoyed Vargas's class, and the professor nods along and smiles gratefully. I can barely hear what they're saying. Mortification swirls in my stomach and pounds in my chest. I close my eyes and a memory hits me with so much force it's difficult to know where I really am.

I'm fifteen and it's Midnight Mass. I am in a pew directly behind the hottest girl in my grade, who I've never talked to one-on-one before and try not to stare at in my algebra class. She smiles at me when we sit down. I smile back automatically, and I have never been more embarrassed in my life.

My parents are on either side of me, and awareness of emotions I don't want to feel in front of them consumes me. My blush is evidence of my true feelings painted on my face. If they look at me, they'll be able to read every thought in my head. How does the normal, straight, God-fearing version of myself act? How does she hold herself? What does she do with her hands?

I can't even look in front of me because that feels unbearably conspicuous. I'm afraid to open my eyes. For all I know, my parents have already looked at me and learned everything I've tried to hide from them for years.

Nat's elbow brushes my arm, and my eyes pop open.

I'm still here. Right next to Nat, close enough for her arm to skim mine as she gesticulates. And the professor is still looking at us. I pull my arms in toward myself, overwhelmed by the desire to disappear. I pick up the sled and take a few steps to the side, moving away from Nat and off the walking path. Nat glances at me for the briefest moment, her brow furrowed, but turns back to the professor and continues talking. I've moved too far now—just far enough away that it's awkward. But I can't seem to make myself go back toward Nat. It was the obvious thing to do. If you're in someone's way, you should move, right? I didn't want to be in her way. I don't want to be in anyone's way. I don't want anyone to look at me at all.

"I'm always really intimidated by, like, *classic* literature." Nat is still enthusing about the class. "So, you making it feel so accessible was amazing."

"I appreciate you saying that, Natalie. I always try to do that, so it's nice to hear it's working."

"It totally is."

Vargas nods and smiles at us. "Well, good to see you both, and I hope you have a great break."

We respond simultaneously.

"Thank you, Professor."

"You too!"

Relief fills me as I watch Vargas resume her walk along the path. *Thank God that's over.*

Nat shoves her hands in her jacket pockets and turns abruptly to walk up the hill. I scramble to keep up as I drag the sled behind me, and almost trip over my own feet.

"Whoa, slow down."

Nat slows her pace to a crawl. "I'm pretty sure she already knows we're friends, Ginny." Her voice is tight, and her gaze is trained on her boots as they crunch in the snow.

"Uh, what?" I can match her pace now, but she still feels five steps ahead of me.

"Vargas. We sat together every class. I don't think inching as far away from me as possible was going to make her forget that."

My embarrassment evaporates, and shame takes its place. I can't handle this. I don't want to think about why moving away from Nat was so automatic for me. The embarrassment had limits, but this shame feels endless.

"I wasn't trying to make her forget anything."

Nat's gaze whips to mine, and the anger in her eyes surprises me. I'm not sure I've ever seen her angry before.

"I don't know what pisses me off more—that you actually expect me to believe that, or that it's not true in the first place."

Lizzie glances at us, and her brow furrows as she watches us climb the hill. She probably can't hear us now, but I know she'll be able to in a moment.

"It *is* true! I just wanted to get out of her way."

"You—"

Nat cuts herself off as we reach our friends at the top of the hill. Beth approaches and asks me for the sled. She either hasn't noticed our argument or wants to break the tension. I pass it to her and watch as she and Mack set up. After a moment, Nat tugs on my arm, and I let her pull me away so we can have some privacy. I don't want to talk about this at all, but I really don't want to talk about it where our friends can hear.

"You shot away from me immediately when Vargas saw us. Like we were doing something wrong."

"We—we were in the middle of the path."

She rolls her eyes, huffing at me with exasperation.

"Come on. That's not all it was. You acted like she caught us making out or something."

"We—I—" I'm overwhelmed by the idea of that alternate scenario. The glare she levels at me makes it impossible to focus on anything else, even my own thoughts. I swallow to recenter myself, but Nat plows on.

"I realize I'm, like, *aggressively* out, but we were sledding, not having sex. I—I don't get it. How is it true that we're not even together and you're still ashamed to be seen with me? Why am I somehow getting the worst of both worlds?"

"I'm not ashamed to be seen with you." *I think.* I have no reason to be ashamed of Nat, but my instincts when Vargas saw us weren't coming from a place of logic.

"Okay, then explain why Vargas looked at you and you immediately moved as far away from me as you could."

I search for another answer, but I can't find one.

"I—I don't know. I just…" The truth is still blurry to me, so my words come out in disconnected bursts. "I'm not used to it yet. To—to everything being so…not subtle."

"If you're so worried about seeming queer by association, I think you've got the wrong friend group. We're not gonna tone it down for you."

Tears prick my eyes, and I stare at the snow. Maybe she'll think I'm crying from the glare off the white surface and not her words.

"Wait. Shit, I—I'm sorry, Ginny. I shouldn't have said that." The regret in her voice is piercing. "I've just had a lot of people tell me to be more subtle about myself. It's kind of a trigger for me."

She shouldn't be the one apologizing right now. I guess I have been hoping that by not really getting involved with Nat, I wouldn't have to expose all the shameful thoughts in my head. I close my eyes, take a deep breath, and force myself to tell us both the truth.

"No, I'm sorry. You're right. I—I moved away because I didn't want her to think we were together. I didn't want her to know about me, so I didn't want her to associate me with you. I was afraid she would see…" *How attracted I am to you. How extremely, undeniably queer I am.* "I was afraid she would know." I pause, overwhelmed by having spoken those words aloud. Saying them shows me how horrible they are—how horrible I just was to her. I squeeze my already-closed eyes even tighter as I wait for her response and try to steel myself for more of her anger.

"Thank you for saying that." My eyes pop open. She looks… fine. Not happy, certainly, but not upset anymore either.

"What?"

"I appreciate you saying that."

"I—What?" I am completely baffled by the gentle smile that forms on her face. "But…it's awful. I was just so awful to you."

"Hey, don't talk about yourself like that. *Awful* is an exaggeration." As relieved as I am to hear her say so, I can't understand how all her anger seems to have dissipated now that I admitted to her accusations.

"But…I was awful. I'm so sorry, Nat."

"It's okay. I just wanted you to say it. I mean, yeah, watching you pull away from me hurt, but then you acted like you hadn't done it at all. I just wanted you to be honest with me."

"I didn't mean to lie, I just…I hate that I reacted that way.

You don't deserve to be wrapped up in all my stupid shameful stuff."

"It's not stupid. I mean, yes, it's stupid in that it absolutely sucks, but I also totally get it."

"You do?"

She laughs and slants her head like I've said something completely absurd.

"Of course, Ginny. I've told you before I haven't always been this confident about my sexuality. I'm still not as confident as I seem, really. I just know the only way I'll ever feel confident about it is if I act like I already am."

"Right." Now I'm embarrassed I've assumed she doesn't ever struggle with stuff like this. Logically, I know Nat must have her own issues with her sexuality, but she always seems so happy to be queer.

The feel of her hand on my arm breaks me out of my head.

"Ginny, you can talk to me about any of this stuff, if you want to. I know your experience has been different from mine, and I never really did the whole closet thing, but I'd never pressure you to be, like, more out or something."

"I'm okay with the students here, but I guess it's different with real adults. Authority figures. There's still something in me that feels like I shouldn't be seen...I don't know...liking you."

She smiles, then shakes her head. "Sorry, sorry, I'm definitely being serious and not getting distracted by you saying you like me." We laugh, but I'm too aware of how close she is to me.

"You know I like you," I say softly.

"I do." She matches my tone. The hand on my arm drifts from my bicep to my wrist. It would be so easy to entwine my fingers with hers.

"Dating me would be full of stuff like this, you know." I either need more distance between us or none at all, and I don't quite know which I'm trying to achieve.

"I know." Her lips quirk into a half-smile. "And dating me would be full of shit like pushing me to talk about myself and calling me out when I lie and say I'm fine."

"I—" I start to respond, but the words stall in my throat,

and I snap my mouth shut. Part of me wants to just go for it and tell her I trust her. Because I think I do. But I don't know if our connection will be strong enough to overcome all our issues. Mostly I'm just scared.

So, I just smile at her and nod, then put my hands in my pockets so I won't be tempted to touch her. She must get my signals because she leads us back toward our friends.

"And, hey, I didn't mean what I said earlier about you being in the wrong friend group. You're in the right one. For sure. We'd love you even if you were straight."

A jagged laugh tumbles out of me.

"Thanks." We smile and I try to ignore the way my heart flips in my chest.

My head bursts with contradictions, like my mind is working against my heart. I was too scared to stand by her side with Vargas, yet I still worship every smile, every look, and every word she gives me.

CHAPTER EIGHTEEN

Natalie

"It's just, like, a normal city." Ginny marvels at the row houses we're passing by. It's been a long day of travel. We took a bus to Albany, a train into Manhattan, and the subway into Crown Heights, the Brooklyn neighborhood I've lived in my entire life. We're both a little exhausted, but I'm happy that Ginny seems energized to finally be here. "I was picturing giant skyscrapers everywhere and hundreds of people on every street, but I guess that's kind of a stereotype."

"That's Times Square. And some of Manhattan. I like to think of Brooklyn as a bunch of tiny little busy villages."

"It is a lot cuter and more village-like than I expected."

"Yeah, that is very dependent on the part of Brooklyn." We each lug a larger suitcase and a backpack, but Ginny doesn't protest when I stop to point out my favorite spots. I show her my go-to bodega, a pottery studio where I took classes when I was a kid, and the park where I joined a youth softball league and sadly discovered that I was horrible at it despite being a lesbian. "I thought I would finally be good at a sport, but alas."

Ginny's dimples pop as she laughs. "Look at you, breaking stereotypes left and right."

"I probably break, like, three lesbian stereotypes. If that. I'm *all* cats and flannel."

"And I'm half and half. Yes, to flannel, but I prefer dogs."

And now I can picture us living on a farm with a bunch of dogs. I've been doing a lot of that lately; imagining us in some fantastical future that I know won't exist for so many reasons.

"I have to admit, cats kinda scare me." Ginny cringes at her own admission.

"Really?"

"Yeah, my grandmother has like eight or nine cats, and I cannot even count how many times one of them has scratched me. They're feral little furballs, but she's obsessed with them."

"Wow, is grandma a lesbian?"

"Super homophobic, actually." She cringes. "Though I guess those aren't mutually exclusive."

"Damn. I'm sorry," I say. Ginny just shrugs. "Well, Moose is sweet. All he wants is someone to pet him. And every bit of food he can find."

"So, he won't scratch me?"

"I didn't say that."

She laughs. "Right. Gotcha."

"This is it." I point to my house as we approach. "We live on the bottom floor."

"Wow. It's beautiful." I root through my backpack for my keys as Ginny takes it in. "Will your family be home?"

I glance at the time. It's almost eight. "My brother, probably. My mom depends on if she decided to close the store early for Hanukkah."

"They know I'm coming, right?" I shoot her a look, and she immediately cringe-laughs. "Stupid question, sorry. Of course they do."

It's almost funny she would ask given how much I've talked to my mom and brother about her in the last week. When I asked my mom if Ginny could stay with us for a couple nights, I ended up talking to her about Ginny for over an hour. Mom even sent me a text about Ginny this morning.

I'm very excited to meet your not-girlfriend!

I begged her to not to say something like that in front of Ginny, even though it would probably be more funny than awkward.

"Are those not your keys?" Ginny points at my hand, where I am one hundred percent holding my keys.

"Uh, yeah." I got so distracted I hadn't realized I'd found them. I unlock the door, hold it open for Ginny, and yell into the living room. "I'M HOME!"

Ginny flinches. "My gosh, that was loud."

"Did you just say *my gosh*?"

"We're in your mother's home."

To my surprise, the woman herself emerges from the kitchen, wiping her hands with a dish towel.

"Mom! I didn't know you'd be home so early."

"Of course I am. You're home on the last night of Hanukkah. Where else would I be?" She embraces me and I melt into the hug—she smells like brisket. She releases me and turns her smile to Ginny. "You must be Ginny."

"Yes, ma'am." Her Southern politeness is in full force. She extends her hand, which Mom shakes immediately despite the surprise on her face. "Thank you so much for your hospitality. Especially over the holidays."

"Of course. It's so nice to meet you."

"You too, ma'am."

My mother blinks, clearly puzzled by someone who manages to call her *ma'am* twice in fifteen seconds.

Noah bounds into the room and gives me an awkward back-patting bro hug, like always. "Finally! What the hell took you so long?"

"It's good to see you, too."

He turns to Ginny. "Hey, I'm Noah."

"I'm Ginny. Hi." She reaches out to shake his hand, and Noah complies with even less ability to conceal his surprise than my mom. "It's great to meet you." She smiles one of those dimpled grins that always gives me butterflies, and my little brother looks shy all of a sudden. I hold in a laugh.

"You have perfect timing," Mom says. "Dinner's almost ready."

She disappears into the kitchen just as Moose winds around my ankles, and I kneel to introduce him to Ginny. She crouches next to me and pets his soft fur carefully. He purrs and butts his head against her shin, and she laughs.

My heart is full. It's odd to see Ginny here, but in a good way. I want to take in every moment of her in my home, with my family. Noah makes a quiet scoffing noise and I glance at him. He gives me a look I can read as clearly as if he said it aloud: *You're a lovesick fool and you're horrible at hiding it.*

I stand to give him another hug. "It is really good to see you."

"You, too." He squeezes me back. "I can't believe she shook my hand," he adds in a whisper.

I laugh as I release him. "It's cute." I look at Ginny, still on the floor with Moose. "Talk later?" At his nod, I take two steps toward Ginny and offer her my hand. "Come on. I'll show you my room." I help her up, then let go of her hand so I can grab her rolling suitcase and my duffel.

"I can take that." She tries to grab her bag from me.

"Shush and let me be a gentleman."

She laughs at the order, but her eyes dart to my brother.

I lead her down the hall. I hope I didn't make her self-conscious. Maybe she would prefer I don't flirt with her in front of my family. I should have told her that I've talked to them about us. I close my bedroom door.

"They both know about our whole…thing."

"Oh." She looks surprised.

"I hope that's okay. It's just, you know, been on my mind. So, I've talked to them about it."

"No, no, of course it's okay. You can talk to whoever about it. I just…I just hope they don't, like, hate me."

"They don't hate you. Why would they hate you?"

"I—I don't know. I rejected you. It's weird."

I step closer and put a hand on her shoulder. "They don't hate you. The exact opposite, actually. I like you, so they've been really excited to meet you."

"They're super nice."

"Yeah. Because they very much don't hate you."

She laughs, shaking her head. "Sorry, I'm being stupid. I should be looking at your room."

She takes it in, and I look, too. I wonder what I would think if I'd never been here before.

It's a tiny room, I guess. The bed, desk, and dresser don't leave much open space. It's messier than I wish it was—I'm messier than I wish I was. Boxes of art supplies are stacked precariously high in the corner. The walls are practically covered with drawings, with no cohesive visual goal beyond hanging them all. The singular plant sitting in the tiny window behind my desk is half-dead; my mother hasn't remembered to water it like she said she would.

"Most of my stuff is at school. This isn't as nice as it used to be."

She sends me a puzzled smile. "Why are you so nervous? I love it. It's so you."

"It is?" I follow her gaze in the hopes that I might be able to see what she does. She goes to the wall next to my bed and ghosts her fingers over the corner of a sketch.

"There's so much of your work. You don't have as much hung up at school." I shrug. I guess I don't. My room at school is more carefully curated—a few favorite sketches and posters—while this room is cluttered with art. "I love seeing your art." She sounds so sincere my heart squeezes in my chest. I sit on the bed, unsure of what else to do, and she sits next to me, so close our knees brush.

I flush at her proximity. We've sat this close many times before, but it's different here—more intimate. True privacy is rare on campus, but my mom has always treated my room as my own space, so no one's going to burst in without warning. Ginny glances at me, then toward the door with a furrowed brow.

"Is it okay that we're in here with the door closed?"

"Uh…is that a real question?" A blush rises on her cheeks, and she laughs.

"Well, not anymore, it isn't," she says.

"Sorry, I'm not making fun of you. That's just very not how

my mom is. I promise you—she couldn't care less about whether my door's open or closed."

"My mom would sooner die than let me have a boy in my room with the door closed."

"What about if you showed up with me, huh? Do you think she'd let me in your room?" I run a hand through my hair and use the other to gesture to the flannel I'm wearing over an old Stevie Nicks T-shirt I stole from my mom. Ginny looks over at me and her eyes crinkle as she smiles.

"I sincerely doubt it."

There's a knock on the door, and Ginny shoots up off the bed.

"Dinner's ready!" my mom calls through the door.

In the tiny kitchen slash dining room, I realize Mom must have left the store super early. She's prepared a giant slab of brisket, two platters' worth of latkes, and homemade applesauce. It's the pink kind full of warm spices, which is probably the most nostalgic food in the world.

She puts a hand on my back. "There's extra applesauce in the fridge."

"You're a goddess." She kisses my temple and directs me to put silverware on the table. Ginny asks how she can help, and Mom gives her a task, too.

We set the table and sit down to dinner. Ginny is almost comically polite at first, but Noah and my mom quickly put her at ease, and it doesn't take her too long to switch from calling Mom ma'am to Ms. Becker. Usually, I do a lot of the talking at family dinners, but today I mostly listen.

Ginny admits she's never had latkes before with a self-deprecating laugh. My mom confesses in turn that she doesn't really know the history behind them, even though she always makes them for Hanukkah. Ginny tells us about learning to cook from her mother, and Mom teases me for not spending as much time learning from her. I roll my eyes and ask her to count the thousands of hours I've spent at her side in the deli.

Noah is quiet at first—he can be shy around people he doesn't know—but when Ginny says she's thinking about majoring in English, he engages more fully. He asks questions about her classes and tells her way more about the poetry elective he's in than I've heard him say about school all year.

I've only known Ginny for about four months, but right now I feel like I've known her forever. I already know most of the stories she tells my family, and the ones I don't know are so perfectly her that I'm almost surprised I haven't heard them before. I'm proud of how well I know her, but a little disconcerted when I realize she definitely doesn't know a single story Noah and my mom share about me. Some of them are kind of embarrassing, but I don't mind. Instead, I wish I'd told her all of them before. I wonder if she wishes that, too, or if she feels the same way I do about her stories—like they're both new and old at the same time, because they're already a part of the way I see her.

When dinner's over, Ginny immediately offers to help my mom clean up. Noah slips away while we clear the table by throwing my mom some bullshit line about the kitchen being too crowded. My mom and I laugh.

"Wow, you're going to let him get away with that?" I ask with as much faux outrage as I can manage.

Mom raises an eyebrow. "You want to talk to me about letting my kids get away with too much?"

"Hard no. But at least my excuses are more creative."

She just smiles and hands me a dish towel.

My mom washes the dishes, Ginny loads most of them into the dishwasher, and I dry and put away the bigger items. Mostly, I continue to listen to them chat and try not to let my smile break my face in half.

"You can call me Joanna, you know," Mom says, while she passes Ginny a plate and a kind smile. Ginny blinks, surprised.

"Oh, I—Okay."

My mom chuckles. "Or Ms. Becker, if you'd rather."

"Okay. I might stick with that for now if that's all right."

Mom nods.

I don't miss the meaning the words *for now* could contain.

I'm in my fantasy world again, imagining Mom teaching Ginny her recipes and watching them bond over the love for classic movie musicals I know they share.

Noah comes back out of his room to light the menorah. We usually fight over the honor, but he hands me the lighter without a word, since it's the only night I've been able to be here. We sing a prayer while we light the candles, then I explain to Ginny what it meant.

Ginny sits with us while we exchange gifts as part of our last night of Hanukkah tradition. Mom tells Ginny she used to give us one gift a night when Noah and I were younger, but that changed when we started wanting things like video game systems instead of toy cars. I give my mom another huge hug for the charcoal pencils she got me that are absurdly expensive for literal pencils. A gift to support my art feels important right now coming from my mother.

"Do you always give your family your art as gifts?" Ginny asks later, after I close my bedroom door behind us. I gave them each a framed drawing I worked on over the last couple weeks.

"Usually." I flop onto the bed and watch her take in my room again.

"That's amazing. I always feel weird buying my parents gifts when I know most of my money comes from them anyway. I'd love to give them something handmade."

"You should do it."

She wrinkles her forehead with an *are you crazy?* look on her face. "I can't draw."

"Everyone can draw." She rolls her eyes. I shrug and change the subject. "Are you going to sit with me or what?"

The furrow between her brows deepens, but she sits next to me anyway. "I know you said it's okay, but it still feels weird. Like your mom could burst in at any moment to check on us."

I laugh at the implausibility of that scenario. "She wants that even less than you do."

"What?" Ginny looks alarmed. "You mean she thinks we're…"

"I mean, I'm sure she thinks it's a possibility."

"Should I sleep on the couch?"

I hesitate. Obviously, I want her to stay here with me, but I don't want her to be uncomfortable.

"If you want to?"

"No, I want to sleep here." She blushes immediately, and I roll my lips between my teeth so I don't smirk at her. "I mean, I'm happy to sleep here."

"I'm happy for you to sleep here, too." So ridiculously happy. If this is the only chance I ever get to share a bed with her, I'm sure as hell taking it. "And I promise my mom doesn't care." She nods and pulls her socked feet onto the bed to lean against the wall.

"Okay."

I smile and parrot her. "Okay."

It's only ten, so we watch a movie on my laptop. I've never been so happy to have a tiny twin bed. Every time Ginny laughs, her arm moves against mine. When she yawns toward the end of the film, I pray she'll rest her head on my shoulder. She doesn't, but we're close enough that I get over it.

When the movie ends, she goes to the bathroom to change, and I slip into my pajamas while she's gone. She returns in a T-shirt and fleecy pajama pants and grabs her toothbrush. I follow her back to the bathroom.

I've never understood the fast-moving lesbian U-Haul stereotype, but now here I am—giddy over a tiny domestic act like making eye contact in the mirror while we brush our teeth together. We're not even dating, and I'm totally mooning over a fantasy of our toothbrushes sitting next to each other in a bathroom of our own.

We settle into my bed—as close together as possible without touching. We talk in hushed tones that remind me of middle school sleepovers. She laughs quietly as I tell her a story about sneaking a girl into my bedroom at night, only to have my mom ask if she got home okay the next morning. When she takes her glasses off, I turn on my side, prop my head in my hand, and stare shamelessly into her green eyes.

As wonderful as the reality of this moment is, it's hard to

be in bed with her without fantastical images invading my mind. I conjure mental sketches of her skin on mine—fingers and lips and legs—and visions of all the parts of her I haven't gotten to see. I close my eyes while she talks, half listening and half imagining hooking my ankle against hers, holding us together in that simple way. I picture our legs entwined and my tattoo leeching into her skin.

It's never been so difficult to not be able to touch her, but when we finally drift off to sleep, all I can think about is how happy I am to be this close to her.

I want to stay like this forever.

CHAPTER NINETEEN

Ginny

Nat's life in Brooklyn is everything and nothing like I imagined. The apartment is small but brimming with personality, and it's easy to see Nat was raised with a lot of love. Her mother is as intensely focused on her store as Nat said, but she's also warm and funny. Noah is smart, endearing, and clearly idolizes his sister. The three of them have a quick, wry rapport I watch with admiration.

Nat doesn't have to work today, but she takes me to the deli for breakfast anyway, where she hops behind the counter to grab us a couple bagels. I've only heard her refer to this place with trepidation, but it's lively, inviting, and I can tell she has a great deal of love for everyone who works there. After we chat with some of her friends and they teach me the difference between lox and smoked salmon, Nat says that for my one and only full day in New York, she wants to take me around to some of her favorite winter attractions in the city.

We go into Manhattan, and Nat tries not to laugh at me as I marvel at all the tall buildings and crowds of people. She does laugh unreservedly, though, when a pedestrian tells me to stop walking so slowly.

We spend a few hours in Union Square, which has an annual open-air market during the holidays, filled with stalls selling all kinds of gifts and food. It's a lot bigger than I imagined given it's smack in the middle of a busy city. We have lunch and Nat helps me choose a couple gifts for my parents. I already have one gift for each of them, but nothing that thoughtful or exciting.

We take the subway to DUMBO, which Nat explains is an acronym for a Brooklyn neighborhood that has nothing to do with cartoon elephants. We get amazingly good hot chocolate and take in the view of the skyline from across the water. Nat buys a tin of hot chocolate mix and explains that it's her mother's favorite thing in the entire world. It's freezing, but we wander Brooklyn Bridge Park for a long time anyway, enjoying ourselves too much to really care about the cold.

Then Nat takes me to her favorite restaurant for dinner. It's a tiny, overly busy Italian place with a small menu of surprisingly cheap homemade pasta, and I spend half the time wondering if the people around us think we're on a date. Probably not, I suppose. Two young women getting dinner together as friends is a common sight. And they would be correct. We are friends having dinner. But it hits me, while we sit at a small candlelit table eating pasta and laughing together, that it feels like a date. I wish it was a date. Everything would be just like it is now, except I could give in to the urge to reach across the table and hold her hand.

This trip has confirmed something I've been slowly realizing over the last couple weeks. Nat is doing exactly what I wanted her to do. I've learned more about her walking around the city together today than I learned in the first couple months of our friendship, and I know how much effort that takes for her. She's making the purposeful choice to share herself with me, and I've never felt closer to her.

The question of trust isn't holding me back anymore. It's *me*. The giddy urge I have for this to be a date is still intermingled with anxiety about other people seeing that desire. Nat doesn't deserve to deal with that. I don't want to make decisions for her, but I'm still assembling my feelings into coherent thoughts.

I will talk to her about it. I will. But today has been amazing, and I'm worried I'll ruin it. My avoidance may be cowardly, but I'm going to give myself this unblemished little trip with her before I bring up the serious stuff.

❖

After dinner, we get on the subway, transfer to another train, then get out and switch to a bus. I've let her lead me around blindly today, not asking where we're going until we get there, but this trek has piqued my curiosity.

"Are we even still in Brooklyn?" I ask after the bus makes yet another stop.

"Yep, Brooklyn is huge. And the next stop is ours, I promise." She leans over me to press the button that signals we want to get off at the next stop.

"Where are you taking me?"

"Dyker Heights."

I hesitate. Sometimes Nat is so sarcastic I can't tell if she's kidding. "Is that, like, a lesbian joke I don't get?"

She furrows her brow at me for a moment before she bursts out in laughter so loud a woman nearby shoots us a look. "I wish. No. It's a real, honest-to-God Brooklyn neighborhood."

"Okay, and what are we doing in…Dyker Heights?"

She snorts. "Now I can't stop thinking of inappropriate jokes. Damn. Well, we're going to Dyker Heights because it's one of my favorite places in Brooklyn in the winter."

"Fitting."

"Yeah, except my lesbianism isn't season permitting." We both laugh, but Nat stops when she sees something out the window. "We're here." She smirks. "Welcome to Dyker Heights."

"Why, thank you." The bus pulls over and Nat leads me out. It looks…like the rest of Brooklyn. A little busy, but otherwise a lot like everywhere else.

"Come on." Nat grabs my wrist to guide me down the block. "It's going to be completely packed, but it's worth it. I come here every year before Christmas. Usually alone, so I'm happy you're here." We share a smile. We walk a couple blocks, then make a turn into another universe—the universe of insane Christmas decorations.

"Whoa." I freeze and stare at the blocks ahead of us, where

every single house is decorated to an otherworldly level. There are countless statues, animatronics, and giant blow-up versions of Christmas-themed creatures—and so many lights I'm surprised there are any left for the rest of the planet.

"It's crazy, right?" Nat surveys the decorations with childlike wonder in her eyes.

"Yeah. Wow. It's amazing." It really is, and she knows that, but she grins at me like my approval means the world to her. A group of people push past, separating us, and she reaches out to grab my arm. "Wow, it's busy." I take in the crowds surrounding us.

"Yeah. Sorry to make you deal with tourists," she says.

"I don't mind. I mean, I *am* a tourist."

She chuckles. "True." Her hand is still on my arm, keeping me close to her in the bustling crowd.

I decide to go for it and link my arm through hers. "Let's look at some lights!"

She laughs and leads us down the block. We walk together slowly, stopping to admire each house.

"So, they do this every year?"

"Yep."

"And you always go?"

"Since I was a kid, yeah."

"Your mom would take you?"

She's silent for a moment, and I turn to watch her throat work as she swallows. I open my mouth to backtrack, but she speaks first.

"My dad."

"Oh. I...I don't think I've ever heard you mention your dad before."

"Yeah, probably not. We don't really have a relationship. He moved to Oregon to get back together with his high school girlfriend when I was seven."

"I'm sorry, Nat."

She shrugs, her shoulder moving against mine. "We weren't, like, close. Even when he lived here, I mean. He was here on vacation, hooked up with my mom, then moved here when she realized she was pregnant. They were sort of on and off for a few years, then called it off for good after they had my brother. My dad stuck around for a few more years, but he always hated New York."

"Do you talk at all now?"

"Once or twice a year. He always acts like we're so close, even though it's obvious he's only calling because it's my birthday or Christmas or whatever. He's got a whole life—a wife and two other kids I've never met. So, it's pretty impossible to pretend we're one big family."

"That sucks, Nat. I'm sorry."

She just shrugs and shakes her head. "Honestly, I'd rather this than having him be a big part of my life. He's not really down with the gay thing." I squeeze her arm. "Sometimes I think that's part of why he liked to bring me here. I didn't even know I was gay then, but he was always freaked by how not-girly I was. He had no idea what to do with a little Jewish tomboy, so he tried to make Christianity seem as fun as possible. I don't know what he thought that would do, really. I guess he just wanted me to be more like him, but it's not like loving Christmas would have translated into loving skirts and the color pink."

I laugh involuntarily, then immediately apologize. "Sorry. It's not funny."

"It's a little funny. I was a kid. I loved the lights, but they were still just lights. They didn't make me believe in God."

"A polar bear made of Christmas lights isn't sufficient proof for you?"

"I'm afraid not. That giant inflatable snowman, on the other hand"—she points, and I almost stop in my tracks at how huge it is—"is almost terrifying enough to make me believe in the vengeful Old Testament God I was taught about in Hebrew school."

We laugh, our arms still linked tightly, and I quell the urge to put my head on her shoulder.

"Well, thank you for bringing me here, especially if it makes you think about your dad."

"I never let him ruin this place for me. It's a nice reminder that I'm still the same gay Jewish girl I was then, and he never changed that. He never could have changed that. I don't have to celebrate Christmas to think this stuff is unbelievably fun."

"I'm honored that you'd share this place with me."

A bright smile blooms on her face. "Thank you for coming with me. I'm glad you liked it." I turn to look into her dark brown eyes. "I know it's kinda silly and cliché, but it makes me feel like a little kid again. In the best ways, not the bad ways."

We walk for over an hour. We take photos of the best houses—the most beautiful ones and the most wildly overstimulating ones. Once Nat says we've seen all there is to see, we stroll leisurely toward the bus stop. We use our phones to compare our favorites as we wait for the bus to arrive.

"I wish I could send this one to my mom." I show Nat a photo of the house we both agree was the prettiest. "She'd get a kick out of it." But I can't do that. When I bought my plane ticket home, I told my parents I was staying a couple extra days to finish my work for the semester. I couldn't update them about my trip to New York without revealing that I'd never wanted to go home in the first place. "Though then I'd have to explain why I'm sightseeing in Brooklyn."

Nat offers a sympathetic smile. "Should we tell your parents there's a huge snowstorm and all the flights got canceled? You could send her a photo of that house with all the fake snow as proof."

I laugh. "I wish."

"Yeah. I wish so, too."

The bus arrives and we find two empty seats together in the back. I give in to the urge I've had throughout the day whenever we've been side by side like this, and I put my head on her shoulder.

"I really don't want to see my parents." I speak in a low voice, frightened to admit it aloud, even though we're miles and miles from Virginia.

"I know." She leans her head on top of mine.

"I kinda hate it there. My parents are so judgmental, and it makes me feel like shit about myself. My mom asks endless questions about whether I'll grow out my hair again, and why I don't wear more dresses, and when am I gonna get a boyfriend. And I know I haven't been at school very long, but I hate not being out now. It feels awful."

"I'm sorry, Ginny. That sounds horrible."

"It'll be okay." I'm reassuring myself more than her. "It's only a few weeks."

"You can call me anytime, you know."

"I know." I hope it will be easier to be myself at home now that I have Nat and all my friends at school to support me. "Do you think...Do you think I should come out to them?"

She takes her head off mine so she can look me in the eyes and says exactly what I knew she would.

"I can't answer that for you."

"Right. I'm sorry. I know that."

"No, don't be sorry. I just—I really don't have an answer."

"Do you have any advice? In case I do?"

She pauses, then slowly shakes her head. "I don't know if I do. All you can do is take care of yourself and say what you need to say, but you know all that already. I know how much you've thought about this, so I'm not sure what I could say that you haven't heard before. It's one of those things I don't know if you can really be prepared for."

"I guess not."

"Just...if you do, know that you can call me after. Even if it's, like, three in the morning."

I smile at her. "I really don't think I'm gonna come out to my parents at three in the morning, but okay. Thank you."

"Of course."

I put my head back on her shoulder and close my eyes. And for a moment I hope everyone on this bus *does* think we're together, because I wish it was the truth, too.

CHAPTER TWENTY

Natalie

I don't want Ginny to leave. I'm sad just watching her repack her suitcase, because I know she doesn't want to leave either.

Yesterday was kind of perfect. I can't remember the last time I spent an entire day one-on-one with someone and was comfortable with them the entire time. We had so much to talk about, and even when we ran out of things to say, I was happy to just be with her.

The nearness is painful, though. I've never felt closer to her, yet there's a distance that we can't cross—an intimacy we can't achieve. Yesterday was like one long beautiful date, but the twenty or so times I wanted to kiss her, I made myself pull away instead. I hope I'm earning her trust. If I'm patient, then maybe someday she'll be the one to kiss me.

But if I'm not changing her mind, then I'm only setting myself up for more heartbreak.

When she's almost done packing, I remember I still have her gift in my suitcase. "Hey, I have something for you." She turns to me with raised brows. "A Christmas present."

"You got me a present?" She sounds dismayed. "I'm so sorry, Nat, I didn't get you anything."

"It's okay! It's not mandatory, I just had an idea I was excited about." I fish the tissue-paper-wrapped gift from my bag and hand it to her. She unwraps it slowly and precisely, as if she's trying to preserve the paper, and pulls out the pair of overalls inside. She stares at the front pouch, which has an embroidered rainbow patch on it.

I stare, too. The patch is stitched in a multitude of light colors. The rainbow curls to form a full circle, like a pastel sunburst. I'm so happy with how it came out. The overalls are exactly how I imagined them when I first drew the idea. That was the first day I ever saw her. I pictured a made-up outfit on the random cute girl sitting across from me in class, so I sketched it, and now I can't wait to see her wearing my imaginary overalls in real life. Even so, when she doesn't say anything for a moment, I worry.

"I've gotten into making patches recently."

Her eyes go wide. "You *made* this?"

"I mean, not the overalls. I got those at Goodwill. I washed them, though, I swear!"

"But you made *this*?" She points to the patch, and I nod. "Wow. That's...wow. Thank you, Nat. This is amazing."

"You like it?"

"I love it!" She hugs me tightly, and I close my eyes, smiling into her shoulder. "Thank you."

"You're welcome."

I watch as she packs them into her suitcase with immense care, as if they're designer fashion instead of used ten-dollar overalls. She's quiet this morning, but I suspect she's nervous about going home, so I don't push her to talk.

She is as gracious and polite as ever, of course, as she says good-bye to my mom and Noah. Then I take the subway into Manhattan with her to make sure she gets on the right platform for her train to Albany.

When it's time to say good-bye, she hugs me so tightly I can barely breathe. We stay there for a minute, holding each other, before I whisper in her ear.

"Thank you for coming all the way down here with me."

"Are you kidding? Thank you for inviting me. I had the best time."

"Me too."

She pulls away and takes a deep breath. She looks toward the platform, and lines of worry form on her forehead.

"Good luck with your parents."

She smiles shakily and nods. "Thank you." She gives me another quick hug, then I reluctantly shoo her toward her train.

Damn. I feel like an idiot watching her go. I miss her already, and I can still see her.

The three weeks of winter break ahead of us seem impossibly long now. We've gotten notably closer in only a couple days. We'll text, I'm sure, but it's nowhere near the same. I just have to hope we'll pick up where we left off when we get back to school.

I go home, but I'm lonely without her. Noah's out with friends and my mom is at the store, so the house is empty and extra depressing. I let myself drown in TV and takeout for the evening.

❖

My mom comes home from the store around eleven, and she knocks on my bedroom door a minute later.

"Come in."

She slips inside and closes the door behind her, which tells me she has something serious she wants to talk about. I pause the show I was watching on my laptop.

"Hi." She's smiling, but her approach still feels pointed. It's not a casual *hey*. It's a *there's something we need to talk about.*

"Hi."

"Ginny get back okay?" I nod. Ginny texted me a little while ago to let me know all was well with her train and the plane ride, and she's back home in Virginia. "She's a very nice girl."

I try not to roll my eyes at how much of a mom thing that is to say. "Yeah."

"You're really not dating?"

"No." I'm frustrated by the question. I wish I could give her a different answer, too. "And you can stop asking me that. I promise I'll tell you if we get together."

Mom nods. "Well, I hope you do. I think a real relationship could be good for you."

"I *know*, Mom."

She frowns at me. "What's wrong?"

"It's not like I don't want that, too. You don't need to remind me."

She raises her palms in a show of surrender. "I'm not trying to nag you, Natalie. I'm trying to say I approve. Not that you need my approval to date someone, but—"

"I know what you mean." An awkward silence descends upon us, and a kernel of guilt blooms in my stomach. Part of me wants to apologize for being blunt, but mostly I want to stop talking about this. I don't need my mother to know all the details about why I'm not in a serious relationship with Ginny.

For a moment I think she might leave me alone, but Mom comes further into my room. She fiddles with random items on my desk—a pine-scented candle, a ceramic dish I made in middle school—then clears her throat.

"So. You haven't said much about the end of your semester. Finals go okay?"

"Yeah, finals were fine. A lot of work, but fine." She watches me without responding, so I try to come up with something else to say. "It kinda took me a while to get back into the swing of things at the beginning of the year, but…yeah. I feel pretty good about the work I did. It was a good term."

"That's great. I'm proud of you." She beams at me, and I grin in return. Even when I'm frustrated with my mom, her praise means the world to me.

"Thanks, Mom."

"And the Student Gallery? How was that? You never told me what you ended up submitting."

Shit. I gushed about the Gallery last year—how cool I thought it was, how excited I was to be a part of it when I got the chance. When she asked about it a couple months ago, I told her I was working on my submission but left out the fact I was terrified I wouldn't be able to pull something together in time. I've avoided the subject since then, but clearly it hasn't slipped her mind.

"Natalie?" Her encouraging smile doesn't wane at all as she waits for my answer. I steel myself with a deep breath.

"Actually…the Gallery didn't work out for me this term."
Her brows pull together, and she crosses the last couple feet
between us to sit next to me on the bed.

"Oh, sweetheart, I'm so sorry. Your submission didn't get
in?" She places a hand on my back.

"No, I—um…I didn't submit anything." I stare at my lap, so
I don't have to see the disappointment on her face. My mom is a
pretty relaxed parent in a lot of ways. She has never been strict
about chores, and never grounds me if I stay out too late with
friends. But when it comes to school, she has always pushed me
and Noah to work our hardest. She'll support me if I try and fail,
but *not trying* is something else entirely.

"You didn't submit? Why not?"

"It's complicated. I wasn't…the timing didn't work."

"Because of your classes? The workload was too much?"

"No, not really. It's just that you have to submit something
you worked on during the term. I had some stuff, but nothing I
really loved."

The reassuring hand on my back falls away. "You could
have submitted *something*, even if it wasn't your favorite work."

"I know. I just—" I swallow all the excuses bubbling inside
me and try to give her the truth instead. "I just didn't get it done
in time. I didn't plan well enough, and when I realized I was
behind, I panicked. Like, really panicked. I got scared and really
negative about my art and the stakes felt too high, like *everything*
was riding on that one submission and I…I just got…stuck."

I have no idea if that made any sense to her or not, but it's the
best way I know to describe how I felt. I wait for her reproach,
my heart pounding.

"Oh," she says, finally. "Well…you'll just have to plan better
for next term, then."

I turn to look at her. She's not smiling, but she doesn't seem
angry either. I was terrified of the stern lecture I'd get when I told
her about my failure to submit to the Gallery, but maybe I didn't
need to worry so much. Maybe she understands.

"I will, Mom."

"I know you will." Relief fills me at the return of her

encouraging smile. "You're far too smart and talented to let some little nerves get in your way. You just have to push yourself a little harder so you don't get stuck like that again. You'll be ready for the Gallery next time, I'm sure." Her words are nice—reassuring and full of confidence—and yet they're the last ones I want to hear. If she thinks I didn't submit because of *little nerves*, then she didn't understand me at all.

"But, sweetheart, you know you really can't let these kinds of opportunities pass you by." Her tone becomes firm, and I am all of twelve years old again. "If you're going into something so unpredictable, you have to be completely committed. Owning a business isn't easy. I put every bit of myself into it because that's what it takes. You'll have to do the same if you want to be a real artist."

My throat feels tight, so I clear it before I answer. "I—I know."

"And you need to appreciate what these opportunities mean. I would have done anything to go to college when I was your age. You get the chance to learn and prepare for the rest of your life. You can't waste a moment of it."

"I'm trying, Mom. I don't want to waste it either."

Mom sighs and squeezes my shoulder.

"I know, I know. I worry about you, that's all. I know how much work and sacrifice it takes to follow your dreams, and I want to make sure you're ready for that." I nod, not sure of what else to say. I don't feel particularly ready right now. "And, you know, when you're finding your footing after school, you'll always have your place at Mim's, just in case."

Of course she would say *that* now. The deli is always there, just in case. I think of the unspoken words at the end of her sentence. *Mim's is there just in case…you fail completely as an artist.* She's trying to be supportive, but it's a bitter reminder. I didn't have time for my art this summer because of the store, and I know Mom will only give me more responsibility as I get older. I don't know how to fit my own dreams in with hers—they're not compatible. But I don't know how to tell her that the deli is only standing in my way.

We sit in silence for a moment before Mom stands, places a kiss on my forehead, and wishes me a good night. Once she's gone, I curl up on my bed and press the heels of my hands into my eyes to try to keep the tears at bay. It doesn't work, of course.

I want to put my all into my art, but so far, I have failed completely in an environment designed to help foster my work. I missed the biggest deadline of the semester, and I have no reason to think I'll be any more successful out in the real world.

I trace a finger over the dahlia on my ankle. There's a similar, far more rudimentary one hanging on the fridge in the kitchen—the one that ultimately inspired my tattoo. It was the first of my drawings Mom put up there, the very first time anyone saw something special in my art, and she hasn't taken it down in over a decade. I inked it on my body last year as a reminder of my artistry and her faith in me.

But I don't feel like much of an artist right now. The original dahlia may still be hanging on our ancient fridge, but it's lost in a jumble of forgotten crap, weathered and stained with splattered cooking grease, pinned up by a magnet from a dentist that closed ten years ago.

I don't know if I should get a head start on next semester's art classes or never take an art class again. I don't know the right path. I don't know what I want. Right now, I don't feel ready for *anything*.

CHAPTER TWENTY-ONE

Ginny

Christmas break in Virginia has been even stranger than Thanksgiving. I feel confined and uneasy, but I understand myself better than I did even a month ago. My bedroom felt like a stranger's space at Thanksgiving. Now, I look around and see the small, varied signs of the *real me*—the bookshelf of classics I still love, the painting of mountains I bought at a flea market for twenty dollars, the clay dog my childhood best friend made for me. The queerness and the sense of freedom are missing, but I can connect the dots back to myself now. This room belongs to an old version of me—still me, but a rendition I'm not trying so hard to be anymore.

The longer I'm here, the clearer it is I need to come out to them. I can tell my mom knows something is going on with me; she senses my discomfort, and she's worried. My dad might be picking up on it too, but I can never tell with him. I've wanted to blurt it out since ten minutes after I got off the plane, when my mom asked if I have a college boyfriend yet. There always seems to be a reason that keeps me from going for it. First, I'd just gotten there, and then it was Christmas, and then it was New Year's, and I didn't want to ruin all the cheery holiday togetherness. For most of the time, I've had no excuse other than *I really don't want to*, but that has certainly proven to be enough.

But now I have less than twenty-four hours before I head back to school, and I still haven't said anything. There's something cowardly about the idea of telling them tomorrow—the day I leave. I shouldn't judge myself for it, but I'll be disappointed in myself if I tell them and then immediately get on a plane to escape the consequences. That leaves tonight. I've just helped my mom clean up from dinner, so there's probably only an hour before they decide to turn in for the night. It's now or never.

Or maybe ten minutes from now.

I excuse myself to the bathroom, and immediately call Nat. It rings and rings, but she doesn't answer.

Damn it. Nat has seemed sad since I left New York, but it's hard to tell over text. I've decided to let it be until I can ask her in person, since she hasn't brought it up. But I'm desperate for a few words of encouragement right now, so I shoot her a text.

Hey, are you around?

I wait for a couple minutes, but she doesn't respond. She's probably having dinner or working at the deli. I can't wait for a pep talk, and honestly, I don't want to. I want to be able to do this right now, without anyone's help. I *need* to be able to do this.

My parents are in the living room, in the exact positions I picture them in when I'm not here. They're side by side in their favorite chairs, my dad reading a book, and my mom knitting socks for my cousin's baby.

"Hey...can I talk to y'all for a second?"

My mom turns to me and immediately puts aside her knitting. Dad glances at Mom, then puts a bookmark in his novel and sets it on the table next to him.

"Of course, sweetie," Mom says. Her smile somehow makes me even more nervous, since what I have to say will probably eradicate it.

Should I sit down? Does that make this seem more serious, or less? And which do I even want to convey? It's serious to me, but I don't want this moment to be any more intense than it has to be. I settle for coming up behind the wingback chair across from them and tracing my fingers across the velvet. I need something to do with my hands.

"I, um, I wanted to tell you…" My brain is empty and moving at light speed at the same time. I've been thinking about how to word this for weeks, yet all the speeches I wrote in my head have evaporated. "I just wanted to let you know—" That sounds way too casual. "Or, not let you know. Talk to you about something." But I definitely don't want their opinions. "Or just—just—I've been doing a lot of thinking about myself recently. And changing—not changing, just understanding myself better, you know?"

I look to them for confirmation, even though I haven't really said anything yet. My dad looks confused, while my mom's face is blank. Usually she's the expressive one, and he's much more impassive, but it's like they've switched their go-to expressions.

I watch my fingers ruffle the chair's dark blue velvet, then smooth it back out again. It's just the truth. All I want to do is tell them the truth—I must be able to manage that. I shift the velvet back and forth. Back and forth. Perhaps if I stare at the chair hard enough, I can pretend it's the only thing that will hear what I want to say. I breathe in while I roughen the velvet, then exhale as I smooth it. *Come on, Ginny. Tell them now and it won't feel like some big, horrible secret anymore.*

"I'm bisexual. That's—I just wanted to tell y'all that. I wanted you to know."

I skim my fingers back and forth over the same spot. I don't want to see their faces. I don't want to know their immediate reactions. I should have sat down. Then my legs wouldn't feel so weak. Or maybe telling them tomorrow wasn't such a bad idea. I could have yelled it in the airport à la *Ellen*, then dashed to the plane.

My mom clears her throat, finally, and my eyes shut involuntarily. I brace myself for whatever she's going to say.

"Bisexual?"

Is that a question? I mean, yes, it is apparently. Her tone definitely doesn't make it a statement of fact. My throat is unbelievably dry.

"Yes."

"Not gay?"

My head snaps up. Why is she asking me that? She looks… hopeful?

"No." My voice is rough and gravelly, and I clear my throat quickly.

"Okay…" The word slips out like a sigh of relief. My stomach clenches. What would her reaction have been if I had said I was gay?

"Are you…dating someone? A…a woman?"

I almost want to say yes just to see how she'd react—but I need to be as honest as I can manage right now. "No. Not at the moment."

"But you were?" Her brows pull together.

"No."

"Oh." There it is again. She's relieved.

"Why—I don't—" I mumble without any idea what I want to say. "That's okay?" *Wait. No.* I don't want to seem like I'm asking permission. "I mean—you're not upset?"

"We're glad you said something."

My dad stays silent but nods once in agreement—short and sharp.

In a lot of ways, this is going so much better than I imagined it would. All the nightmares I'd concocted filled with Bible quotes and tears and yelling would be so much worse. But I can't accept their quiet approval. It's false. I know it's false. They don't believe me.

"I—why did you ask me all those questions?" I demand in a tight voice.

Mom crosses her arms over her chest. "Well, this is news to us, Virginia. You don't expect us to have questions?"

"No, but—why *those* questions?"

"We just want to understand, sweetheart."

"What if I'd said yes? What if I'd said I *was* in a relationship with a woman?" My mom shakes her head quickly.

"We understand that things are changing for you, that it's important for young people to have new experiences. We can understand that."

"It's not…" There are too many problems with what she said to pick from. "It's not an *experience*. It's an identity."

"We know identity is so important to your generation." Still silent, my dad nods, like this is the truest thing that's been said in this ridiculous conversation. "We can support that."

"But—"

"Sweetheart, we're not fighting with you."

I rub my eyes in frustration. We've been talking about this for less than five minutes, and I'm already so unbelievably tired of it. I want to leave. I want to lock myself in my room until it's time to go to the airport. But I look at my mom's small, encouraging smile and my dad's completely calm and unbothered stare—and I can't let it go. I can't let them leave this conversation thinking this isn't real.

I smooth the velvet out one last time, then put my hands at my sides, stand up straight, and look my mom directly in the eye.

"You don't think I'm being serious."

"Of course you're being serious," my dad says, like he's exhausted by this topic, even though it's the very first thing he's said. "Your mother has made it very clear that we're listening to you. We hear you."

"But you don't. Not really. You're just rationalizing it away."

"Virginia…" My mom sighs. "We do hear you. But we also *know* you. You're figuring out who you are, and you're trying new things, but we know you're still you."

How am I supposed to argue with that? It's the exact point I'm trying to make, twisted to somehow mean the opposite.

"I am still me. But I'm bi. I've always been bi."

"Okay. We hear you."

An angry, disbelieving laugh bubbles out of me. They've already decided what they want me to be saying, and now my words don't make any difference to them. I could repeat myself a thousand times, but they just don't want to believe me.

"You're upset," my father notes.

"Yes, thanks, Sherlock." I spit out the words before I can filter myself.

His jaw clenches, and Mom purses her lips.

"Virginia!"

"Sorry." As much as I don't want to apologize for any of this, I'd rather do it now than after he guilts me into it.

"I don't know why you're so upset." My mom's tone is now small and defensive. "You can't possibly expect us to have no reaction."

"I didn't. I don't."

"Would you rather we were angry?" Dad asks.

"No, I—"

"It's not fair to be upset that we're having a reaction." Mom sounds like she's going to cry. She knows I won't attack her if she starts crying. "We know this doesn't change you—doesn't change who you are. Isn't that what you want?"

"It doesn't change me because it's always been true. But it does—"

"Right. You're still you. You still want the same things you've always wanted. I know you still want to get married and have children. You've always wanted that, since you were a little girl, and you pretended your dolls were your babies—that was always your favorite."

I could tell her that I only did that because she bought me those dolls and encouraged me to play that specific kind of make-believe, but I don't want to upset her any more than I have to right now.

"That's not related. I don't—I can be bi and get married. I can still want and have children."

"Right. That's exactly what we're saying. You've been away, in a new place, at a new school, and having new experiences. But we know you."

"But I could do all that with a woman. You understand that's what I'm saying, right?"

She breaks the eye contact I've been trying so hard to hold. I wait—I need to hear their response. I won't just back down and let that question go unanswered.

I watch my mom's fingers clench and unclench on her knee. I see my dad turn his gaze briefly to his book. He glances to my mom, blinks, looks to his book, blinks, then turns to my mom again in a slow, agonizing cycle. My mother keeps her eyes trained on her lap. Everything about her is tense—her shoulders, her eyes, her mouth—but she doesn't say a word.

I guess this silence is my answer after all. *No.* They can't comprehend what I'm saying. They'd rather chalk this conversation up to a phase and bet on me marrying a man like they always have. I'm not in a relationship, and I'm not telling them that ending up with a man is out of the question, so they don't believe this is something real and serious.

It could be so much worse. I know it could. But I thought I'd at least get some sense of closure out of this conversation. I hoped that even if they were awful about it, I'd be able to take comfort in finally being out to them, like I've wanted to be for years.

But I don't know how to find closure in this. The conversation still feels unfinished, like I was halfway out of the closet and they decided to freeze me there. I could continue to repeat myself—but I don't think it would make a difference. My words aren't big enough to break the wall of denial they've built for themselves. They aren't able to believe me right now. They just can't do it. Coming out to them will have to be a war, not a battle, and I'm too tired to keep fighting tonight.

"I..." I clear my throat when I hear my voice tremble. I refuse to sound anything but confident in front of them right now. "I'm gonna go pack."

My mom nods. My dad reaches for his book. I go back to my room.

It's only once I'm alone that I notice how shaky I am. *I can't believe I did that.* After years of agonizing about when to tell them—how to tell them—would I ever be brave enough to tell them—I actually did it.

I check my phone in the hope that Nat texted me back, but the screen is free of notifications. I toss it onto my bed next to me with a sigh.

This isn't about her. It's about me. And now that I'm alone again I'm...relieved. Angry and sad and so much other bad stuff, but mostly relieved. Not because of their reaction, but because of mine. I said it. I held my ground and said it again when they pushed me. I tried to make them understand why I was upset, even though it didn't work.

Six months ago, I wouldn't have pressed my mom about the questions she asked me. I would have accepted their disbelief. It would have felt natural then, I think. I would have been fine with them thinking it was a phase, because hey, maybe I'd end up with a man and it wouldn't matter anyway. But after four months at school—in a community where being queer is not only accepted but loved—I can't go back to thinking my sexuality doesn't matter. It matters to me so much. Even if I never date a woman. Even if I meet a guy tomorrow and fall in love and we're together for the rest of my life, it matters to me that I don't keep this part of myself a secret.

A tear rolls down my cheek. But I'm smiling, too, because I can't believe I'm actually here. Out to my parents or not, I can't believe I'm out to myself, and I'm happy about it. I've never let myself try to feel that way before. I've never let myself want that, because it felt so far away. But tonight—vocally fighting for my queerness for the first time ever—I let myself admit how important it is to me.

That means everything to me.

My phone vibrates. It's a text from Beth saying how excited she is to get back from break and see everyone tomorrow. I consider texting her back but decide to do what I really want. I call her.

"Hello?" She sounds confused.

"Hey, sorry for calling, I don't know if that's weird—"

"Of course not! I know it's not very Gen Z of me, but I'm always down for a phone call."

I laugh, reveling in the release of tension. I tell her about it all—everything I said, everything my parents said, everything they didn't say but I could see on their faces and hear in their silences. She's tentative and apologetic at first, but once I tell her I'm not in the middle of a total meltdown, she's bursting with happiness for me.

This is exactly what I needed—to talk to someone who's been through the same thing, who shares her experience with me and relates to me but doesn't impose her feelings onto mine. Beth is serious yet funny, and I appreciate her friendship in this moment more than ever.

"Have you talked to Nat yet?" she asks after we've been talking for an hour or so.

"I texted her, but she must be busy." She emits a little humming noise that makes me laugh. "What? Why do you ask?"

"I just know this has been weighing on you." After the sledding incident a couple weeks ago, I'd mentioned to Beth how my newness to being out was one of the worries I have about being in a relationship.

"Yeah…" I want to find the right words, and I trust Beth will let me take my time. "I know we haven't talked about my trip to Brooklyn with Nat, but honestly that made me feel like I'm being a total idiot."

"Ginny. You're not an idiot."

"What was it Mack called me? A dope."

She laughs but chides me anyway. "You're not a dope."

"I'm a little bit of a dope. I'm—I'm crazy about Nat. We all know that, including her. And going home with her…it was all kinda amazing. There were like thirty tiny moments I look back on now and have no idea why I didn't just kiss her."

"Because you're nervous, probably?"

"And that's the dope part."

"Come on." I can almost see her rolling her eyes at me. "It's beyond normal to be nervous about doing something like that."

"Right. But I know she feels the same way. She literally could not be more clear about how she feels. If I kissed her, I know she'd kiss me back."

"It's still new. And it's always a little scary to kiss someone for the first time."

"Well…" I close my eyes and smile into my empty room. "Second time would be more accurate."

"Wait, wait, wait! You've kissed her before? *Excuse me?* How do I not know about this?"

"She kissed me, if you want to get specific about it."

"I absolutely do."

"It was just once. After Thanksgiving."

Beth hums, thinking. "After Thanksgiving…"

"Like, right after. The night we all got back from break."

"Huh. I remember that night. Nat seemed really intense and upset, and she ran out of the room, and you followed her. Then later you ran out and…and there was a lot of running out of the party between the two of you."

"Yeah, exactly." It still surprises me just how much other people have paid attention to our interactions. "She was in a bad headspace. We talked, and she kissed me. It was weird, and confusing, and I reacted badly. I had a hard time believing it wasn't just because she was drunk and sad."

"Oh, Nat." Beth chuckles. "*That* is a dopey move."

"We were both dopes. That's why I didn't tell you about it."

"Well, that makes kissing her now even more nerve-wracking, actually. Last time it was a whole confusing thing. And now the ball's in your court, and you have to initiate it."

"Yeah…I'm not the best at initiating things."

"You could just go up to her and be like *Okay, you can kiss me now.*"

I groan, and she laughs at me. "I think I would die of embarrassment."

"I'm pretty sure Nat won't mind how you do it. She just wants to be with you."

I nod, even though I know she can't see me. "I know you're right. I just…it'll make it all real, you know?"

"Yeah. That makes a lot of sense."

I've been holding myself back, hoping I'd somehow get confirmation that me and Nat being together is the right decision, so I could go in without being afraid. But that's never going to happen. I'll be nervous to jump into a relationship with her, no matter when I do it, so that's no reason to keep us in this weird limbo when I know a real relationship is what we both want.

Even if we're shitty girlfriends, I just want us to be each other's.

I stare up at the ceiling with determination. "I just need to do it."

"Right!" Beth immediately switches from quietly supportive to excited and encouraging. "Just go for it!"

"I will. When I see her tomorrow, I'm gonna go for it."

CHAPTER TWENTY-TWO

Natalie

This is exactly what I needed on my first night back at school. My friends and I dance in a group, sing along to the music playing on someone's speaker, and laugh at nothing. I'm two drinks deep, teetering on the line between tipsy and drunk. I'm loose and giddy, the tension that's been living in my body throughout the break finally easing.

I haven't felt this free in weeks.

A couple dozen people are squished into the common room of Lizzie's dorm for this welcome back party. It's the ideal size—small enough that you can talk to your friends without yelling, but big enough to create a good-sized crowd of dancers.

I'm so happy to be with my friends again. Lizzie, Mack, and Beth dance with me, while Raf stands off to the side, chatting with Isaiah. Ginny isn't here yet, but she texted a while ago to say she was off the plane and on a bus, so she should walk in any minute now. I keep one eye on the door while I dance, in the hopes that I'll see her on the threshold. Every time it opens, her arrival plays like a movie in my head.

The door opens, Ginny silhouetted by moonlight before she enters. She comes into the light and searches the room. Her eyes land on mine and she smiles. The curve of her mouth, the glimmer in her eyes, the half-moon dimples piercing her cheeks—perfection.

I'm desperate to see her. In New York, everything clicked into place between us. I think—or hope, at least—that I've finally earned her trust. We didn't talk much after she left, but the anticipation of seeing her in person again has grown every day.

And there's the door again. I slow my dancing to a sway as I watch it open. Moonlight spills in and—*damn*. Still not Ginny.

"Nat!" I blink at Lizzie, who raises her eyebrows at me in question.

"Sorry, what?" I lean in, as if distance was the reason I didn't hear what she said, not distraction.

"Do you want to take a break with me? I need some water."

I look to Mack and Beth, but they're in their own world, dancing close together, not noticing anything but each other.

"Sure, I could use a break." I follow Lizzie to the other side of the room, where she rummages behind one of the couches to find where she stashed her water bottle.

The rush of energy from the dancing subsides as I stand still for the first time in an hour, and I'm left a little light-headed and wobbly. I lean against the wall to steady myself.

"You haven't told me about your break yet," Lizzie says when she straightens, water bottle in hand.

"It was…not great." I don't want to talk about it, but I let the words flow anyway. "A lot of tension between me and my mom. I don't—um—I don't really know what I'm gonna do about all of that yet." My head isn't clear enough to explain any better.

Lizzie frowns. "I'm sorry. That sucks."

"Yeah." Memories of Ginny's eyes shining in the glow of Christmas lights come back to me. "It wasn't all bad, though. Ginny staying with us was amazing."

"Oh, right. So, it was good? Having her in your home, with your family? Not awkward, or, like, too close, or whatever?"

"No, it was great. I showed her around my neighborhood, and we went to some of my favorite places in the city. My mom and Noah really liked her. It was all kind of perfect, actually. I know it was only a couple days, but we got closer. I think…" A grin forms on my face. "I think maybe she's ready to be together."

Her brows rise. "Really?"

"Yeah, really."

"Wow."

The surprise on her face is unnerving, but I try to laugh it off. "You don't have to look quite so shocked, Liz."

"Oh, come on, I'm not shocked. Her feelings for you are beyond obvious. It's just new. I'm not used to this committed-settled-relationship version of Nat, so I'm still recalibrating. It's gonna be so crazy to see you in a relationship."

I sink back against the wall behind me. Lizzie finds the idea of me in a relationship *crazy*. I can still barely picture it myself, but my best friend's lack of endorsement doesn't feel very promising.

"Are you okay, Nat?" I look up into Lizzie's concerned brown eyes. "You look…spooked or something."

"Yeah, just…um…I'm a little light-headed." It's not a lie—I am a bit dizzy.

"Do you want me to walk you home?"

"No, no, I'm okay. It's not that bad, and I can't leave. Ginny should be here soon."

Lizzie frowns. "Are you sure you're ready for that right now?"

I hear uncertainty in her voice, and I feel ten times worse.

"What? Why would you—I mean, do you think I'm not ready?"

"No, I wasn't saying that. You just seem freaked out."

The movement of the door behind Lizzie catches my eye. My heart starts beating out of my chest as I watch someone walk into the light and…it's a tall, red-haired girl. Not Ginny. I'm not sure whether I'm disappointed or relieved, but I can't keep standing here watching the door.

"I—um…" I swallow when my words come out choked. "I need a moment."

Lizzie's brows pull together. "Do you need—"

"I'm not going to throw up or anything. I—I just need a moment alone." I ignore the churning in my stomach and speed-walk from the common room, down the hallway, and into the bathroom. A breath rushes out of me the moment I close myself inside. I shut my eyes, my head swimming.

I shouldn't be terrified to talk to Ginny. I've been waiting weeks to see her in person, mostly excited and a little bit anxious. But now the eagerness has evaporated, and the nerves have turned into full-blown panic. I'm afraid she'll reject me again—afraid she'll tell me she's ready and I'll mess it up somehow—afraid of anything and everything that could happen when we finally see each other again.

Lizzie's words echo in my head. *Are you sure you're ready?*

No. I'm not sure. I hope I'm ready, but I don't know how to be sure.

I look in the mirror. My eyes are red and misty. I wipe away a tear and notice my hand shaking. *I'm such a mess.*

I need to go to my room. I'll talk to Ginny tomorrow, when I'm better. I cannot speak to her like this. I hurry back through the hallway, but Lizzie catches me the moment I reach the common room.

"Nat, I really didn't mean to—"

"I know. It's okay, I just—I don't feel very well. Can we please talk about this tomorrow?" She frowns. "Please, Lizzie?"

I'll talk about whatever she wants tomorrow, but I can't handle it tonight. I'm far too out of control to have a conversation right now. She nods reluctantly.

"Okay, I guess. Do you need someone to walk you home? You do look kinda pale."

No. I just need to be alone.

"No, no. It's two minutes away, I'll be fine." I turn toward the front door before she can say another word. I just need to make it out the door, a few houses down, and— *Fuck.*

Ginny.

She steps inside and the door closes behind her. I'm watching one of my sketches come to life. Everything is how I pictured it, but real, solid, and only a few feet away. Her dark hair is half up, and little tendrils dangle as if someone designed them to frame her face. Beneath her unzipped puffy jacket, she's wearing the overalls I gave her, and they look even better on her than I hoped they would. She turns her head, her eyes find mine, and she smiles. She's a dream, floating in to make everything better. *She's perfect.*

And I'm a total mess.

My head spins. Tears push at the back of my eyes as she walks through the crowd. I swear they are the same tears I've been holding in since that conversation with my mom the night Ginny left Brooklyn.

I'm back at the party after Thanksgiving—tipsy, upset, and unwieldy—about to fuck things up even worse than I already have. I'm going hurt her somehow if I talk to her like this. I need to leave *right now*.

I try to go around her, but she's right in my way, that adorably dimpled smile on her face.

"Hi!" She comes closer, like she's going to hug me, but I step away.

"No. I—no. Can you just—can you please just not talk to me right now?"

She blinks, the smile drops from her face, and I feel like a complete piece of shit. But there's no backing out now.

"Seriously." I look her right in the eyes. "Please leave me alone."

CHAPTER TWENTY-THREE

Ginny

I blink.

I don't know what else to do but hope that closing my eyes for the briefest moment will change the expression on her face or erase her words from my memory. I don't think I heard her wrong, and she doesn't look like she's joking, but I don't know what I could have done for her to be so upset with me.

"What?" I am at a loss for anything more specific to say.

"I need you to leave me alone." It doesn't hurt any less the second time, but now I push her on it immediately.

"Why? What's going on?"

"I really don't want to talk right now."

"Did I—did I do something wrong? Or did—"

"Of course you didn't." She looks pale and her eyes are watery. She must be drunk. But I still don't understand what's happening.

"Are you okay, Nat? You seem—" She cuts me off with a groan, and she rubs her eyes with the heels of her hands.

"Please don't ask me questions. I can't do this right now. Can you just let it go?" She tries to step around me, but I stop her.

"Did something happen at home? Do you need to talk or—"

"Ginny!" She yells over the music, drawing attention from the people around us. "Stop asking me that! I'm telling you what I need—and I need to not talk to you right now!"

Lizzie is at Nat's side suddenly, concern and anger weaved together on her face.

"Jesus, Nat," she says in a low, tense voice, putting a hand on Nat's shoulder. "You need to calm down."

Nat pulls away and turns her anger on Lizzie. "Just leave me alone! Both of you." She pushes past me and disappears into the crowd, leaving us both in stunned silence.

What the hell just happened?

"I'm sorry, Ginny," Lizzie says, even though we both just got yelled at. "She wasn't feeling well, and I...I think maybe I made things worse."

"It's okay, I—" I cut myself off, because it's not okay. I'm about to cry.

"I'm gonna make sure she gets to her room okay. Or, you know, safe, at least."

"Good idea." I nod. We exchange a tense smile, and she leaves.

I'm left in the middle of this overly crowded room, tears building in my eyes. I turn around and go back outside as quickly as I can, not to follow Nat and Lizzie, but to escape—escape that conversation—escape that feeling. The cold air is bracing and keeps my tears at bay.

Her outburst can't be my fault. I haven't seen her in weeks. Something else must be going on with her, but that doesn't make her harsh words hurt any less. And I know she doesn't hate me, but that doesn't stop me from wondering why she might. I hear the door open behind me and move out of the way.

"Sorry, I—"

Oh. It's Beth, Mack, and Rafael. Concern is written on every inch of their faces.

"Hey," Mack says in a soft, gentle tone. "Are you okay? We saw that, uh, conversation with Nat."

They saw her yelling at me, they mean. I nod, not necessarily to answer their question, but because I need time to find the right words. I'm afraid to admit how deeply hurt I am aloud. If I do, they'll see every bit of my jumbled, fervent feelings for Nat.

"She's kinda drunk, I think," Rafael says.

"Yeah, I—" I choke out a laugh, even though nothing feels funny. "I was getting that."

"I'm sure it's not about you." Beth offers a reassuring smile, but that just makes my last bit of resolve disappear, and I start to cry. "Hey, it's okay."

She pulls me into a hug, but I'm too tense to take comfort in it. I pull away and brace my hands on her arms. I saw them all inside—Mack and Beth dancing together and Raf making out with his ex. I don't want to ruin their nice night with my bad one.

"Y'all are sweet for following me out, but I'm fine, I promise."

Rafael puts a hand on my arm. "You're not fine."

"I'm not *great*, but—"

"We all know how much you care about Nat." Beth ducks her head to hold my gaze. "It's okay. Whatever happened, we're here for you."

All three of them gather me in one big hug, and the tension leaves my body in a rush, pain taking its place. My tears shift into full-fledged, no-holds-barred sobs.

"I—" I suck in a breath of air, struggling to breathe, talk, and cry at the same time. "I thought we were finally on the same page, but she told me to leave her alone. She told me not to talk to her."

"*What?*"

I pull out of the hug to see Mack's face slack with shock.

"*That's* what she said?" Rafael raises his brows. "Wow. I mean, I saw her yelling, but I'm still surprised she would say *that*."

"You—" Beth shakes her head, like she doesn't believe what I'm saying. "You told her how you felt, and she—"

"No! I barely said anything. I said hi."

Mack squints at me. "Was she, like, joking or something?"

"No! I don't know why, but no. She told me to go away, and when I pushed her on why, she yelled. She said to leave her alone, and she meant it."

Raf puts a comforting hand on my back, but Mack shakes their head in disbelief.

"I just—I can't believe she would do that."

Anger bubbles in my stomach, and I snap at them. "Well, she did!"

Mack's eyes widen. "I believe you."

"*Of course* we believe you," Beth says.

"I just—It's just crazy. I don't understand it."

Something clicks in me at Mack's words. I do understand it, at least a little. I know how negative Nat can be when she's upset. In a way, I'm familiar with this version of her. The sad, self-sabotaging girl who desperately wants to pretend she's not feeling all the things she doesn't know how to handle. It's kind of like the way she was with me before Thanksgiving, when she would never quite tell me what she was feeling.

This was different, though, because she wasn't pretending to be happy like she would then. Tonight, all the feelings she didn't want to deal with were right at the surface, no matter how much she didn't want them to be there. And those feelings were directed at me.

Does she not like me anymore? Does she feel like I've been wasting her time? Is she disappointed in me for not being brave enough to be with her?

I want so badly not to take her anger to heart. The last time I saw her, everything seemed right between us. I couldn't have done something to offend her that badly in the last three weeks.

I want to believe she's not upset because of something I did, but I can't stop seeing the anger and disappointment in her eyes when I spoke to her.

"Ginny?"

I blink into Beth's questioning gaze. "What if I waited too long?"

I explore each of their expressions as if one of them might contain the answers to all the questions and anxieties I have right now.

"What if she's pissed that she's been so open with me, and I've been holding myself back from her?"

Mack shakes their head but says nothing. Beth just presses her lips together and watches me with sad eyes.

"What if she's changed her mind, and she feels like I've been stringing her along? She wouldn't really be that wrong."

"Nat's smarter than that," Mack says. "She wouldn't reject you just because you were taking some time to figure things out."

All three of them send me soft, comforting smiles. I must look pretty damn sad right now.

"Look..." Beth hesitates, and I can tell she's choosing her words carefully. "Even if she is frustrated with you for some reason, it doesn't mean her feelings have changed."

Logically, I know Beth's right. Nat cares about me. She could be upset about a million different things that have nothing to do with me.

Maybe I should go after her. I could find her and force her to talk to me.

But no, that's an awful idea. She did not want to talk to me, and I doubt that's going to change tonight. Lizzie said she'd make sure she was safe. As desperate as I am for an explanation, I need to wait until she's ready to talk to me. Or at least until tomorrow.

"I just—" I swallow and brush the tears out of my eyes. "I think I just need to go to bed. If this is her way of rejecting me, I can't deal with that tonight. And if it's not, I'm gonna drive myself crazy asking questions I can't answer."

Beth smiles at me. "That sounds like a very good idea."

"Let's get you back to your room," Raf says, as he slips his arm through mine and turns us in the direction of my dorm.

I shake my head half-heartedly. "You don't have to do that. Y'all should enjoy the party." I shoot him the most playful glance I can manage. "I saw you with Isaiah. You don't want to miss that."

He rolls his eyes as Mack and Beth pretend to be shocked. "Isaiah can wait. C'mon." He tugs me forward, and the four of us start down the path together. They exchange random funny stories from their holidays, and no one pushes me when I choose to listen instead of talk.

They really are good friends. The best. I need to take comfort in the support I have from them. They will be here for me with or without Nat.

They walk me all the way to my door, each giving me a tight hug before they leave.

Jess pulls me into another hug the moment I open the door to our room. "Hey! It's so good to see you! How was your break?" She pulls away to look me in the eye, and her face falls. "Hey… are you okay?"

"Yeah, I, um, I'll be fine. I just had a weird semi fight with Natalie."

She frowns, sympathy in her eyes. "I'm sorry. That sucks."

I offer as much of a smile as I can muster, then turn to slip off my jacket and hang it.

"Hey, I love your overalls!"

Her words have the exact opposite effect than a compliment should. Tears threaten to pour out again, and I close my eyes to brace against them.

"Oh!" She approaches me tentatively, like she's afraid one wrong move will cause me to explode. "Hey, hey, I'm sorry. I didn't mean to—"

"It's okay, Jess. It's not you, I promise."

"Okay…Why don't I go make you some tea?"

I smile. I made her tea once when she saw pictures of her ex with a new girl on Instagram.

As embarrassed as I am to be a crying mess in front of her, it's nice to be reminded again of my strong support system here. My friends are ready for anything, even *girl drama*, a concept I never imagined I'd be comfortable enough to talk about before college.

"That would be amazing. Thank you."

"Of course." She grabs a mug and some tea, then rushes toward the kitchen.

Once the door closes behind her, my head fills again with all the questions my friends tried to chase away.

Is she okay? Are *we* okay?

I must have waited too long, right? Why else would she be so angry with me?

The look she gave me when she saw me walking toward her…She looked like the last thing in the world she wanted was to see me. I have absolutely no idea what was going through her head in that moment, and that is beyond frightening. Maybe I don't understand her half as well as I think I do. Maybe she has more walls than I'm capable of tearing down.

No. She wants me to get to know her. She wants to let me see her without pretenses or barriers. I know that. Something bad must have happened at home. That makes more sense than anything else.

This worrying is pointless. I can't possibly understand the reason she was so upset on my own. I need to talk to Nat.

Chapter Twenty-four

Natalie

I have *the worst* timing. If I have any particularly special talent, it's doing the exact wrong thing at the exact wrong time.

I need to make a list of all the reasons why I should never drink alcohol ever again:

1. Alcohol doesn't make me feel better.
2. It makes my decision-making skills even worse than they usually are.
3. It brings out my most destructive tendencies.
4. Hangovers suck.

There's no new information for me, but I'm feeling the consequences more than ever this morning, so I'm committing them to memory for good.

The alcohol isn't responsible, though. I probably would have panicked sober, too, but maybe with less drama. I gingerly sip my coffee and nibble on some toast in the dining hall. I hope the food—along with the ibuprofen I took the moment I woke up—will help me feel better.

But feeling better physically is so far from my biggest problem. I'm way more worried about everything I said to my friends. *Ugh.* I cannot believe I acted like that.

I woke an hour ago to three texts from Lizzie. She followed me to my room last night, told me to talk to her in the morning, and closed the door behind me. I guess I slept later than she wanted, because the messages all echo her desire to speak with me ASAP.

There were no texts from Ginny, but of course she's the one I can't stop thinking about. I've undone all the effort I put into our relationship. I promised I'd be open and honest with her, even when I was feeling awful, and I did the opposite last night. I followed the exact patterns that she told me were the reasons she didn't want to be with me. And I yelled at her.

I can't blame her for not trusting me now. I haven't earned it.

The last half hour here has helped me put a lot of things in perspective. I've been trying to be better for Ginny, but if I really want her to trust me, she's also going to have to see me at my worst. Last night I was afraid I would hurt her if I couldn't control myself, but I ended up hurting her because I was so desperate to contain those feelings.

I don't want to be the person who yells at her friends instead of asking for support. I don't want to take such a passive approach to my own life anymore. I can't wait around for a life I don't want. I need to choose to pursue the things I love wholeheartedly. I have to believe in myself first, and I'm the only one who can change that.

"Hey." I look up from my food and right into Lizzie's eyes. She looks hesitant, but she's also here, with a plate of scrambled eggs and bacon in her hands. She gestures to the table. "Can I sit?"

"Of course." She sets her plate at the seat across from mine. "I'm sorry." I start talking before she even sits down. "I'm so sorry. I yelled at you, and I ran away instead of talking to you. I was childish and rude, and I'm sorry. You were just trying to be a good friend."

"It's okay, Nat. I mean, I appreciate the apology, but honestly the only thing I'm mad about is you not telling me what the hell happened. We were talking, and clearly something I said freaked you out, but you didn't want to talk to me about it. I really wish you would—"

"You said it would be crazy to see me in a relationship."

Lizzie blinks at me. "That's what freaked me out. I know how you meant it, but in the moment, it felt like you were saying I was crazy to even try to be with Ginny. And then you asked me if I was ready to talk to her, and I didn't feel ready anymore. I'd been waiting to see her in person again for weeks, building it up in my head, and it felt like the entire possibility of our relationship was at stake. So, one word from you and I just panicked."

Lizzie reaches across the table to grab my hand. "You know I never meant to make you doubt yourself, right?"

"I know, Liz. Honestly, you could have said just about anything, and my brain would have found a way to spiral over it."

"It's new to see you so into someone, but it's not unimaginable or something. It makes sense, actually. You're a good friend, Nat. You're loyal and thoughtful. I'm sure you'll be a great girl-friend."

Lizzie's encouragement is exactly what I need. She may be right. Maybe I can be a good girlfriend. Maybe the idea of earning Ginny's trust—deserving her trust—isn't so implausible after all.

"Thank you." I squeeze her hand. "That means a lot—like, so much." Lizzie smiles and squeezes my hand back. "I love you, Liz."

"I know. I love you, too." She pulls her hand away. "Ugh, we need to stop this before I start crying in the dining hall. I'd never recover from the embarrassment." We laugh, but then she fixes me with a stern look. "As happy as I am to be talking to you about this, why are you here? Have you talked to Ginny yet?"

"No. I was getting up my courage. And trying to dull my hangover."

"And stalling." She pops a brow in challenge.

"Yes, and stalling. I can admit that."

"I understand wanting to be less hungover, but…the longer you wait, the longer she has to be mad at you."

She's right. I'm terrified of what Ginny's going to say when I see her, but I shouldn't wait a moment longer to start fixing what I broke last night. I look from my empty plate to her full one.

"Are you gonna be pissed if I leave right now?" I ask, but Lizzie smiles and shakes her head.

"I'm gonna be pissed if you *don't* leave right now."

I hop up from my chair, nervous energy already coursing through me, and button up my jacket with slightly shaking hands. After I loop my scarf around my neck, Lizzie stands and pulls me into a tight hug.

"Good luck, Nat. Whatever Ginny says, I'm happy for you, for putting yourself out there like this."

A lump forms in my throat. I've never given her the opportunity to support me like this before—never been honest enough for her to know exactly what I needed to hear—but I won't make that mistake again.

"Thank you. You're the best, Liz."

"I know." She pulls away, grabs my shoulders, and turns me to face the door. "You got this."

I give her one last smile over my shoulder, then rush out the door. I jog outside, then stop to take in a deep breath of the cold winter air. The food and ibuprofen have turned my headache from jackhammer intensity to more of a light buzzing, and the sun starts to feel invigorating instead of blinding. I take another breath.

I'm going to be okay.

I don't know if Ginny will forgive me. It's entirely possible that I've fucked things up beyond repair. But I'm not going to beat myself up over it without talking to her first. I need to take action, not wallow.

Maybe I should start by texting her. I can apologize for my behavior last night and assure her I wasn't angry with her. Or maybe I should call.

No.

I have to find her so I can talk to her in person. The idea of having my apology rejected to my face is way more terrifying than having it rejected over the phone, but I don't want to make decisions out of fear. I have to do this right.

I should walk back to my dorm, change into something

slightly nicer than the sweatpants and flannel I threw on to go to the dining hall, then go to her room to grovel.

There. Now I have a plan. She may still reject my apology, but I have to give it my all.

I push my door open gently, because Payton was still sleeping when I left to get breakfast. I see immediately she's not in bed anymore.

"Hi."

"Holy shit!" I whip around to see someone sitting on my bed—*Ginny*.

"Sorry." She slips off the bed to stand. "I didn't mean to scare you."

"No, I—no. It's okay." I place a hand on my chest and will my heartbeat to slow. It's racing now—not because I'm surprised someone's here, but because I'm delighted she's here. She came to my room, just as I was about to find her. That must be a good sign.

"I knocked on the door and Payton let me in, then she left."

"Right." I nod at her explanation, but she continues.

"She said I could wait for you here, but maybe it would have been better to have waited in the hall. Also, maybe I shouldn't have come by without texting first, in case you were sleeping, but I figured noon seemed like late enough to check."

"It's fine, Ginny." She nods and presses her lips together. "Also, hi. Sorry I didn't return your hi earlier, I was surprised."

"That's okay."

"I'm so happy you're here." I take a step closer so there's only a couple feet between us. I want to look her right in the eye when I apologize. "I was just about to head over to talk to you."

"You were?"

"Of course. I have to apologize for last night. I can't believe I was so mean to you. I'm really sorry." Some of the tension in my chest releases when she nods, but I barrel on before she can reply. "I just—I was having a bad night. At home after you left…I had this…weird conversation with my mom. I felt like I'd disappointed her, and I'd disappointed myself, and I spent most of the break feeling like shit about it." The words flow out so quickly I can barely breathe. "And then last night I freaked out over something Lizzie said—not that it's Lizzie's fault, it's not, it's completely my fault—but I felt so terrified to see you, like I could absolutely never deserve you. And I felt super mixed-up and out of it and kinda drunk and I just wanted to go home and not see you until I was feeling better. But then you came in and you were wearing your overalls. Your *overalls*. The ones I gave you."

Her brow furrows in confusion. "The overalls upset you?" Her voice is entirely earnest, and a strangled groan mixed with a laugh escapes me, because that is absolutely not what I'm trying to convey.

"No. Not at all. It was just so damn good to see you. I missed you, and there you were looking all perfect in your overalls when I was feeling like shit, and I wasn't ready for it. Just seeing you across the room made me feel real, and grounded, and more in touch with my emotions than I had been in weeks. I panicked, and I didn't trust myself not to ruin things completely. Which, I guess, I may have done anyway. I was so terrified I'd hurt you, I felt like I had no idea how to talk to you."

Her eyebrows shoot up over the rims of her glasses, and she blinks at me, surprised.

"You—you yelled at me because you didn't want to hurt me?"

I laugh, because even though I already know how stupid I was last night, I sound even stupider when I hear her describe it. "Yeah. I realize that's completely idiotic and self-sabotaging, but—"

"No." She shakes her head and takes a step closer to me. "I mean—yes. It is self-sabotaging, and it's not a good long-term plan, but I get it."

"You do?" There's so much compassion in her eyes, but it still feels hard to believe.

"Yeah. I'd like to think I know you well enough by now to understand that kind of stuff about you. And…I guess sometimes I worry about a similar kind of thing. I get scared that being closer to you means I might hurt you with the messed-up crap in my head."

"Oh. I—I thought you'd be mad at me." I'm still not sure why she isn't. She must be at least a little frustrated.

"Well, I'd love it if you didn't yell at me to leave you alone again, but I'm not mad."

I bury my head in my hands, and my cheeks heat with embarrassment. "I can't believe I yelled at you."

"It's okay."

"It's really not. It was awful. I'm so sorry, Ginny. You totally deserve to hate me."

Her fingers encircle one of my wrists, and she gently pulls my hand away from my face. Even though she said she wasn't mad, I'm still surprised by the soft smile on her face.

"It's *okay*. I don't hate you—not at all. I'm just glad we can talk about this."

I stare at my feet. I need to be honest about what I'm thinking, but I'm terrified something I say will make her smile fade.

"But I…" I could just accept that she says she's not angry, but I need to understand why she doesn't hate me for how I acted last night, or I'll never stop hating myself for my mistakes. "I broke the promise I made you. How are you okay with that?"

She doesn't say anything for a moment, and the hand on my wrist releases me. When I risk a look back at her face, her smile is gone. But she doesn't look angry, like I feared. Instead, she looks completely baffled.

"What are you talking about? What promise?"

I stumble over my words for a moment. How can she not know what I'm talking about? "I—I told you I was going to be open with you, and I wasn't going to push you away. And I've been trying so hard to do that, but last night I—"

"Listen to yourself, Nat!" Ginny laughs like she can't believe what I'm saying. "That was last night. And we're already here talking about it. I don't need you to always be in the mood to tell me everything. Everyone has days where they don't want to talk stuff through. It's about how you deal with that."

"I dealt with it pretty horribly last night."

She just laughs again. "Well, yeah. And like I said, it would be great if next time you could say something more like *I don't want to talk about it right now* instead of yelling at me but—"

"I promise I won't do anything like that again. It was awful."

"It's okay. I forgive you."

"You don't have to. I mean—it's okay if you're still mad. You have every right in the world to—" I slam my mouth shut at the feel of her hand slipping into mine.

"I'm not mad. Honestly, I'm a little bit happy it happened." Her smile proves it—dimples and all—but I still have to understand.

"You're happy I yelled at you?"

"No, but I realized something. When I woke up this morning, I knew this would happen. I knew we'd talk about it, and we'd figure it out." She tugs my hand gently so I'm only inches away. "Because I…" She tilts her head up to meet my gaze, and I watch her throat work as she swallows. "I trust you. I know you want to be open with me, and that even if you push me away for a moment, you'll let me in again soon. I would never give up on you over one fight, or you not wanting to share one time. That's not how this works. Last night freaked me out, sure, but I trust you."

"Really?" My voice is barely above a whisper. She's so close.

"Really."

I close the distance and kiss her, because there's nothing else to do when she says the exact words I've been wanting to hear for weeks. I hold her face in my hands just like I did the first time I kissed her, and it's just as magical as it was then. Better, really, because this thing between us feels real and it's been voiced aloud by both of us, instead of a fantasy that hadn't existed anywhere but in our own heads.

Actually—*damn it*. This has been spoken aloud by both of us, but not today. And even though I feel like something's changed between us recently, I don't know that this is what she really wants.

I pull away and take a couple steps back. I let the words

tumble out of my mouth before I can process them. "Shit. Sorry. I didn't…You said you trust me. But that doesn't mean you wanted me to kiss you. I shouldn't have done that. I'm sorry."

She smiles and shakes her head. "Oh, shut up. Of course I wanted you to kiss me."

We laugh and she loops her arms around my neck to draw me back into another kiss.

Fuck. Yes.

I pull her as close to me as possible, my arms around her waist, like maybe I could combine us into one person if I hold her tightly enough. Her tongue touches mine and I feel light-headed.

"This is what I was coming to tell you yesterday." Her lips brush against mine as she speaks. "I just want to be with you, even if we're bad at it. I'm sorry I took so long to figure that out."

"Well, damn. I can't believe that was the day I chose to act like a total idiot."

She laughs into another kiss, and I take her face in my hands again. I trace one of her dimples with my thumb, feeling it appear and disappear as she kisses me.

I am a little crazed. Finally being here. Finally being with her. Finally knowing this is as real and big and important as it felt inside my head.

I'm usually calm and purposeful when I'm kissing someone—trying to ensure we're both having the best time possible, and struggling to get fully out of my head like I wish I could. I'm not capable of that right now. I'm rushed and clumsy as I kiss her with months of built-up desperation. I'm so far from being stuck in my head that I can barely think. This is my whole world right now. Her. The soft skin at the small of her back when I slip my fingers just under the hem of her shirt. The way she fists her hands in my hair. It's too much and not enough all at once. I kiss her so hard she stumbles backward and almost falls onto my bed. She pulls away with a laugh.

"We should probably lock the door," she says.

I nod, my nose bumping hers. "Right."

"I mean, I don't know exactly what I'm ready to do right now, but whatever it is, we should probably lock the door."

"Right." I can't seem to access any other words with her so close. I release her slowly and resist the urge to run to the door and back as fast as possible. My head clears a bit as I walk over. I never would have remembered this if she hadn't said something. "I always forget to lock these doors."

She laughs like I've made the greatest joke of all time. I turn to her and narrow my eyes playfully.

"What's so funny?"

"You said something like that the first time we talked." I furrow my brow at her as I flip the lock, my head too full of this moment to remember anything else. "When I walked in on you getting dressed after you hooked up with Jess."

"Oh!" I burst out laughing as the shock on her face at the sight of me half-naked comes back to me. "Right. That feels like forever ago."

"It does." She reaches out for me as I approach her again. I settle my hips against hers, bracing my hands on the bed behind her.

"You were very surprised. It was a little bit funny."

"You were half-naked. More than half—like eighty percent naked. I'd never seen a half-naked girl in reality before."

"You'd seen them elsewhere?"

She wrinkles her nose at me. "TV. Movies. You know what I mean."

"I do. Well, I'm honored to have been the first, even if it was an accident."

"As you should be."

I kiss one of her dimples, then the other. The freedom to stare without limitation or awkwardness is amazing.

"Look at you all up close," I murmur.

She frowns thoughtfully, and I kiss her frown, too.

"You've been up close with me before. It was in this very room, even."

Our first kiss feels like it happened in a different universe, even if it was only a few feet away from where we are now.

"It was dark," I say. "We were rushed and had no idea what it meant. This feels so different. This is…everything I've wanted."

She nods slowly and her nose traces against mine.

"Me too." She smiles, and her dimples pop again.

"Your dimples are overwhelming up close."

She coughs out a confused laugh. "Sorry?"

"You should know now that I'm obsessed with your dimples."

"I'm starting to sense that."

I shrug and my shoulder brushes hers. "I'm only human."

She looks down and I follow her gaze to watch her play with the corner of my shirt.

"Well, I'm obsessed with a lot of things about you, too."

I look into her eyes. Her glasses have slipped down the bridge of her nose just enough that she can watch me over the rims. Her eyes are so green up close.

"Oh yeah?"

"Yeah."

I kiss her again, slowly this time, savoring the ability to be this close to her, basking in the knowledge that she wants me here. She moves a hand to the back of my head and plays with my hair. Maybe she's thought about doing that as much as I've thought about tracing her dimples.

She pulls back, her fingers still toying with the hair at the nape of my neck. She looks me right in the eye, but I can see concern in the furrow of her brow. "I'm happy to be up close with you, Nat, but I'm a little nervous about this stuff, too."

I smile at her confession—half to comfort her, and half because I'm happy I could tell.

"Me too." I look back and forth between her green, green eyes as they widen.

"Really?"

"Yeah, really." I laugh at the incredulity on her face. "Of course, I'm nervous. It's *you*. It's important."

"Right. I just mean…I've never done this before."

"I know." I hesitate. I want to tell her she doesn't have to be nervous, but I don't want her to think I don't understand.

Before I can find the right words, she says, "You don't—I don't think you're going to make me feel uncomfortable, or expect something, or anything like that. I trust that we've built better communication than that. I just…It feels important. Like you said."

"It is important."

"Yeah. It is. I guess that's kind of the point." She glances down, and a strand of hair falls into her eyes. I tuck it behind her ear.

"I don't think I can help you feel completely un-nervous, but I hope you know that I just want to be with you, whatever form that may take."

She nods. "Yeah. I do know that."

"I think it's kinda good that we're nervous." She raises an eyebrow in silent question. "There is so much here that neither of us has ever done before. We should be a little nervous. It means we want this to work."

She beams at me. "As much as I love all the words coming out of your mouth, I feel like we could—"

I kiss her, and she loops her arms around my shoulders again. I try my best to kiss her slowly. A reminder to us both that there's no rush for anything.

She's here with me. She wants to be with me. *She trusts me.*

I don't want to rush. I don't want to turn this into something stressful, where all the good stuff seems like it's on a timer. I just want to be in this moment with her. And for the first time in a while, that feels easy.

So, I take my time and appreciate the hell out of every fraction of this moment.

Chapter Twenty-five

Ginny

The first day of the new semester greets me with warm sun streaming through Nat's windows. My eyes blink open, the familiar room in soft focus without my glasses. I feel the weight of Nat's arm around my waist, the heat of her body curled against my back. My eyes slide closed again, not to fall back asleep, but to bask in the glory of this moment.

I can barely believe I'm here—in Nat's bed—in a fantasy I've dreamed of for months.

Last term I woke up alone before my first class, grateful Jess was gone so I could have a moment to myself. Today, as I drift into consciousness with Nat's arm around me, I've never been happier to *not* be alone.

Nat's chest rises and falls with slow, even breaths against my back. She must still be asleep. I reach for my phone where it rests on Nat's desk, careful not to jostle her arm too much. I squint at the bright screen. It's just after eleven. We're lucky neither of us have class until the afternoon. I never forget to set an alarm, but last night all my focus was on Nat.

Yesterday was so amazing, it almost feels like a dream.

Nat and I spent most of the day in her room. We sat on her bed together for hours and snacked on the Goldfish she keeps in her desk and the black-and-white cookies her mom made her take back to school. We talked about serious things and nothing at all. I told her about coming out to my parents, she recounted a tough conversation she'd had with her mother after I left Brooklyn, then we debated the merits of holiday foods for an hour.

At around seven she said that if this was going to be our anniversary, then she wanted to take me out on a real date. My heart squeezed in my chest at her confidence in our six-hour-long relationship. She was amusingly serious about making it official, putting on a nice outfit and asking her roommate if she could borrow her car so we wouldn't have to take the bus into town. She took us on a thirty-minute drive to a Thai restaurant a couple towns away that she'd been to once before, and I teased her for how nervous she was about it being as good as she remembered.

I had not realized how much she'd been thinking about all this—how intently she'd been waiting and wishing for us to get here—until last night. The earnest, deliberate thought she put into each moment humbled me. I've never been more aware of how much I mean to someone.

On the drive back to school after dinner, I pointed out that we could have been together for almost two months now if I'd trusted her when she told me how she felt after Thanksgiving. She insisted this was better, and I think she's right. Not only do we trust each other so much more than we did then, but we both realize how important our relationship is to us.

After a discussion about whose roommate was around less, we went back to Nat's room. I felt a little pressure when she confirmed Payton wasn't coming back for the night, but it faded quickly. We didn't directly discuss me staying over, but it felt like an unspoken agreement by the time she asked if I wanted to borrow pajamas.

Sleeping in the same bed was completely different than the nights I'd stayed with her in Brooklyn. She didn't hesitate to pull me into her arms, and I didn't feel awkward being so close. I felt relieved, like all the tension of the last few months could finally slip away. And now that it has, I'm in no rush to wake up and leave this cozy, intimate cocoon we've created.

I return my phone to Nat's desk and nestle back into her arms. I release a contented sigh and— *Damn.* Nat stirs and a sleepy little groan rumbles out of her. Her arm tightens around me and she pulls me even closer. She mumbles something incoherent.

"Go back to sleep, Nat."

"Why?" Her voice is far away and confused. I stay quiet, hoping she'll drift off again. "Why would I do that…when you're here."

Oh.

I turn in her arms so I can face her. Her eyes are still closed, but the corners of her mouth are turned up in a soft smile.

"I didn't mean to wake you," I say. "We don't have anywhere to be yet. You can go back to sleep, if you want."

She opens her eyes. "I don't want. Do you?"

I shake my head. Maybe it's the novelty of waking up with her like this, or her mussed hair, but I can't resist leaning in to kiss her sleepy smile. I mean for it to be a quick kiss, but the moment her lips move against mine, I want anything but quick. I cup the back of her head, bringing her as close as I can. She follows my touch and lifts her head off the pillow to hover over me.

I want to pull her on top of me. Maybe I can.

But she pulls back with a low chuckle. "Wow," she says, voice thick and gravelly with sleep. "You're friendly in the morning."

"Sorry, I kind of attacked you there."

She grins and props herself up on one elbow, her head in her hand. "I'm not complaining. You can wake me up like that anytime."

"I may have to if you're always this cute in the morning." I reach up to ruffle her wild hair, and she laughs. I lower my hand to trace the edge of her strong jaw. She turns her head, placing a soft kiss on my palm.

Just like last night, I'm surprised by how normal it feels to be so close with her. My nerves of inexperience go out the window when her skin touches mine.

"What are you thinking right now?" she asks. Her eyes search my face.

"I'm thinking that this is so…easy." I skim my fingers over

her stomach and play with the hem of her shirt. "When I stayed with you in Brooklyn, it was weird to be so close. I wanted to touch you, but I was scared, and I had no idea what I would even do if I got the chance. I felt awkward, self-conscious. Now…"

"Now?" She raises an eyebrow.

"Now I don't think my brain remembers how to be self-conscious when you're so close."

The answering smile on her face is so huge it must hurt.

She leans in and kisses me again, slow and sweet.

❖

After we finally pull ourselves out of bed, Nat gets ready, then walks me to my room so I can do the same. As we stroll toward the dining hall for lunch, hand in hand, it occurs to me for the first time that we'll have to tell our friends we're dating.

"What?" Nat asks as she studies me out of the corner of her eye.

"What?"

"You made this little sound. A hmm kinda thing." She makes the noise back, and I laugh at the way she squints as she pretends to be thinking deeply.

"Well, I'm thinking."

"About what?"

"We have to tell our friends." I glance at our joined hands. "Or they'll probably figure it out before we say anything." Her brow furrows.

"Is this okay?" She squeezes my hand. "And stuff like this? PDA or whatever. I should have asked first." It's a loaded question. She isn't casually gauging my comfort with PDA. She wants to know if I'm ready to walk through the campus with her and leave no question as to our relationship status, or my queerness.

"I don't think I'd be comfortable, like, making out in public. Not because you're a girl, just because that's not a level of PDA I'd ever be really comfortable with. But beyond that…" I shrug.

"I'm comfortable with you. I'm comfortable here. So, yeah." I squeeze her hand back. "This is okay." She grins and leans over to kiss me, but pulls away before she reaches me, eyes going wide.

"I'm so sorry. We were literally just talking about not doing that. I was just happy, and you were smiling with your dimples, and I wanted to kiss you. I'm sorry."

"It's okay. I'm okay with that, too." I kiss her once. Twice. "This is not what I meant by making out."

"Thank God."

I laugh, resisting the urge to break my own rule already. Nat's grin shifts into a thoughtful frown.

"Are you nervous about telling everybody?"

"No, not nervous, really. I just hope it doesn't change anything with the group dynamic, you know?"

"I don't think it will. Not in any big ways, at least. There will be a lot of *finally*, I bet, but beyond that I think they'll be happy for us."

"How much does Lizzie know?" I ask.

"About us getting together? Yesterday?" She tilts her head at me. "When would I have talked to her about that?"

"No, us in general. Before yesterday."

"Oh. She knows a lot. Like, most of it." She frowns. "I hope that's okay."

"Of course it's okay."

"Why'd you just ask about Lizzie? Not worried about everyone else?"

"Well, she's your best friend, for one. And I—um…I've talked to Beth and Mack about us. And Raf a bit, too, actually."

Nat's mouth falls open. "Really?"

"Yeah. I hope that's okay."

"Of course, it's okay. It's just—I didn't realize. It's nice." But her brows are still halfway up her forehead.

"Are you sure?" I ask her with a tentative smile. "You look more than a little surprised."

"Yes, absolutely. It's great, actually. I didn't realize you were comfortable enough to talk about us so openly. I mean, they know you're queer, obviously, but…I guess I wasn't sure if you were ready for that kind of visibility."

"I wasn't, for a while, but Beth and Mack asked me what was going on with us, and then it wasn't so hard anymore."

She grins and bumps her hip into mine.

"Of course they did. I guess it's not like we were ever that subtle, anyway."

I scoff in mock outrage. "Excuse me? *You* weren't that subtle. I wasn't the one flirting at every possible opportunity."

"*Please*. You walked into a desk. We're even."

I laugh and lean in to kiss her quickly. "Fine. Even."

The dining hall is especially crowded since it's peak lunch time, but Rafael texted our group chat twenty minutes ago to say he got a table, so I'm sure most of our friends are here by now. We grab food, then wander around to find the table. Nat tugs my hand, and I turn to see her pointing at them.

"Hey!"

Mack turns at the sound of Nat's voice first, and they let out a scream at the sight of us. A *screech*, really. They run over at full speed and bring Nat and me into a crushing group hug. It's a miracle that neither of us drop our food. I let go of Nat's hand to hug them back.

"I'm so happy for you!" Mack pulls away, excitement brightening their blue eyes. "This is insane. Oh my God. We need to go out on a double date. This weekend! How about this weekend?"

"What the hell is going on over there?" Lizzie asks.

Mack moves out of her line of sight and gestures to Nat and me with a flourish, like they're introducing us to an adoring crowd. Nat grabs my hand again and holds it up, a gigantic grin on her face. Our friends break into spontaneous applause, but I immediately start shaking my head. I'm still an introvert. Even happy and proud to be holding Nat's hand, I don't want people clapping for me in the dining hall for any reason.

"Please, no. Before the entire student body joins you."

They laugh and make room for us at the table instead. There's only one empty chair, so Nat and I put our food down and glance around for another.

"Frankly, that was even less fanfare than I was expecting," Nat says.

"What would be more fanfare than applause in the dining hall?" I shudder to think of the possibilities.

Nat reels off suggestions as her eyes flick around the room for a chair. "Betting pool? Surprise party? Giant banner that says *Thank God we don't have to deal with the angst anymore*? These are just off the top of my head."

"How were we supposed to throw you a surprise party when we didn't know this happened?" Beth asks.

"Mack did bet me it would happen, like, two weeks into last term." Rafael smirks at Mack. "But I said that was way too soon."

"There's one." Nat points to an unoccupied chair all the way on the other side of the room.

"Oh, I'll—"

"I'll get it." She shoots me a smile before she starts maneuvering around the crowded tables.

"What a gentleman!" Mack calls after her.

Lizzie stands to pull me into a hug. "I'm really happy for you two, Ginny."

"Thanks." Beth hugs me, too. I'm a little embarrassed by how excited everyone is, but I'm relieved by the lack of awkwardness.

Nat appears behind me with another chair and makes a show of offering to pull it out for me. Everyone teases us for being painfully cute for a couple more minutes, but soon the conversation switches to Rafael and Beth's first classes.

It's wonderfully normal. I thought I'd feel like an entirely different person just by existing out in the world with a girlfriend, but it's a meal like any other we've had before. I'm calmer with everything out in the open, and I'm still a bit giddy from yesterday, but more than anything it all feels surprisingly normal.

And normal is amazing for me. I never imagined a normal like this before I came here. I have friends I am truly comfortable around, a community where I'm not anxious to be myself, and a girlfriend I'm absolutely crazy about.

Nat leans against me as she laughs at a joke Lizzie makes, and that feels kind of normal, too.

Or maybe *normal* isn't the best way to put it. *Right* is better. Something feels notably right about the sensation of Nat's hand squeezing mine as I listen to our friends laugh. Everything about this moment feels right, natural, and true.

I feel right, in a way I never have before.

I feel like myself.

EPILOGUE

Natalie

After all our worry about being shitty girlfriends, Ginny and I are actually damn good ones. We've only been together for a couple months, but our communication is free and comfortable, and we're getting better and better at knowing how to best support each other.

We were both surprised, at first, by how simple it is to be together. Our relationship feels so natural, even the tough stuff. It's not always easy for me to be open with her, and Ginny struggles with people's perceptions sometimes, but we both want to be at home with each other, and that makes all the difference.

Just about everything has been easier since we started dating. I can talk to Ginny about anything—really, absolutely anything—and her extensive support is a kind of comfort I'm not sure I've ever felt before. I am a million times lighter knowing I have her to talk to when I'm overwhelmed. The restless sense of unease about my future is still there sometimes, but it's quieter now, more manageable.

It helps that things are a lot better with my mom now, too. I've called her more often this term to talk about Ginny, my classes, and my art, and she's much less worried about me as a result. I told her last week that I need to cut back on my time at the deli when I'm home, and that I won't work there after I graduate. Ginny sat next to me, holding my hand, while I told my mom how stuck I feel when I'm working there, despite all the love I have for the store. The disappointment was palpable in her voice, and I still have some lingering guilt for not following the path she worked so hard to build for me, but I think she's happy to see me going after what I want.

I have much more confidence in my art now that I've committed fully to it. I push myself harder, I like my work more, and inspiration comes more easily, like it used to when art was just fun, not something with endless expectations attached to it.

I started my Student Gallery submission way in advance this term so I don't miss a chance to show my work again. I'm planning a mural composed of handmade pins and embroidered patches, which I'm really excited about.

Now I'm looking through a pile of my old sketchbooks and notebooks to find a particular drawing I want to incorporate into my mural, while Ginny reads a giant novel next to me. We're in my room today, since Payton's been really busy recently, and we like to take advantage of the privacy.

Ginny glances with a frown at the growing pile of books I've searched. "Haven't found it yet?"

"Nope."

"Want me to help you look?"

"Don't you have a whole bunch of chapters to read?"

"I'm done." I laugh as she slips a bookmark into her novel. She's a freakishly fast reader.

"Of course you are." I hand her a couple notebooks. "It's a bicycle. It looks kinda like that one that's always outside Lizzie's dorm, but not really."

She chuckles at my description. "Gotcha." We search in silence for a minute. Ginny gets through one notebook and opens another.

She takes a sudden, sharp breath, and I turn to look at her. She's staring at a page of the notebook, eyebrows raised high above the rims of her glasses, mouth open. I crane my neck to see what she's gawking at, but there's more space between us than usual because of the gigantic stack of sketchbooks. Her head snaps up and her wide eyes lock on mine.

"What?" I don't know what she could have found that would

be that shocking. I rack my brain for any risqué drawing I've made in a school notebook.

"It's me," she says.

"Oh." I laugh. *There's more where that came from.* "Yeah. You're definitely in a lot of these. A lot of times. A lot." She just blinks. "Is that weird? They're private, I promise. I wouldn't show them to anyone without asking you. Or maybe that makes it pervier. I guess I drew a lot of them before we were together, so that probably is weird. I'm sorry."

She shakes her head. "No. It's—" She looks at the drawing again and a soft smile blooms on her face as she studies it. "I love it."

I grin at her. I wonder if she realizes that's the ultimate compliment.

"Aw, I'm glad. Thank you." I shove some of the books out of my way so I can scoot next to her and see which sketch it is.

Oh. Damn.

"What's funny?" she asks. I must have laughed.

"Not funny, just wow. This one…" I trace my finger around the sketch of her, careful not to touch it directly. "I drew this one the first day of Gothic Lit."

"The…" Her eyebrows inch up again toward her hairline. "That was the first time we ever met. Or barely met. We'd never even talked to each other then."

I shrug. "I thought you were cute."

She laughs and leans in to kiss me. "I thought you were cute, too."

"Thank God." I flip to the next page of the notebook and point to the overalls sketch I'd made that day, covered in all the patches I could imagine. "When I realized it was kinda creepy to draw a stranger in class, I drew these instead. I thought maybe they'd be your style."

Her green eyes glitter at me as she smiles.

"You were right."

We both glance at the overalls she's wearing—the ones I gave her. I ghost my fingers over one of the straps, then curl my hand around it so my knuckles brush her collarbone.

"I should make you a couple more patches for these. For your birthday."

She groans good-naturedly. "My birthday's in the summer. At least let me think of a gift for yours next month first."

"True. I need to see what you get me first, so I can outdo you."

She laughs and kisses me again, then turns back to the notebook. The look in her eyes as she stares at the drawing makes my chest feel tight in the best way. It means a lot to her, I can tell.

I mean a lot to her.

And that's the best thing in the world. Because she means a lot to me.

But that's not quite right. Words and phrases like *means a lot* have become more and more inadequate by the day.

Maybe now is the right time to change that.

I watch her as she puts the notebook down on her other side, then gently pulls my legs into her lap.

She plays absentmindedly with a rip in my jeans, skims her fingers over my ankle, traces my tattoo without having to look at it, all while she glances through the sketches.

I'm still getting used to how happy I am when she initiates physical stuff, especially the way she's touching me now, like it's second nature. I adore those little, silent reminders that she feels as close to me as I feel to her.

I slip a hand into one of hers, hoping that the feel of her fingers intertwining with mine will ground me.

"Hey, Ginny?"

She turns to me and pops a brow in question. "Yeah?"

I take a deep breath and focus on the words I've wanted to say for a while now.

"I love you."

Her smile makes her eyes crinkle at the edges and her dimples pop—a sight I could watch endlessly.

"I love you too, Nat."

And *that* really is the best thing in the world.

About the Author

Maggie Fortuna is a writer and theater artist born and bred in Brooklyn, New York. She is a lover of Victorian literature, genre television, and snowy weather. Maggie has a passion for telling stories that deal with the complex reality of being queer but still provide the kind of positivity that queer people don't get to see often enough.

Books Available From Bold Strokes Books

A Case for Discretion by Ashley Moore. Will Gwen, a prominent Atlanta attorney, choose Etta, the law student she's clandestinely dating, or is her political future too important to sacrifice? (978-1-63679-617-8)

Aubrey McFadden Is Never Getting Married by Georgia Beers. Aubrey McFadden is never getting married, but she does have five weddings to attend, and she'll be avoiding Monica Wallace, the woman who ruined her happily ever after, at every single one. (978-1-63679-613-0)

The Broken Lines of Us by Shia Woods. Charlie Dawson returns to the city she left behind and meets an unexpected stranger on her first night back, discovering that coming home might not be as hard as she thought. (978-1-63679-585-0)

Flowers for Dead Girls by Abigail Collins. Isla might be just the right kind of girl to bring Astra out of her shell—and maybe more. The only problem? She's dead. (978-1-63679-584-3)

Good Bones by Aurora Rey. Designer and contractor Logan Barrow can give Kathleen Kenney the house of her dreams, but can she convince the cynical romance writer to take a chance on love? (978-1-63679-589-8)

Leather, Lace, and Locs by Anne Shade. Three friends, each on their own path in life, with one obstacle…finding room in their busy lives for a love that will give them their happily ever afters. (978-1-63679-529-4)

Rainbow Overalls by Maggie Fortuna. Arriving in Vermont for her first year of college, an introverted bookworm forms a friendship with an outgoing artist and finds what comes after the classic coming out story: a being out story. (978-1-63679-606-2)

Revisiting Summer Nights by Ashley Bartlett. PJ Addison and Wylie Parsons have been called back to film the most recent *Dangerous Summer Nights* installment. Only this time they're not in love, and it's going to stay that way. (978-1-63679-551-5)

All This Time by Sage Donnell. Erin and Jodi share a complicated past, but a very different present. Will they ever be able to make a future together work? (978-1-63679-622-2)

Crossing Bridges by Chelsey Lynford. When a one-night stand between a snowboard instructor and a business executive becomes more, one has to overcome her past, while the other must let go of her planned future. (978-1-63679-646-8)

Dancing Toward Stardust by Julia Underwood. Age has nothing to do with becoming the person you were meant to be, taking a chance, and finding love. (978-1-63679-588-1)

Evacuation to Love by CA Popovich. As a hurricane rips through Florida, so too are Joanne and Shanna's lives upended. It'll take a force of nature to show them the love it takes to rebuild. (978-1-63679-493-8)

Lean in to Love by Catherine Lane. Will badly behaving celebrities, erotic sex tapes, and steamy scandals prevent Rory and Ellis from leaning in to love? (978-1-63679-582-9)

The Romance Lovers Book Club by MA Binfield and Toni Logan. After their book club reads a romance about an American tourist falling in love with an English princess, Harper and her best friend, Alice, book an impulsive trip to London hoping they'll both fall for the women of their dreams. (978-1-63679-501-0)

Searching for Someday by Renee Roman. For loner Rayne Thomas, her only goal for working out is to build her confidence, but Maggie Flanders has another idea, and neither is prepared for the outcome. (978-1-63679-568-3)

Truly Home by J.J. Hale. Ruth and Olivia discover home is more than a four-letter word. (978-1-63679-579-9)

View from the Top by Morgan Adams. When it comes to love, sometimes the higher you climb, the harder you fall. (978-1-63679-604-8)

Blood Rage by Illeandra Young. A stolen artifact, a family in the dark, an entire city on edge. Can SPEAR agent Danika Karson juggle all three over a weekend with the "in-laws" while an unknown, malevolent entity lies in wait upon her very skin? (978-1-63679-539-3)

Ghost Town by R.E. Ward. Blair Wyndon and Leif Henderson are set to prove ghosts exist when the mystery suddenly turns deadly. Someone or something else is in Masonville, and if they don't find a way to escape, they might never leave. (978-1-63679-523-2)

Good Christian Girls by Elizabeth Bradshaw. In this heartfelt coming of age lesbian romance, Lacey and Jo help each other untangle who they are from who everyone says they're supposed to be. (978-1-63679-555-3)

Guide Us Home by CF Frizzell and Jesse J. Thoma. When acquisition of an abandoned lighthouse pits ambitious competitors Nancy and Sam against each other, it takes a WWII tale of two brave women to make them see the light. (978-1-63679-533-1)

Lost Harbor by Kimberly Cooper Griffin. For Alice and Bridget's love to survive, they must find a way to reconcile the most important passions in their lives—devotion to the church and each other. (978-1-63679-463-1)

Never a Bridesmaid by Spencer Greene. As her sister's wedding gets closer, Jessica finds that her hatred for the maid of honor is a bit more complicated than she thought. Could it be something more than hatred? (978-1-63679-559-1)

The Rewind by Nicole Stiling. For police detective Cami Lyons and crime reporter Alicia Flynn, some choices break hearts. Others leave a body count. (978-1-63679-572-0)

Turning Point by Cathy Dunnell. When Asha and her former high school bully Jody struggle to deny their growing attraction, can they move forward without going back? (978-1-63679-549-2)

When Tomorrow Comes by D. Jackson Leigh. Teague Maxwell, convinced she will die before she turns 41, hires animal rescue owner Baye Cobb to rehome her extensive menagerie. (978-1-63679-557-7)

You Had Me at Merlot by Melissa Brayden. Leighton and Jamie have all the ingredients to turn their attraction into love, but it's a recipe for disaster.(978-1-63679-543-0)